F
GAR

GOOD MOON RISING

FARRAR
STRAUS
GIROUX

Good Moon Rising

NANCY GARDEN

FARRAR · STRAUS · GIROUX
NEW YORK

Library of Congress Cataloging-in-Publication Data
Garden, Nancy.
Good moon rising / Nancy Garden.—1st ed.
p.   cm.
[1. Lesbians—Fiction.   2. Theater—Fiction.   3. High schools—Fiction.
4. Schools—Fiction.   5. Identity—Fiction.]   I. Title.
PZ7.G165Go   1996   [Fic]—dc20   96-11836   CIP   AC

For the company of the world premiere of
the stage version of
Annie on My Mind,
especially
Kim Smith Aaronson, adapter and director,
and actors:

B. J. Backman, Lea Burgess-Carland, Anna Chappell, Julie Chappell, Brooke Emerson, Lanya Fent, Charis Gibbs, Ashley Griffin, Lakin Griffin, Sarah Cipriana Heivonimus, Juanita of the Buffalo People, Jill Jurado, Lijia Lyles, Martin Martin, Jon Eric Narum, Cory Poul, Keith Scott, Jeremy Shawl, Myka Small, Catherine Ushka

GOOD MOON RISING

ONE

THE DREAM AGAIN:

A bright circle of light on a dark stage and the three of them tightly in it: Jan herself and her fellow apprentices, Raphael and Corrin. No audience, no set, no other apprentices or actors from Jan's recently completed first season of summer stock; no sound or motion—just the three of them. Only . . . only . . .

Only Jan had no sense of why she was there, though she'd dreamed the same dream at least three times since she'd been home in the small town of Southview, New Hampshire. No idea, either, why Corrin, who'd been her roommate, and Raphael, her new friend, were watching her oddly. In the dream, Raphael's kind green eyes were uncharacteristically mocking, and beautiful Corrin seemed both startled and cold. It was as if they'd been bound into silence at the moment they'd tried to tell her something, or as if they'd been about to warn her of something they saw and she didn't . . .

Covered with sweat, Jan woke in her small square room, reassuring herself with familiar objects: the battered pine

3

desk where she'd struggled harder each year to do homework that meant less to her as her certainty about acting deepened; the script for this year's junior-senior play, Arthur Miller's *The Crucible*, on her bedside table; the bright rag rug that always slipped a little, as it did now, when she put her feet on it.

"Jan—Janna!" Her mother's rich voice, though it called insistently, was also reassuring.

It's only a dream, Jan told herself, trying to ignore the dread it had left with her. Not even a dream, really: a disturbing, plotless image. Just a picture, that was all.

"Jan! It's time! You don't want to be late on your first day of senior year!"

"Okay, Mom."

Jan pulled off the T-shirt she wore for sleeping, and fumbled in the still-dim room for her clothes. The image began to recede.

"Jan, your eggs are freezing. And Ted's here."

Guiltily, Jan let her eyes close for a moment, then opened them and sat down on her bed to put on her Nikes. Of course Ted would pick her up the first day of school, even though she'd written him only once all summer and hadn't called him since she'd been home. Good old loyal Teddy Bear, just about her best friend since fourth grade—until a certain awkward scene in his car last spring, which was one reason why she hadn't felt eager to get back in touch with him.

"Coming!" she called again. Then, reluctantly, "Hi, Ted!" She tugged her brush through her short unruly blond curls. "I'll be right down."

What a contrast Ted would be to Raphael, and the girls at school to Corrin! Not that she'd really gotten to know Corrin, in spite of rooming with her. Raphael was different. They'd become close so quickly that Jan had barely been surprised

4

when he'd confided in her that he was gay and in love with Don Jeffords, one of the actors; it seemed to fit, to be right for him. But with Corrin, despite the intensity of their talks about theater, there had always been an odd distance, perhaps partly because her beauty had sometimes made Jan stare at her, until Raphael pointed out that the other apprentices might notice . . .

"Hey, Janna, Janna Montcrief!" came Ted's familiar impatient voice, with a grin in it, and close, as if he'd come partway up the stairs. "How's the great actress? Any big contracts yet?"

"Not yet," Jan called down. "But the season's young." At least, she thought, putting the brush down and tucking her shirt into her jeans, I can still kid around with him, and he doesn't sound mad about my not having written. "Hot or cold out, Ted?" she shouted.

"Cold."

"So're your eggs," her mother called mournfully. "You could ski on them."

Jan grinned. Mom's funny comments had made Jan smile for as long as she could remember. "You should've been a comedian," Jan's now married and pregnant sister Anita had often told their mother. But "I *like* being a housewife" had always been Mom's reaction to any suggestion she be more than that. It was a good thing, though, Jan had thought sometimes, since for years their father had worked night and day building up his law practice, and was often out of town. This time he'd been away since the middle of the summer.

"Be right there," Jan shouted.

The dream image gone now, Jan tugged her old green sweatshirt over her head and started for the bathroom. Then she stopped: should she take the script to school?

5

Tryouts weren't till the following week, but she picked up *Crucible* anyway and propped it against the mouthwash bottle while she brushed her teeth. She didn't have to turn to the big scene between Elizabeth and John; she'd worked on it so often during the summer that the script fell open there by itself. Even if the play was basically John's—and hence Kent Norris's, who everyone knew would get the part—Elizabeth was an excellent role. Most girls at school, Jan knew, would want to play Abigail, the villain in this play about the seventeenth-century witch-hunt in Salem, Massachusetts— or they'd want Mary Warren, who'd almost but not quite had the courage to stop the terrible accusations that had led to so many cruel, unjustified hangings. Both parts were openly dramatic, calling for a good deal of hysteria and weeping. But quiet, withdrawn, moral Elizabeth Proctor, falsely accused of witchcraft—that was a part for a real actress. Mrs. Nicholson, Southview High's drama coach, had even said so herself last spring when she'd announced what the play would be, and she'd been looking right at Jan when she'd said it.

" 'The town's gone wild, I think,' " Jan whispered around the toothpaste in her mouth to an imaginary John Proctor, Elizabeth's husband—not so imaginary, since he had Kent's face. " 'She speak of Abigail, and I thought she were a saint, to hear her.' " She repeated the line, trying to make the old-fashioned words sound smooth and natural, then said it again.

A firm knock interrupted her. "Jan," said her mother, just a hint of testiness in her voice, "the neighbors' cat is eyeing your eggs."

Good-naturedly, confident of getting cast as Elizabeth, Jan flung the door open, grabbed her small, plump mother around the waist, and twirled her around. "Mother, I come," she intoned, kissing her.

Mom laughed fondly and then tweaked the sleeve of Jan's sweatshirt. "Even the great French actress Sarah Bernhardt washed her clothes once a year or so," she remarked without reproach.

"Yeah," said Jan, darting back for the script and tossing it into her bookbag, "but sweatshirts take too long to dry. Hey there, Ted!" she shouted before her mother could point out that she owned more than one. This was the one she'd had in stock, and so was good luck.

Applause greeted her from the foot of the stairs. Jan waved and did a curtain-call curtsy, thinking, as Ted answered with a sweeping bow, of a line from the sentimental song she'd learned years earlier in camp about new friends being silver, but old ones gold. It was good to see him after all.

"La Montcrief at last," Ted said with the familiar slow grin that started with just a twitch of his wide mouth and gradually spread till it put a twinkle deep in his brown eyes. "La Divine Montcrief, fans. And such an entrance," he added as she deliberately thumped clumsily down the stairs. "Such a costume!"

"Sarcasm," said Jan, ducking around the corner into the kitchen as he bent to kiss her cheek, "will get you everywhere." He caught her hand and kissed her anyway.

"How've you been?" she asked, avoiding his eyes.

"Not bad." He let her go.

"What's the matter? My head on crooked?"

"Your head's fine." The breeziness was gone; he looked like a whipped dog.

She went into the kitchen with him following, and to the stove, wishing she knew what to say. The congealed yellow mass that was her eggs stared up at her from the frying pan on the front burner. "Yuck."

Ted stood there watching her, then draped himself with exaggerated carelessness on one of the four green stools at the long kitchen counter that doubled as a table. "Meet anyone interesting this summer?" he asked, a little too casually.

"Well, yeah." Jan scraped the eggs onto a plate and pushed down the bread her mother had left for her in the toaster. "A few people. But not—not what you think. How about you?"

"Nope."

"Too bad." Jan wondered briefly what Ted would make of Raphael. Raphael, she felt sure, would be drawn to Ted, who was, she had to admit, pretty good-looking, especially now that the acne was almost gone from his strong, square face.

"Your face has cleared up," she said, thinking that might make him feel better.

"You noticed. I figured I'd surprise you. It took a whole drugstore full of glop and nine visits to that creep Dr. Zolotow. But"—he ran his hand over his chin—"at least I can get within ten feet of a razor without ending up looking like something Dracula bit in all the wrong places."

Jan laughed.

Ted rearranged himself on the stool, seeming more relaxed. "You going to eat that mess?" he asked as she put the plate on the counter.

Jan shrugged.

"We could stop for pheasants' tongues," he said, like the old Ted again. "What matter if we be late the first day? Nary a whit, I say, if lateness lets me serve you, lady."

"Nay, gracious sir, nay." Jan, relieved to return to banter, tried not to gag as she bolted down the eggs and toast, then poured herself a cup of coffee; that, at least, was still hot. "Lateness likes me not on such a day."

"What day, madame?" Ted shifted again on the stool. His

8

too long legs jutted out grasshopper-like at the knees; she'd envied him his height since fourth grade. "Surely the—er— noted academy we have good fortune to attend has such a day in every year, nay, in every month . . ."

"Yea, verily," said Jan, over her coffee mug. "But . . ."

"Yea, verily, indeed!" Jan's mother came into the kitchen, a pile of laundry in her arms. "If you two don't hie yourselves to yon noted academy instanter, you will . . ."

"Instanter?" asked Jan. *"Instanter?"*

"Just what it sounds like." Her mother kissed her and pushed her toward the door. "You have exactly ten minutes before the first bell, and I don't want to hear you've gotten a speeding ticket, Ted."

It was two late slips they got instead of a speeding ticket, because Ted turned morose again about Jan's not writing or calling, and Jan's attempt at explanation took closer to fifteen minutes than ten. But later, sitting in her usual back-row seat in English, Jan knew she hadn't even begun to make him understand. How could she, when she herself really didn't understand and when she felt she'd changed over the summer and he hadn't? Obviously, the easy banter was still there. And so were the quick improvisations they'd fallen into spontaneously since freshman year when Jan had first gotten involved with theater and Ted had tagged along, sometimes acting, sometimes working backstage. But Jan felt those things weren't enough anymore, and she wondered how she and Ted would be together if Ted got a part in *Crucible*, for which he'd told her that morning he was trying out.

"Janna Montcrief, I asked you a question."

There was a faint wave of tittering; heads turned as the teacher walked toward Jan.

9

"I'm sorry, Ms. Smathers," Jan said calmly. "I guess I was daydreaming." *The Crucible* slipped out of her notebook and onto the floor.

"Ah, yes." Ms. Smathers picked it up. "Our actress. But tryouts, I believe, are not until next Wednesday. In the meantime, kindly turn your attention to the task at hand. In a short story . . ."

The day did not improve. When math let out, Jan got her paper-bag lunch out of her locker and took it and *Crucible* to her favorite corner table in the huge cafeteria. It was a sterile, noisy room, with ugly chrome-and-vinyl furniture, but she'd found even as a freshman that the chairs were uncomfortable enough to keep her awake if she wanted to study and the noise, with a little extra concentration, could become its own insulation.

Jan unwrapped her tuna sandwich and opened *Crucible* again to Elizabeth's first scene with John. It was an uncomfortable scene, in which it becomes obvious there is tension between them, partly because John is attracted to their servant, Mary Warren—and not long after it, Elizabeth is arrested for witchcraft. Jan decided to reread the whole play that night, and then the next day write an autobiography of Elizabeth, starting with Elizabeth's earliest memory and going up to the time of the play. The apprentices' acting teacher in stock had recommended that as a good way to give depth to a characterization, and Jan had found that it worked well for her, at least in the scenes she'd done in class there.

"Hey, Sarah Bernhardt, beware. Competition stalks, methinks."

Annoyed at the interruption, Jan slid her lunch over to make room for Ted's.

"Oh, yeah?" she said, her eyes still on the script. "How come?"

Ted poked her in the side with his elbow, and then gestured toward a girl who was just coming out of the lunch-buying line, somehow managing to balance her tray, a load of books, and an enormous shoulder bag without looking awkward. "New kid," Ted explained. "Junior. Kerry Ann—um—Socrides. Just moved in with her aunt. Signed up for tryouts. Looks like an Elizabeth type to me."

Reluctantly, Jan glanced up.

"Well, maybe she can't act," she said brusquely, pretending to return to the script. But her mouth had gone dry, and she had to admit Ted was right. The girl's clear pale skin and her long black hair—which she'd have to wear up, of course, as Elizabeth would have—the precision of her delicate features, the dignity with which she carried herself—all exactly matched Jan's own picture of Elizabeth Proctor. But more than that—oh, much more than that—was the girl's air of quiet strength, the sureness she'd radiated even in the short moment Jan had watched her.

"More like Elizabeth than Elizabeth," Ted whispered. "Wow! You're going to have to give one heck of a reading to convince Mrs. Nicholson she shouldn't cast that one! But I know you'll do it, Jan—hey, remember, you're the school star." He turned slightly. "And here's the other school star. Hiya, Norris."

Kent Norris plunked his tray down next to Jan's, and again Jan thought how perfect he'd be for Proctor. His longish brown hair, edged with new sideburns, was still tied back in a severe ponytail as it had been last spring. The ponytail, plus his thin straight mouth, which remained solemn even when his dark eyes smoldered, made him look like the men in many

11

pictures Jan had seen of early New England settlers. According to Miller, *Crucible*'s author, John Proctor was "not easily led," and that certainly worked for Kent, though another part of Miller's description—"even-tempered"—did not. Jan had seen Kent's rage more than once when he hadn't gotten his way.

"So, Jan," Kent said, ignoring Ted, "how was stock?"

"Great," Jan answered amiably. She didn't like Kent much and was pretty sure he felt the same way about her, but they did share the same professional goals and she enjoyed working onstage with him when he was at his best as an actor. "How was your summer? You did some community theater, right?"

"I did Stanley Kowalski in *A Streetcar Named Desire*." He tossed it off as if it didn't matter, but Jan could see he was proud of it. "At the beach. You know, the Marlon Brando part." Kent thumped his chest with his fist. "Stella!" he bellowed, and Jan recognized the super-macho attitude Marlon Brando had made famous in the old black-and-white movie of *Streetcar* that she and Ted had seen twice.

Startled eyes looked up from lunch trays at Kent's outburst; he stood up and bowed.

"Yeah," he said, sitting again, "it really was great. We got terrific notices and the girls were all over me. So were a couple of fags, but I got rid of them pretty quick."

"Oh?" Jan said noncommittally; Ted raised his eyebrows.

"Yeah, you know," said Kent. "Kept following me around and staring. Just couldn't resist my gorgeous hard-muscled bod, I guess." He shivered. "Creeps."

"This has to be my cue to leave," Ted announced, picking up his tray. "See you."

"Later," Kent said with an indifferent wave. He turned

12

back to Jan. "So stock was great, huh? Man, I'd like to do it next year, but after the fags this summer, I don't know. That's the one thing I like less and less about this business, you know what I mean?"

"No," said Jan coldly, thinking of Raphael. "I don't know what you mean. One thing I learned this summer is that the important things in theater are talent and hard work, not who people like to sleep with. Besides, I call them gays, not fags."

"Well, excuse me!" Kent gave her an odd look. "Gays, spays—hey, that's pretty good!—what's the difference?"

Jan stood, picking up her tray. "The difference," she said, "is that it's the same as calling someone a nigger instead of calling them black or African-American or a person of color. I'll see you at tryouts, Kent." She walked briskly to the counter, slammed her tray down, and was about to leave when she saw the new girl again, alone in a corner with the *Crucible* script propped up against her milk carton. "More like Elizabeth than Elizabeth," Jan muttered reluctantly, and headed for the girls' room, where she studied herself in the mirror. She tried to convince herself that looks didn't matter, especially to Mrs. Nicholson; talent mattered.

But Mrs. Nicholson, she knew, was as much a pro in her way as were the people Jan had met in stock, and Jan herself knew enough about real theater to know that looks *did* matter. Could she play Elizabeth convincingly despite her curly hair and the short squarish body that one of the professional actresses in stock had told her would limit her to character parts once she was out of school? How could solemn Elizabeth Proctor have a tipped-up nose like a little kid's, or greenish-blue eyes that, for all the misery in them now, could never, never look as self-assured as that new girl's had, even at a distance? Especially at a distance. If Kerry What's-Her-

Name could project that quality across the school cafeteria, she'd have no trouble at all projecting it from a stage.

"Are you an actress or aren't you?" Jan whispered to her reflection, throwing her shoulders back and making her eyes flash into the mirror. There! That was better. " 'John,' " she said in Elizabeth's voice, " 'it come to naught that I should forgive you, if you'll not forgive yourself. It is not my soul, John, it is yours . . .'

"And, oh, please, Mrs. Nicholson," Jan prayed, turning from the mirror as a group of girls came loudly in, "it's my soul, too. It's my last part with you, my last big show here at Southview. It's my soul, too!"

TWO

༒

THE AFTERNOON OF tryouts was crisp, but with a trace of summer's humidity to remind one that it was still only September. Jan had spent most of the intervening time working on Elizabeth, and now she sat at her homeroom desk, *Crucible* open inside her Western Civ book, but her eyes staring blankly outside. Her stomach was jumpy and her hands restless; she finally picked up a pencil and began doodling on the cover of her notebook. Then she noticed she was sketching *Crucible* characters, and stopped. If only the bell would ring; if only it were six o'clock and tryouts were over; if only it were tomorrow, next week, next year!

When the bell did ring, Jan, seeing Ted waiting for her at the door, got stiffly to her feet, picking up *Crucible*. What was it Raphael had said last summer? Something about how playing Elizabeth would "stretch" her as playing Abigail never would? And yet she'd been working on Abigail, too, a little, just in case.

The classroom Mrs. Nicholson always used for tryouts was crowded when Jan and Ted got there, even though they arrived early. Books and sweaters were strewn on the floor and on chairs, and an excited buzz, shot through with bursts of laughter, rose from the clusters of juniors and seniors that filled the room. Jan sat in the back near the door, after telling Ted she wanted to be alone. She closed her eyes, trying to use her cafeteria trick to shut out the audible bits of conversation, but it didn't work; they came through anyway:

"Yes, but Jack didn't call last night."

"What did Clarendon say about the social studies homework? How many pages?"

"Look, jerk, we've got to beat Northern. There's no way we can get through the season if we don't."

Don't be snobby, Jan admonished herself when the chattering annoyed her; don't be stuck up; stop making yourself into some kind of elitist. But the interest the others seemed to have in everything but the play made her miss Raphael and Corrin, who would be talking about *Crucible* if they were waiting to try out, or who would be wrapped in silence as she was, trying to feel their way into it. Except for Ted, Jan had never had a close friend at Southview, and coming back after a season of stock made that clearer to her than it had ever been before . . .

"Sorry. Hi."

Jan felt her legs being tripped over and pulled them back, grabbing for her books. Then she opened her eyes to see Brenda George, a brittle senior with a tough manner that would make her a good Abigail. Brenda's brown hair, Jan saw, was bushier than she remembered it, and was streaked with silvery blond.

"Hi, yourself," Jan said reluctantly; Brenda had never been one of her favorite people. She was part of a clique Jan and Ted called The Cheerleaders. Some of them—not Brenda—

actually were cheerleaders, and all of them spent most of their time aggressively seeking dates, clothes, and popularity.

"It's okay," Jan said. "I mean, if I kept my eyes open I'd know when to get out of the way, wouldn't I?"

"Yeah. But you said it; I didn't." Brenda moved on to sit with her friends, and Jan heard her ask, "Like my mane? Mom and I went to Mr. Jerome's in New York in August. He does all the stars. I sure hope Kent notices." She dropped her voice, but Jan could still hear. "He is so-o-o gorgeous," she gushed. "And guess what? He actually asked me to try out for the play. Oooh, look, there he is now!" Brenda stood up and gave a flirtatious wave in Kent's direction as he walked to an empty seat in front, acknowledging Jan with a characteristically aloof nod. Will Omlin, a somewhat clumsy but earnest boy who wasn't a very good actor, followed worshipfully in his wake.

Jan wasn't surprised at Brenda's reaction to Kent, for almost every girl in Southview had a crush on him. But she was surprised he'd asked her to try out; Brenda wasn't known for her acting ability.

The door opened again and Jan heard someone ask in a low, musical voice, "Is this the right room?" She turned around to see Kerry Ann Socrides walking uncertainly toward her. "The right room for the play tryouts?"

No, Jan was tempted to say; *no, this is band practice. Tryouts are in the basement, Room 005.* Or even: *Tryouts are cancelled.*

But something in Kerry's face—maybe it was the unexpected uncertainty, hinting that perhaps she wasn't always as confident as she'd seemed at lunch that first day—made Jan smile and say, "Yes, it's the tryouts; you're in the right place." The next minute, though, Kerry was sitting beside her, ar-

17

ranging her books on the floor, and pushing up the sleeves of her deep-red turtleneck; the room was getting hot with so many people in it. "Wow, am I nervous!" Kerry exclaimed. "Aren't you?"

"Yes," Jan said. She wanted to bury herself in *Crucible*; she didn't want to talk at all and certainly not to Kerry, but she found herself noticing things about her even so. They were Elizabeth things, mostly, but not exclusively: the calm behind her eyes, warring with nervousness; the laughter that seemed ready to spill over; a certain infectious eagerness.

"I've never been in a play before," Kerry confided to her, "but I've always wanted to be. Have you? Been in plays, I mean?"

It was funny, having someone at Southview not know the answer to that; that was Jan's first thought. Her second thought was that it was nice. And only then did she realize how relieved she was that Kerry had no experience. "I've been in a few," Jan told her modestly.

There was a rustle behind them and Mrs. Nicholson— Elvira Nicholson—pushed open the door. Her straight, stout figure was heavy with jewelry as usual, and her hands and arms were full of director's paraphernalia: scripts, pencils, a huge clipboard with a thick legal pad fastened to it, the now grimy sign-up sheet, covered with names.

Jan leapt up to hold the door open.

Mrs. Nicholson gave Jan the special smile she reserved for the few she called "her" actors: Jan, Kent, a kind, plump girl named Nanny Davis whose talent was only average, but who was reliable, worked hard, and always helped with costumes and makeup. "Thank you, Janna," Mrs. Nicholson said, her vibrant, husky voice automatically set to reach Jan's ears and no one else's. She bent toward Jan, her heavy gold earrings

18

and pendant swinging. "You look as if stock agreed with you. We'll have to have a talk later."

"Sure," said Jan. "I—I hope you had a good summer." She wondered if she had. Somehow, under the thick but well-applied makeup Mrs. Nicholson always wore, her face looked strained and pale, and close up she looked as if she'd shrunk a little, though it was hard to tell under the voluminous paisley tent dress that floated around her body.

"Splendid summer, splendid!" Mrs. Nicholson emphasized her words with a beringed hand. "A trifle dull, perhaps, now and then"—the hand turned gracefully onto its side—"a little trying somewhere in July"—the hand dropped—"but"—and went up again—"some good theater, oh, very good. We *will* have to talk. Nevertheless—well, it's good to be back." Mrs. Nicholson bent closer; Jan could smell heavy but not unpleasant perfume. "I suspect *you* hate being back, though, don't you?"

"Yes, some," Jan admitted.

Mrs. Nicholson patted Jan's hand, murmured "Never mind," and swept majestically to the front of the room as if she had just come down a gracefully curving staircase into a glittering hallway lit with crystal chandeliers and crowded with elegantly dressed, partying people.

Despite the photos from ancient *Theater Arts* magazines that adorned its walls, the room was used for English classes and had the usual yellow-brown teacher's desk and plastic bolted-down desk-armchairs. But, as always, as soon as Mrs. Nicholson faced her students, the scarred floor in front became a stage, the walls were transformed into a set with the blue-green chalkboard for a skydrop, and the students into a waiting audience.

Jan knew that many Southview students thought Mrs.

19

Nicholson was both bizarre and superficial, but even so, most also admitted she was the most exciting teacher there and certainly the best thing that had ever happened to their rather stuffy English and Speech Department. Twenty-five years earlier, the story went, Mrs. Nicholson had left the Broadway stage and moved to New Hampshire to marry her beloved Robert, a banker, who couldn't bear the idea of a wife who faced the public every night. But by the time their son Robert Junior, who now did TV commercials with an embarrassing lack of talent, had entered Southview High, Robert Senior had mellowed enough to agree to his wife's teaching. She'd stayed on ever since, despite threatening every year to resign because no one, neither students nor teachers, took producing plays seriously enough to suit her.

Kent had straightened up in his seat, Jan saw, as soon as Mrs. Nicholson's commanding figure had reached the front of the room. "Kent," stated Mrs. Nicholson, nodding at him. It meant "Hello."

"Mrs. Nicholson," answered Kent in the same way.

"Whoa," Kerry whispered. "Isn't she something? Is she always that regal?"

"Pretty much always."

"Someone," Kerry said, "told me the best thing about doing plays here is that the teacher who directs them is really good. She *looks* like a housewife who's trying to be elegant, but she acts like she just stepped off a stage or out of the movies or something. She's so powerful!"

Jan studied Kerry with growing interest. She didn't know anyone except Kent and herself who hadn't laughed at Mrs. Nicholson at first and grown to respect her only after working with her. But before she got a chance to say anything more to Kerry, Mrs. Nicholson held up her hand and everyone knew tryouts were about to begin.

Jan's mouth went dry, as usual, as soon as Mrs. Nicholson, all business now, called her and Kent to read the first Elizabeth–John scene. A few kids grumbled, but everyone else in the room settled back to be entertained. Ted mouthed "Good luck" from across the room as Jan went up to the front. She mouthed "Thanks" back, and then smiled at Kent, aware that both of them knew some of the kids felt Mrs. Nicholson would always cast them as leads whether or not they read. "But why shouldn't we do leads?" he'd said to her once. "We're good and it means more to us than to the others. Besides, we need the practice. You don't think we're going to get big parts right away in New York, do you?"

Jan and Kent sailed through the scene; Jan was calm, as always, the moment she started reading. Kent reacted to every nuance of her voice, just as he always did; she concentrated on his every line as if she were hearing it for the first time. When they finished, most everyone clapped, although Mrs. Nicholson held up her hand for silence immediately.

"Thank you," she said, not a twitch betraying her reaction. "Kent, you may sit down for a minute, but I'll call you again soon. Janna, stay here, please, and read the same scene again with Will Omlin."

Poor gangling Will tried, but he stumbled over every line and his face shone with nervous sweat. He never failed to try out for every play Kent tried out for, and he never failed to get a good small part, as if being rewarded for the agony he suffered at tryouts and would continue to suffer at rehearsals and in performances. No matter how hard the others tried to calm him down, he had never gotten through a rehearsal or performance without blundering. This time he messed up the line "I know I cannot keep it. I say I will think on it," saying instead, "I know I cannot think on it. I say I will keep it." Everyone laughed, but Jan squelched the laugh quickly, stepping on it with her next line, which she revised to "Good, then. Let you keep it," covering Will's mistake as she would have in a performance.

"Thank you." Mrs. Nicholson again betrayed no reaction, except to say, "Good recovery, Jan. Don't leave; I'll call you later. But now I'd like to hear you again, Kent, in the same scene with"—her bracelets clanked as she reached for the sign-up list—"Kerry Ann Socrides."

Jan walked back to her seat, more nervous now than when she herself had been called to read. She felt she should say "Good luck" as she passed Kerry, then wondered if she could avoid it, and finally said it anyway.

"Thanks," Kerry breathed nervously.

Jan sat down, her palms damp. Easy out, she promised herself. Easy out.

Kerry waited, as had Jan, for Kent to indicate his entrance, then read, " 'What keeps you so late? It's almost dark.' "

Her voice was clear, gentle, and strong, with just the right hint of reproach—less than Jan had put in hers, but enough to communicate instantly that Elizabeth had been both worried and suspicious when John had come home late.

" 'I were planting,' " Kent answered, obviously surprised she read so well, " 'far out to the forest edge.' "

" 'Oh, you're done then,' " Kerry responded. Another subtlety: this time, a perfect shadow of a smile.

Jan groaned inwardly, but she leaned forward in her seat, noticing as she did that everyone else was doing the same. She stayed leaning forward till the scene was over. Every line was a gem, or nearly.

When he'd put down the script, Kent ran his hand over his skinned-back hair and gave Kerry a dazzling smile. From the audience there was silence, then applause. This time

Mrs. Nicholson was too busy scribbling on her pad to hold up her hand. Finally, when the applause had died away on its own, Mrs. Nicholson stopped writing and said, "Thank you, Kerry Ann. Is it Kerry Ann or just Kerry?"

"Just Kerry, usually."

"Kerry, then. I'd like you to do the last scene now, just a bit of it, with Kent, but with more authority. I'd like to see Elizabeth a little surer of herself. She'd like to seem that way to John in that scene, even though she doubts herself. Do you understand?"

"I—I think so," said Kerry.

She looks scared, Jan thought, scared but determined. It was a difficult scene, in which Elizabeth refuses to tell John whether or not he should sign a confession that would, if signed, save him from hanging.

"Splendid," said Mrs. Nicholson. "Let's try it, then."

Kerry sounded even more convincing this time.

"Some people are good readers and lousy actors," Ted remarked on the way home; Jan was driving her mother's car this time, having borrowed it for the day. "You've said that yourself, often."

"Yeah." Jan slowed down at an intersection, then speeded up again. "That's true, but I don't think this kid's like that."

"You never know."

"Maybe, but I'd cast her if I were Mrs. Nicholson. She's so good I can't even dislike her! I want to hate her; I want to cut her up in little pieces and—and . . ."

"And throw her to the lions or flush her away. I know, Jan, I know." Ted put his arm around her.

"Don't do that while I'm driving," Jan said testily.

"How about stopping driving then?"

"Oh, come on, Ted!"

"Come on yourself," he said, his mood changing. "It's time we had a talk anyway."

"I don't want to talk," she said irritably. "I just want to go home."

"Jan, you'll get some kind of part; you always do. I've been wanting to have a real talk with you ever since you got back from stock, and I haven't because of tryouts. But tryouts are over."

"Can't you at least wait till the cast list goes up tomorrow?"

"I've got a dentist appointment after school tomorrow."

Jan sighed. He sounded so forlorn she suddenly felt sorry for him. "Okay. Where to?"

"The park. Down by the river. Anywhere. Doesn't matter."

Jan drove in silence to the wide river that flowed behind Southview, linking it to a medium-sized port city ten miles away. The air was even crisper now that the sun was beginning to set, and near the river the few prematurely red and orange leaves glowed brightly against the green ones. But Jan was too miserable to care.

She pulled the car to one side of the road and switched off the ignition. A small powerboat, in great need of paint, was chugging slowly downstream. She watched it, to avoid Ted.

"Hi." He touched her shoulder gently. "Hey, I'm sorry about that girl. But, like I said, you'll get something, even if you don't get Elizabeth. And aren't you going to have to get used to competition?"

"That's not what you made me come here to talk about," she said gruffly, shrugging his hand away. How could she tell him that it wasn't so much the idea of competition that bothered her as it was the nagging thought that she might not have as much talent as everyone had always told her she had?

"Jan, why do you always move away from me?"

"Do I?" she asked, startled. "I hadn't noticed. I've hardly seen you since I got back."

"Yes, you do. I know you've hardly seen me, believe me! And this year we don't even have any classes together."

"Is that what you wanted to talk about?"

"Sort of." Ted put his hand under Jan's chin and turned her face toward his.

She started in surprise. They'd never touched much, except for that one awkward time last spring. He'd kissed her and then tried to go further, and she'd bolted—but this time she was so startled she let him turn her. His eyes were as troubled as she'd ever seen them, and she tried to concentrate on what he was saying, but it was too soon after tryouts. Lines from *Crucible* were still repeating themselves in her head—Elizabeth's lines, in Kerry's voice.

"Jan, we're seniors," she finally heard him say, smoothly, as if he'd rehearsed it. "Don't you think it's time we started talking about going steady?"

She felt herself blink in astonishment. "Going—going steady?" she repeated stupidly. "But we're not even 'going' at all!"

"We see each other nearly every day. We did most of last year, anyway. It could be nights, too."

Jan shook her head vigorously, surprised at the strength of her sudden panic. "No!" she told him, not meaning to say it so emphatically. "No."

"But—but why?" Ted fumbled. "Why, Jan? We've known each other so long, we're friends, we care about each other. Don't we? I hardly dated anyone else last year; you didn't date at all. I thought—well, I . . ." He broke off, his face red and miserable.

This is Ted, this is Teddy Bear, Jan thought, miserable

25

herself. She put her hand lightly on his arm, though she couldn't think what to answer. "I'm sorry," she said at last, trying to be honest. "I do care about you, Ted. But I guess I don't want to date anyone."

Ted took her hand and stroked it as if he had wanted to for a long time. She, surprised again, let her hand lie limply in his, embarrassed and uncomfortable, but not wanting to hurt him anymore.

"Why?" he asked again. "Why don't you want to date?"

She watched the powerboat again. Except for feeling left out once in a while on weekends when she knew everyone else was partying, it had never bothered her much. When it did, all she had to do was read a play and she'd forget.

Maybe that was it.

"Theater," she answered tentatively. "I don't have time, or room, I guess, for anything else."

Ted turned her face toward his again, and before she realized what was going to happen, he'd pulled her close the way he had last spring. He kissed her, first gently, then hard.

She felt her body stiffen; she wanted to pull away, but he gripped her shoulders firmly, so she waited, feeling trapped and struggling for air.

Abruptly, Ted let her go. "Okay," he said, facing the river. The powerboat, Jan noticed as she surreptitiously wiped her damp mouth, had moved around a bend and was nearly out of sight. "I don't think that's it," he said, "but okay."

She heard the pain in his voice, felt sorry for him again, and said so. She wanted to touch him, comfort him, as a friend, but didn't dare now. Had he always thought she meant something else whenever she'd squeezed his hand or patted his shoulder?

"Ted, you're—we've been so close," she began hesitantly. "It's . . ."

"I know," he said ruefully. "It's incestuous, right? We're like brother and sister, or something."

"I'm sorry."

"Yeah, okay."

"Ted . . ."

"It's okay, Jan. Let's go, huh?"

Jan turned the car engine on again and drove Ted home in silence.

The next morning, the cast list went up.

It was a few minutes before Jan could ease her way through the crowd around it. Will Omlin, right in front of her, muttered, "Cheever? That must be the smallest part in the whole play!" Then, giving Jan a look she couldn't read, he bolted down the hall.

Jan had to skim the list twice before she could find her name, though she had no trouble seeing Kent's name after John Proctor's. Ted was to play eighty-three-year-old Giles Corey; Nanny, gentle, elderly Rebecca Nurse; Brenda, Abigail, as everyone had expected—she'd read surprisingly well—and Kerry, Jan saw through suddenly rising tears she immediately struggled to blink back, Elizabeth Proctor.

"*Janna Montcrief*," she saw finally, at the bottom, below the cast and heading the crew. "*Stage Manager/Assistant Director.*"

No part. No part at all.

THREE

❧

IT WAS DARK AND silent on the stage, as in an empty church. On the other side of the thick act curtain, a chorus rehearsal was in progress. Jan could just hear the muffled voice of Mrs. Dunson, the music teacher, preparing to warm up her singers. There was no set on the stage yet, just a pile of wood-framed canvas flats leaning against the blue back wall, painted that way so it could double as a cyclorama. The tormentors, heavy curtains on each side of the stage masking the backstage area, swayed softly; a window was open near the old-fashioned light board. There'd been talk for years about replacing it with a computerized one, but the school committee kept allocating the money to other things.

Jan closed the window, thinking dully that it wouldn't be good for rain to come in on the board. If it should happen to rain.

She put her hand on a dimmer handle, saw that the main switch was off, moved the handle slowly as if she were taking a light cue, then returned it to its original position. Her introduction to theater, back when she'd been a freshman, had been at this board, when she'd run lights for the dramatic

28

club's spring one-acters. It had been like playing music to dim the big Lekos and the smaller Fresnels down slowly, making the stage gradually dark, or to bring a single dramatic spotlight up on an important character.

"Magic time," Jan whispered.

She went over to the sound console and ran her hand over its controls. She'd have to learn about them if she was going to stage manage.

Not that there were a lot of sound effects in *Crucible*.

" 'I cannot think the Devil may own a woman's soul, Mr. Hale,' " she said softly, quoting her favorite speech of Elizabeth's, " 'when she keeps an upright way, as I have. I am a good woman, I know it; and . . .' " Jan's voice strengthened as she walked onstage, oblivious to the chorus, who had now begun vocalizing—" 'and if you believe I may do only good work in the world, and yet be secretly bound to Satan, then I must tell you, sir, I do not believe it.' "

"You wanted Elizabeth," said a voice behind her.

Jan wheeled; it was Kerry.

"I'm so sorry." Kerry's eyes met Jan's and she reached out sympathetically. "I didn't know, I . . ."

"It's okay," Jan said thickly, turning away. "You were good. You deserve it."

"You were good, too," Kerry said to her back. "The kids say you were in summer stock, that you're almost a professional. It must be awful, Jan—Montcrief, isn't it?"

"Right," Jan answered, but she wished Kerry would go away. It made it worse, knowing that she understood.

"Jan, it's not fair. I just did it for fun. I bet the only reason I got it, really, is that I look like Miller's idea of Elizabeth, a little. Or someone's, Mrs. Nicholson's. I'm not at all like her inside. I . . ."

Jan faced her now, noticing again Kerry's clear skin and

her softly shining hair, twisted today into a single braid that fell over her shoulder. "Don't," she pleaded. "Please don't. I'll be all right. There's a saying that there are no small parts, only small actors. I'm just up here trying to remind myself of that."

"But you didn't get a part at all!" Kerry cried indignantly. "That's not fair. You're better than any of us; you have more experience. Nanny, that girl who got Rebecca Nurse? She said everyone was sure you'd get Elizabeth—that Mrs. Nicholson almost promised you would last spring. I—I feel awful about it, really, I . . ."

"Don't feel awful. I told you that you were good. Actually, you were almost perfect."

"It was luck," said Kerry. "I'm terrified of it now. I even tried to read it again at home and it sounded terrible. I wish I could give it back to you." Quickly, Kerry left the stage.

Jan buried her head in the soft velour of a torm. It's all going away, she thought, falling apart. First Ted, then Elizabeth. Or maybe the other way around. I don't know . . .

Mrs. Dunson played a loud chord on the auditorium piano. The chorus, released from their exercises, burst lustily into song.

After school the next afternoon, Jan watched Mrs. Nicholson let herself heavily down into the chair at her desk in the English and Speech office. Her hands, as they sorted through a pile of scripts, seemed thinner than Jan remembered them; they shook slightly, making her rings slip. The words "villain, villain, smiling, damned villain" from *Hamlet* popped into Jan's head, but she suppressed them quickly, determined not to show disappointment or anger.

"Do you know how to make a prompt book out of these

silly acting editions?" Mrs. Nicholson asked, handing Jan two scripts.

"Yes."

"Good. I want you to be a real stage manager, not just a high-school prompter, you know. That means hard work—writing down blocking and all tech cues and scene changes; it means cueing the crew during performances and being in charge backstage, et cetera, et cetera, et cetera. I'm sure you know." She handed Jan a ring binder and a stack of three-hole paper sheets on which to paste the acting-edition pages. "You'll be my brain, in other words," Mrs. Nicholson said, looking through the window at the thin rain that was now falling outside. "You'll know everything I do about the show, technical and otherwise. You'll keep track of how each character develops so you can take over for me if I miss a rehearsal. Any time an actor's absent, you'll read that part."

Not Elizabeth, Jan thought. Please not Elizabeth.

Mrs. Nicholson turned away from the rain. "It'll be so *good* to have a proper stage manager. You're the first student I've dared trust with the job in all my years of teaching. I know, Janna," she said. "I know you're disappointed, and maybe very, very angry. I probably shouldn't have let you read, but until I saw and heard Kerry, I didn't know this—er—arrangement—would be possible." Her eyes were unnaturally bright, as if with unshed tears. "If I told you this will strengthen you, you would tell me, rightly, that you'll have plenty of time to be strengthened when you're pounding pavement in New York looking for jobs that don't come. But, Janna, this is a school with others in it besides you, and there are still dramatic club's one-act plays in the spring."

"They're not *Crucible*," Jan said bitterly before she could stop herself. "They're not even a major production. They're not Elizabeth. And last year you almost said . . ."

"I know. But that new girl is the image of Elizabeth. And she's good."

"Better than I am."

Mrs. Nicholson studied Jan closely. "Don't ever doubt your talent," she said. "You have the makings of a fine actress. I'm going to tell you something you won't believe, but that I want you to remember. Someday you won't be satisfied with just acting. You'll want something more, something more creative. This will help you prepare for that."

"Stage managing!" Jan exclaimed. "That's not creative, that's . . ."

"It's one step removed from directing, Janna. And . . ." Mrs. Nicholson fingered her pendant, a heavy green stone set in gold. "I need you to help me on this show. Also, just to make for good cast-crew morale, I think I should tell you that Kerry Ann Socrides came to me this morning and asked me to give you Elizabeth, and that I refused."

Jan stared at her. "But why?" she managed to ask finally. "Why did she do that?"

"Oh, my dear, I don't know her reasons! But I refused because I gave her the part, not you, and because I made you stage manager, not her. It sounds stubborn, I know, but— you'll understand someday, perhaps. And now," she said, pushing her chair back heavily and reaching into a drawer, "I have to work out a rehearsal schedule. Even though the play's not till nearly Christmas, it's a difficult one and we're going to need all the time we can wangle. I anticipate more than the usual number of arguments with academic teachers about homework, and—Janna, dear, trust me. Please."

Jan didn't—couldn't—react. She didn't want to argue with

32

Mrs. Nicholson; she knew she'd either lose or say something she'd be sorry about later. But she didn't want to pretend to agree with her when she didn't. "May I go now?" she asked thickly.

"Yes, of course," said Mrs. Nicholson, and Jan left.

And, unknown to Jan, when the door was tightly closed again, Mrs. Nicholson put her head down on her desk and wept silently for a minute before she returned to her scripts and her schedules.

FOUR

MONDAY WAS WET AND windy, fitting Jan's mood. She overslept, forgetting that she couldn't count on Ted anymore to
drive her to school; at least she assumed she couldn't. She'd
arranged to borrow her mother's car several times a week and
to take the bus the rest of the time. Because she overslept,
she left without breakfast. Then she realized she'd forgotten
a book, and when she went back for it, she tramped mud all
over a rug her mother had just vacuumed—which reminded
her that her father was coming home from his long business
trip that night and that her sister and brother-in-law were
coming for dinner. An evening with Anita, Hal, and Dad was
the last thing Jan wanted to come home to after an afternoon
of seeing someone else play her part.

But it's not your part, she scolded herself all morning, trying to concentrate on her classes; it's not your part. She
thought it again as Kerry walked cheerfully by, carrying her
new script on top of her books. *Not my part,* she thought,
too, when Kent waved laconically to her at lunch—waved
but didn't go over to her and say he was sorry or even congratulate her for being stage manager.

34

"Hi, green eyes," Ted said when she went into the auditorium for rehearsal that afternoon.

Jan, recognizing his reference to "jealousy . . . the green-ey'd monster" from *Othello*, bit her lip to keep from saying something cutting to him, and walked two rows past him to sit down. Another time she might have asked, "Does it show?" and he'd probably have said, "No, just to me. It must be awful for you." Another time—but now she couldn't be sure what he meant anymore, or how he felt.

Kerry came in with Kent and Will; Kent, with unusual animation, seemed to be pointing something out in the script. Jan pretended to hunt for a pencil, then went to the back row to ask Brenda if she could borrow one.

"You poor thing!" Brenda gushed as she held one out. "What's a stage manager do, anyway?" But Jan sensed that she didn't really want an answer. Brenda's eyes were on Kent, devouring him.

"Helps the director during rehearsals," Jan said, trying to make light of it. "And runs things backstage during performances. It'll be kind of neat, actually. I've never done it."

"We'd both better keep an eye on that Kerry." Brenda gestured toward where Kerry and Kent were still deep in conversation. "I don't know about you, but I have no intention of letting her get her mitts on Kent the way she did on your part. Look at the way she's watching him!"

Jan looked, but it seemed more to her that Kent was trying to impress Kerry and Kerry wasn't buying it. Then Kent focused on the back of the auditorium, and Jan knew Mrs. Nicholson was about to make one of her famous first-rehearsal entrances. She sat down quickly next to Brenda, determined to enjoy that, at least.

"Good afternoon," boomed Mrs. Nicholson from the auditorium door. Then, with a swirl of long red plaid skirt, she swept down the center aisle, again carrying scripts, papers, pencils, and clipboard, talking as she came, welcoming them to the first rehearsal, saying the usual things about working hard and being on time and letting her know if they were going to be absent and telling them there might be a couple of extra rehearsals after Thanksgiving. Then, reaching the stage, she sailed onto it via a step unit that had been set up on the auditorium floor, put her books and papers down on the table that was waiting for her center stage, and with another swirl of her skirt pivoted around to face them.

The effect was electric; no one in the auditorium moved.

"This," intoned Mrs. Nicholson dramatically, holding up a script, "is a great play." She paused long enough to lock eyes quickly but piercingly with each of them in turn. "We have never done a great play in this school. It is a play about misguided power and the cruelty of falsehood, and about the sin of blindly following the common herd. I trust we will all be equal to the task before us."

She looked piercingly at them again, giving Jan goosebumps, and then stepped back with one foot, turning her body slightly upstage and making her full skirt swing sharply around her legs in a flash of red. Gesturing at the double circle of chairs behind her, she said, "On stage, please. Cast in the inner circle, crew in the outer. Janna, you sit in the inner circle next to me."

The first reading began.

And when they got to the end, where Elizabeth watches John's unjustified execution through a window and cries out, "He have his goodness now. God forbid I take it from him!" Jan felt limp with the play's power. Mrs. Nicholson's right, she thought, about its being a great play. Everyone was silent; even Kent seemed moved, the thin line of his mouth unusually taut. Jan glanced out of habit at Ted and saw he was looking at her. "Hi," he mouthed, so she went to him as soon as Mrs. Nicholson said quietly, "Let's all take ten minutes."

"Truce?" said Jan, following him to the fire exit.

"Always," he answered, gazing out at the rain. "You know that. For what it's worth, it was dumb of me to say 'green eyes.' I'm sorry. It's just that I don't know quite how to react to you now. And I guess I have to convince myself I don't care. But I know saying crummy things isn't the way. Okay?"

"Okay."

He faced her then. "I've always kind of liked Nanny Davis anyway. And since she's in *Crucible*, too, I ought to be able to get to know her. Think she'll go out with me?"

"She's not going with anyone else, I'm pretty sure," Jan said. And Nanny, she realized, would be perfect for Ted. Her gentleness hid a quiet strength, Jan was sure; she had a sense of humor—yes, Nanny was a fine choice. She was well cast, too, as Rebecca Nurse.

"I'm glad you're playing Giles Corey, Ted," Jan said. "It's a good part."

Ted laughed. "Well, since I'll be hidden behind a ton of makeup and have lines drawn all over my face and white glop in my hair, it shouldn't matter too much. No one'll know who I am anyway."

Jan laughed, too. "There's always the program," she said.

"Yeah, but there's always pseudonyms. I'm thinking of calling myself Reginald Spotswoodie. Like it?"

Jan pretended to consider it. "Not quite right," she said. "Spotswood, I think. The *ie* part seems too frivolous for Giles. After all, he may be a grouchy old man, but he ends up a hero of sorts."

"Oh, right! Pressed to death offstage, with a ton of rocks on his chest. Ugh!" He shivered.

"Be glad it's *off*stage. Come on, Teddy, it's a great part."

"It's a great play." Ted leaned against the fire door. "As Mrs. Nicholson said. I just hope she can do it. She seems kind of tired or something. Old, maybe. Older, anyway."

Jan turned, studying Mrs. Nicholson as she spoke earnestly with Nanny and Ms. Grillo, the art teacher, who would be supervising the work on the set and costumes. Now that Mrs. Nicholson wasn't actually directing them, Jan had to admit that she did seem older, and she remembered her face had looked strained and pale at tryouts. But except for maybe being a little thinner, and for her hands shaking once or twice, she'd seemed fine since then, and fine when she'd been talking about the play or taking notes while they read.

"So what?" Jan said stubbornly. "I bet none of us will be as lively as she is when we're her age."

"She's only fifty."

"So what?" Jan repeated. "How do you know how old she is, anyway?"

"Kent looked her up in an old *Who's Who* or something, and told me. But fifty's not old. I bet your own mother's close to fifty."

Jan studied Mrs. Nicholson again. Anita was twenty-two and her mother had had her when she'd been twenty-three, which made Mom forty-five, not fifty—but that wasn't the point. She knew perfectly well that fifty wasn't old enough to *look* old, and again she wondered about Mrs. Nicholson's summer: had something bad happened?

"Jan," said Ted as Mrs. Nicholson slowly stood and called them back to the stage, this time to discuss their characters. "Jan, I'm not going to give up, you know. If it takes me all year, I'm not going to give up on you and me, Nanny notwithstanding. Nanny's just for fun."

He walked away before she'd had time to absorb what he'd

said, and by the time she did absorb it, it was too late to call off the truce.

Her father's craggy face beamed at Jan from the door, and he hugged her, dripping slicker and all.

"Sorry I'm late," she muttered against his chest.

"I can't even be mad," he answered, pushing her gently back by the shoulders, the deep vertical wrinkles in his cheeks crinkling deeper with his smile. "How are you? Here —let's get rid of that sodden garment." He helped her out of her slicker, flung it carelessly on the hall chair, where it would be sure to drip on the floor, and reached down—he was over six feet tall—to put his arm around her. Apparently not remembering he'd just asked her how she was, he asked her again as he led her into the living room, where her sister Anita, a flowered maternity smock billowing over her swollen belly, sat on the sofa across from her husband, Hal.

"Look what I found out in the rain," Dad said, still beaming. "The family actress, fresh from her latest triumph!"

Does he know, Jan wondered as she bent to kiss Anita and Hal, that I didn't get Elizabeth? Does he even know what play we're doing?

"Look how big I am, Jan," Anita said proudly, patting her belly. "Remember you said last June you didn't believe I was three months pregnant? Believe me now?"

"I sure do." Jan grinned; she was fond of Anita, even though there were too many years between them for them to have been really close.

"Sit next to me, Jan." Anita made a little-girl pout with her palely lipsticked lips. "I'm sick of talking to these boring men. Let me tell you the latest names for your new niece or nephew."

"Not," said Hal, "before she fills us in on her summer, eh, Jan? People have babies all the time, honey, but they don't go to summer stock. Right, Jan?"

"Right," Jan answered. Hal was sweet, really, and he meant well, but sometimes she wished he wouldn't try quite so hard to be chummy.

"Hey"—Hal leaned forward—"pretty good crop of boys there in stock, huh? I bet you gave them quite a time."

"Not really." She couldn't resist adding, "Most of them were gay."

Hal looked shocked, his conspiratorial wink stopped halfway.

"Jan," said Anita, "that's not nice. Those people are to be pitied, not laughed at."

"Who's laughing?" Jan said, now annoyed. She thought of how ludicrous it would be to pity Raphael, and, her bad mood deepening, she added, "Some of my best friends are homosexuals. I think I'll go see if Mom needs any help. Excuse me."

Jan had two cups of strong coffee at dinner, and they kept her awake till after two. Toward morning, she had her summer-stock dream again, except that the characters in it changed from Raphael and Corrin to Ted and Kerry and back again.

It must have been the coffee, she thought, waking in the familiar miserable sweat.

FIVE

꒦꒷꒦

"ALL RIGHT, KENT; good. Hold it there." Mrs. Nicholson leaned against the stage-right side of the proscenium, shifting her script from one hand to the other. It was the next week, and they were blocking out the movements in Elizabeth's first scene. Jan had expected to have trouble watching Kerry, but she found that she was so busy she felt only an occasional pang at being out front instead of onstage. Mrs. Nicholson had already let her go over some complicated first-act blocking with the cast. And she'd been pleased when Jan had made a suggestion that cleared up an awkward move, so Jan was paying careful attention now, trying to be alert to potential problems.

"Kerry," Mrs. Nicholson was saying, "turn away left on your line—no, no, not yet, *on* the line, as you say it, on . . ." The script fluttered to the floor and Mrs. Nicholson bent, oddly graceless, to pick it up. "Damnit," she said through clenched teeth, though Jan had rarely heard her swear. "I've lost the place."

" 'Good, then, let you think on it,' " Jan prompted quickly, giving both Mrs. Nicholson and Kerry the line.

Jan saw Kerry nod and then rub her shoulders after she'd made a mark in her script. No wonder, she thought; her shoulders must be stiff, the way she's been hunching them. It was becoming more and more clear to her that although Kerry's voice and line readings suggested Elizabeth perfectly, her body did not.

"'Good, then, let you think on it,'" said Kerry, forgetting to move till after she'd said it. Then she made a tense, awkward turn, in the wrong direction and not like Elizabeth at all.

Kent shot his arm out in obvious exasperation. "*Left,*" he snapped, spinning Kerry around roughly. "*Left,* for Pete's sake."

"I'm sorry," Kerry gasped. "I get mixed up between left and right anyway, and stage left and right mix me up even more. I'm sorry."

Jan was suddenly angry; Kent could be such a jerk sometimes. It was one thing for someone who was professional enough and confident enough to give it right back to him, but . . .

Mrs. Nicholson had sat down and still seemed to be hunting for her place in the script, so Jan vaulted up onto the stage. "Kerry," she said, glaring at Kent, "stage left and right are from your point of view, as you face the audience. And" —she searched Kerry's hands for a ring or some other thing that would help her tell the difference at least till she learned the move—"and your left wrist's the one with the watch. Elizabeth turns this way," she said, demonstrating. "Toward your watch. Okay?"

"Very clever," Kent said dryly.

Kerry smiled gratefully as Jan jumped down off the stage, ignoring Kent. "Okay," Kerry said. "Thank you."

"Take it again," said Mrs. Nicholson as Jan returned to her seat in the first row. "A few lines back. Jan?"

"How about from Proctor's line 'I'll think on it'?"

"Good," said Mrs. Nicholson, and Kent shouted, " 'I'll think on it!' " before Kerry was in position.

" 'Good, then, let you think on it,' " said Kerry, jumping two lines and turning first the wrong way, then the right one.

Kent rolled his eyes and strode dramatically downstage. "Shall I skip to where she skipped to, or go back, or what?" he asked Mrs. Nicholson with a long-suffering grimace. "Seems to me we *both* ought to get this scene right."

"Seems to me," muttered Jan under her breath, "that you could be more patient."

"I agree," Mrs. Nicholson muttered back. "We'll break here," she announced, "for a few minutes. Ted, Will, the rest of you, we'll go right on with the remainder of Act Two when we finish this scene, so don't go away. Kerry and Kent, come over here, please." Then, turning to Jan, she said in an undertone, "Do you think you could calm Kerry down a bit while I tell our male prima donna he's not quite Kevin Costner yet?"

"Sure," said Jan.

"If you could find some time to coach her on how to move," said Mrs. Nicholson, "it might help. All her stage presence is in her voice, heaven help us. I should have realized that," she added apologetically to Jan. "If I had, then maybe . . ."

"She's nervous," Jan said quickly; she didn't want to think about that now. "She'll probably be okay once she gets used to what she's doing."

"I hope so." Mrs. Nicholson got up as Kent and Kerry approached, and, taking Kent's arm, she led him to the back of the auditorium.

Kerry sat down despondently beside Jan. "As an actress," she said, "I make a pretty good biologist."

"Is that what you want to be?" Jan asked, realizing that Mrs. Nicholson was leaving it up to her to broach the subject of coaching Kerry. She wondered how she could do that tactfully.

"No," Kerry answered. "I just said it because I couldn't think of anything else. I like biology, but not that much. About Elizabeth—tell me what to do."

"Just try to relax, first of all. It's only a rehearsal. No one expects you to be perfect."

"Kent does."

"Kent's a bag of wind sometimes."

"Yeah."

"And try to loosen those shoulders a bit." She touched Kerry's left shoulder lightly and then drew her hand away, surprised to find even more tension there than she'd expected. "Waggle your arms around before you go on, or bend down and swing them, anything to get the kinks out. And look, here's an easy trick. Never move when you're not talking, unless the director tells you to, or unless you feel it's really right. In other words, as a general rule, move only while you're actually saying a line, not before or after. Okay?"

Kerry sighed. "Okay. I feel like such an oaf up there."

"You shouldn't," said Jan, liking her. "You're not clumsy offstage."

"No, but when I get up there I feel like the whole world's staring at me. Dumb, I know, but there you are."

"Would it help," asked Jan in as offhand a way as she could, "if we—you and me, I mean—went over your scenes sometime, maybe ran through your blocking? It might make you feel more comfortable about it."

"Sure! That'd be great! I was hoping you'd want to do that, but I didn't dare ask. I know I'm playing what you wanted to play, and . . ."

"Maybe that's what's hanging you up, Kerry. Look, I don't care that much anymore. I like doing this, stage managing and stuff. It's fun."

"You're sure?"

Jan realized then that the last of her resentment had vanished. She'd always wish she could have played Elizabeth, she knew, but it didn't hurt anymore. "Yes," she told Kerry. "I'm sure."

"Okay."

"You're so good at reading lines. It's just a question of the rest of you catching up."

"Okay," Kerry said again. "When can we start?"

"Tomorrow after school? Mrs. Nicholson has a doctor's appointment, so there's no rehearsal."

"Sure."

It was odd knowing she was going to be working with just one person instead of with a group as she'd done during the first-act blocking rehearsals, and it would be especially odd working without Mrs. Nicholson there. Jan couldn't figure out, as she went into the auditorium and switched on the houselights, whether the boiling in her stomach meant she was excited or nervous.

After a few minutes of waiting for Kerry, she got up from her usual front-row seat and climbed onto the stage. She stood for a moment down center, head bowed, then snapped her head up and, lifting her arms high, felt the tragic strength of Medea, one of the great classical parts she'd been told by the acting teacher at stock that she was too short to play. Her clear voice filled the auditorium:

I will look at the light of the sun, this last time. I wish
     from that blue sky the white wolf of lightning
Would leap, and burst my skull and my brain, and like a
     burning babe cling to these breasts . . .
Someone is here? I did not know I had visitors . . . Women
     of Corinth:
If anything has been spoken too loudly here, consider
That I believed I was alone; and I have some provocation.
     You've come—let me suppose
With love and sympathy—to peer at my sorrow. I under-
     stand well enough
That nothing is ever private in a Greek city; whoever with-
     holds anything
Is thought sullen or proud . . . undemocratic
I think you call it. This is not always just, but we know that
     justice, at least on earth,
Is a name, not a fact; and as for me, I wish to avoid any
     appearance
Of being . . . proud. Of what? Of affliction? I will show you
     my naked heart . . .

Then she switched to Medea's nurse, a part she'd played in
scene class in stock, and liked almost as well:

I wish the long ship Argo had never passed that perilous
     channel between the Symplegades,
I wish the pines that made her mast and her oars still
     waved in the wind on Mount Pelion, and the gray
     fishhawk
Still nested in them, the great adventurers had never
     voyaged

46

Into the Asian sunrise to the shores of morning for the
    Golden Fleece.

For then my mistress Medea
Would never have seen Jason nor loved and saved him, nor
    cut herself off from home to come with him
Into this country of the smiling chattering Greeks and the
    roofs of Corinth: over which I see evil
Hang like a cloud. For she is not meek but fierce, and the
    daughter of a king.

A muffled thump in the auditorium broke her concentration and made her angry at herself because nothing should ever be able to do that. Then she noticed Kerry standing halfway down the center aisle, her long braid over one shoulder and her eyes riveted on Jan. "Go on," she said quietly. "That was beautiful. I dropped a book," she added apologetically. "But please go on."

Jan crouched, her hand on the stage floor, and jumped lightly down. "Nope," she said. "I was just killing time."

"You—you're so good."

"But so are you!" Jan exclaimed, meaning it. "Look, I'm not the most graceful person who ever walked across a stage either. I sure wasn't at first; I was just as awkward as you. It takes practice and confidence, that's all."

"I hope so," said Kerry. "I do want to be good, Jan. It's more than just fun now; I want you to know that. I want to be good partly to justify getting the part in the first place, and partly because—well, I guess I just want to be good for my own sake."

"That's a fine start," Jan said briskly. "Okay. Let's walk through your blocking. Come on." She jumped back onto the stage and held her hand out to Kerry, pulling her up. "I'll read John."

They worked for more than an hour and by the end of that time Kerry was moving as if she'd begun to feel she had a right to be on a stage.

Playing opposite her, Jan realized after a while, was as satisfying as playing opposite Kent—maybe even more, as Kerry's self-consciousness diminished and her confidence grew. Kerry, unlike most inexperienced actors, seemed instinctively to know how to listen and react.

At around five-thirty they stopped, and suddenly Jan was the one who felt awkward, as if there were nothing to say.

Kerry sat on the apron, dangling her feet over the edge of the stage. "It's like sitting on a giant curbstone," she said. "We're three inches high. Look, there goes a car!" She followed a gigantic imaginary car with her eyes. "Oh," she squealed. "It splashed me! Help, I'm drowning!"

Jan, mentally shrinking herself to three inches high, too, grabbed Kerry's hands and pulled her to center stage; Kerry gurgled dramatically and lay still. Jan rolled her back and forth, as if to get the water out. "Careful," she said, as Kerry came to dizzily, "you'll bump into that twig. Wait—there's a daisy over here. Better lean against it for a minute."

Kerry pretended to lean against the daisy. She seemed perfectly relaxed now, as much at ease as she'd been that first day in the cafeteria when Ted had pointed her out.

"Here's a petal," said Jan, watching her closely. "Fan yourself with that."

Kerry took the imaginary petal carefully by one end and waved it back and forth at just about the right distance from her face.

"You know," Jan told her, surprised and pleased, "you're doing fine now. Perfect control. No awkwardness."

"You almost made me drop the petal," Kerry said, still fanning.

"Here." Jan held out her hand. "I'm giving you an acorn."

But Kerry refused it. "You grew," she said reproachfully. "Get small again."

"You're right." Jan adjusted in size, holding the "acorn" in both hands now, as if it were heavy. "Here you are. I bet if we could get it open we could eat some of the inside. I'm hungry."

This time Kerry took the acorn, and they continued the improvisation, developing it into a story with a squirrel for a villain, until the custodian switched off the houselights from backstage and they both shouted in indignation. "Hey," Jan yelled, "don't lock us in!"

"Sorry, miss," came an elderly voice from somewhere behind the stage-right torms. "Didn't know you were there. Turn the lights off when you leave, would you?"

A few minutes later, outside, Jan walked Kerry in silence to the rack where Kerry had left her bike. The leaves were crunchy underfoot, the darkening sky just slightly pink.

"Today seems important." Kerry leaned pensively against the rack. "I don't know why. It just seems important."

Jan nodded; she felt it, too. "There's only one other person outside of theater I've ever been able to do improvs like that with," she said, thinking of Ted. "And he's not as quick as you. Are you sure you never wanted to act?"

"I want to do everything," Kerry said, "not one thing. I want to feel everything, be everything. Like Faust. Did you ever read *Faust*?"

"No," said Jan, deciding that she would.

"He's the main character in this long German play, by Goethe. He wants to experience everything there is to experience—good, evil, everything. I'm like that, I guess." Kerry looked quizzically at Jan. "What are you like?"

This is weird, Jan thought; people don't talk like this. I don't talk like this to people I don't know—to Raphael, maybe; once to Ted—but somehow this is different . . .

Still, she found herself answering with complete honesty. "I want to act, to be in theater. Theater is—it's all I am. I'm nothing without it."

Kerry touched Jan's arm, then moved away. "That's why," she said.

"Why what?"

"Why today is special. Important. Because we're both strange. Strange in different ways, but strange. Not like the others." Kerry put her hands behind her on the bike rack and jumped up, sitting on it. "Everyone in my family *does* something. My mother used to be a microbiologist and now she's just graduated from divinity school. She and my father are in Europe, traveling around to celebrate. My father's head of a plastics company. 'Fantasies in Plastics,' they say in their ads. He's always inventing new novelties. I've got an uncle who's mayor of a town in the Midwest, and his wife's a big-deal lawyer. My other aunt—she's who I'm staying with till my folks come back in January and we go back to Boston, where we live—my aunt's kind of silly and eccentric, but she runs a gift shop. Do, do, do—no one *is*, everyone just does. You're another doer. But," she added, "you're not like them. You seem to care more about what you do—to love it. I don't think any of them really cares, not deeply. With them— maybe not my aunt so much—it's the doing itself that seems important, not *what* they're doing."

"I care, all right," Jan said emphatically.

"Too much?"

Jan shrugged. She was still thinking how strange the con-

50

versation was. But she was drawn to it nonetheless, to Kerry's intensity, and to Kerry herself. And she didn't want them to stop talking, so when Kerry fell silent and jumped down to strap her books onto her bike carrier, Jan said, "Did you really mean that, about experiencing everything? I mean, how about things like murder and war and insanity—rape—things like that?"

"Maybe I draw the line at rape and murder," Kerry said after a minute in which Jan realized she was actually considering them. "But yes, I think I do. At least enough to become a person."

"If I did any of those things," Jan told her, "it would be for a part or to become a better actress."

"Quite a pair," said Kerry, "aren't we? Can we work together again, on Elizabeth?"

"Yes, I'd like to." Jan realized she was already looking forward to seeing more of Kerry. "You don't need much more work, though. But I could cue you, help you learn your lines."

"Sure." Kerry straddled her bike seat, then threw her head back, tossing her long braid loosely behind her. "Look." She pointed to the now dark sky. "The moon's rising. We met by the rising of the moon."

"Dreamer!" But Jan felt herself smiling. "We met in Room 206, at tryouts. I first saw you in the cafeteria the first day of school."

"Pedant!" Kerry cried. "Hopeless, hopeless pedant! For an actress, you have no sense of poetry—poesy, whatever." She threw her head back again, shoulders, too, this time. Jan found herself noticing the curve of Kerry's throat, and she turned away, her face suddenly hot in the cool air.

"I love fall," Kerry said. "Don't you? Well, do you?" she asked. "It's important."

"Why?" Jan laughed self-consciously. "Sure, I love fall. Re-

OUT-OF-DOOR ACADEMY
444 REID STREET
SARASOTA, FLORIDA 34242

ally," she insisted, when Kerry seemed skeptical. "Honest."

"Good." Kerry pointed to the sky again. "Then it's a good moon rising." She touched Jan's arm lightly again and said, "I have to go. Work with me again tomorrow? At lunchtime? I don't think Mrs. Nicholson's doing any of my scenes, but I'll probably go to rehearsal anyway. The more I know about the play, the better."

"Sure." Jan felt like shouting, running—dancing, even. "Tomorrow, at lunch."

SIX

❧

AS THE FALL PROGRESSED, Jan saw more of Kerry and less of Ted, even during rehearsals. By mid-October she found herself thinking of Kerry at odd moments during the day, writing notes to her, storing up things to tell her, jokes and anecdotes to laugh about with her. They began reading plays aloud together, and Kerry read Jan some of *Faust* late one night over the phone, then lent her the book. "Only one good woman's part," Jan joked when she returned it.

"If Sarah Bernhardt played Hamlet," said Kerry, "surely you or I could play Faust. Especially you."

So they took turns reading from *Faust*, after rehearsals on the darkened stage, using the slowly growing *Crucible* set as a background.

Toward the end of the month, when the ground was covered with red and gold leaves and pumpkins began appearing on porches, posters went up around school announcing what was billed as a "Junior–Senior Get-Acquainted Dance" in November. "It should be called a Veterans' Day dance," Ted explained, "since that's when it is. 'Get-Acquainted Dance' was someone's idea of a joke. You know, since the freshmen and sophomores have one in September."

"Blagh," said Jan.

But the day after that, Ted sauntered over to Kerry and Jan in the cafeteria. "Hi," he said, sliding a chair between them. "The show looks pretty good now, don't you think?"

Kerry, forced to move her chair to make room for his, murmured noncommittally.

"Yeah, not bad," said Jan. "You're doing great as Giles, by the way."

Ted bowed in his chair. "Why, thank you, madame stage manager–assistant director. Which doesn't really bring me to my next point, but hey, why not?" He turned to Kerry. "Kerry, would you excuse us for a sec? I'd like to talk to Jan, and I never get a chance at rehearsals anymore. And last night when I tried to call the phone was busy. I tried eight times."

"Talk," said Jan, annoyed; she'd been on the phone with Kerry, but that wasn't any business of Ted's. Besides, he could have asked to sit down instead of just barging in between them.

"It's kind of private."

"I don't have any secrets from Kerry," said Jan.

Kerry raised her eyebrows at Jan; Jan winked.

Ted's eyes went from one of them to the other. "What's going on?" he asked. "You two got some kind of secret society going or something?"

"Sure," Kerry said lightly. "It's called the SSS—Secret Society Society."

Ted was the only one who didn't laugh.

"Come on, Teddy," Jan said when they'd stopped. "Whatever it is, Kerry can hear it, too."

"I'm not used to asking girls out with other girls around," Ted said angrily.

"Other guys do," Jan said to Kerry, ignoring the mild feeling of dread that was worming its way into her stomach. "Don't they?"

"Sure," Kerry answered promptly. "Why, just the other day, that big creep on the football team—what's his name?"

"Creep Jones—no, Charley Jones," said Jan.

"Yeah, that's the one. He came right up to a whole bunch of junior girls and he said, 'Okay, women'—someone's told him not to say 'girls'—'Okay, women, which one of you is going to the dance with me?' "

"What aplomb," said Jan.

"Dash and panache." Kerry fluttered her eyelids and put on a phony voice. "I mean, like totally awesome."

"Of course everyone jumped at the chance," Jan said.

"Oh, absolutely. Simply leapt. But our hero lost his nerve, I guess, because he did a twenty-five-yard dash out the door. Of course the fact that Katy Jenkins was swinging at him and the rest of us were laughing hysterically had nothing to do with it."

"Nothing," Jan said solemnly.

Ted pushed his chair away from the table. "Look," he said, "send me a fax or something when this meeting of the SSS breaks up, okay?"

"Hey!" Jan caught his arm as he stood up. "Ted, I'm sorry."

"Yeah," said Kerry. "I am, too, Ted. That was mean. Jan and I just got carried away."

"Oh, I don't mind. Much."

Kerry got up. "Come on, Ted. Sit down. I give you Jan, okay? At least for now. I've got a class." She blew an exaggerated kiss at them both. "Farewell."

Ted watched her leave. "That is one weird kid," he said. "You sure pick 'em."

"She's doing okay in the play," Jan said defensively.

"Yeah, she's doing great. She ought to. She spends all her time with you, these days. Pretty weird for a junior."

"You know I'm coaching her," Jan said, angry again. "And she's our age—but you don't know that. I didn't either till she told me the other day. She missed a year because her parents were in this village in Turkey and the school there wasn't any good."

"Turkey! No wonder she's weird." Ted made a noise like a turkey.

Jan neither laughed nor made a noise back. By the time she realized that was what Ted expected, and knew it was what she'd usually have done, it was too late. "Her mother was working for some government health department or other," she told him. "She was a microbiologist."

"Oh." Ted sounded as if he were trying hard to stay interested. "She dead or something? You said 'was.' Maybe that's why Kerry's weird. Growing girls need their mothers, I hear."

Ted, Jan thought as she answered him testily, seems like he's growing down, not up, these days. "No," she said. "She's not dead. She's just not a microbiologist anymore."

"Look," said Ted, "I could make this conversation last all afternoon by asking what a microbiologist, who I happen to know usually sits in a lab all day surrounded by Petri dishes and electron microscopes, was doing in Turkey on a health project, but I've got a class, too, and I don't want to be late because I'm talking about your nutty friend. I want to ask you to the dance."

Aplomb, thought Jan. Dash and panache. Aloud she said bluntly, "I'm not going. Why don't you ask Nanny?"

"Of course you're going. Everyone's going."

"Ted, don't bully me!" Jan said, furious. Surprised at her own reaction, she got up and slammed her chair back into the table. "I said I'm not going, and I'm not."

Leaving an openmouthed Ted staring after her, she ran from the room, forgetting her books. He was still staring when she ran back and snatched them up.

"Well," said Kerry after rehearsal that afternoon, when the others had gone home, "you were pretty rotten to him, from what you say. Maybe you ought to apologize, for openers. I'd say that's a note from a hurt person who's trying not to show it."

Jan, who'd been talking about Ted while Kerry helped her put away the props the actors had been using, read the note again over Kerry's shoulder; she'd found it stuck to her clipboard after a break in rehearsal, during which Ted had left. "Madame," it said, "I do not wish to offend, but I would deem it a matter of infinite joy if you would honor my humble self with your presence at the dance we have, I believe, discussed. I miss you sore. Yr ob't etc., Ted."

"He likes you a lot, Jan."

"Yes, but I don't like him a lot. I mean, I do, but not that way."

Kerry raised her eyebrows. "What way, then?"

"He's a friend, that's all."

"Not to him, apparently." Kerry handed the note back to Jan. "Oh, heck, Jan, why don't you put the poor beast out of its misery and go to the silly dance?"

"You and I are going to the movies that night. Olivier's *Hamlet*, remember?"

"I sure do."

"Well, I'd rather do that."

"Would you?" Kerry asked.

"Yes," Jan answered defensively. "Is that so weird?"

"Some people would say so." Kerry faced Jan again. "Don't you know that?" she asked.

Jan fought not to let the thought through. "What? I—I . . ." she sputtered. "I don't know what you're talking about."

Kerry picked a small speck of dust off her suede jacket. "Are you sure? Don't you think some people would think it's weird that you'd rather be with me than with Ted?"

"No," Jan answered stubbornly. "You're my—friend. Aren't you?"

"Yes, of course," said Kerry. "But Ted's a boy. You're maybe saying you'd rather be with a girl than with a boy. At least some people would think that's what you're saying."

Jan closed her eyes. The thought came through after all, and her dream-image was suddenly there with it. "Yeah," she said after a moment. "Yeah, I do know." The dream-image stayed, and she opened her eyes again. "I know. Look, I've thought about it—or, rather, I've *not* thought about it. I don't want to think about it, I—oh, I don't know!"

"It's only fair," said Kerry quietly, "to tell you I've thought about it, too."

Her face was open, unsmiling, but her eyes hid nothing as, her voice very low, she said, "A good moon rising. I wonder."

SEVEN

COLD NOVEMBER SUN slanted dimly around the edges of the thick auditorium drapes. Jan shivered in spite of the wool blazer she wore on top of her sweater, and saw that Kerry, who sat hunched in the second row, had her coat over her shoulders. "ANYONE KNOW WHY HEAT'S OFF?" Jan scrawled on her clipboard notepad and without thinking showed it to Ted, who was sitting two empty seats away from her. By the time she realized maybe he'd still be too hurt about the dance to want to talk to her, he'd answered.

"Boiler's busted," he whispered. "I heard the custodian say so when I went past the office on my way over here. The secretary said there'd be no school tomorrow if it doesn't get fixed, and if it's cold enough out. Which it's supposed to be."

"Terrific," Jan whispered back sarcastically, glad that he seemed just about normal again. "With Kent being such a jerk, we need all the rehearsals we can get. What's with him, anyway?"

"Maybe his brain's cold."

"Something sure is." Jan shifted her attention to the stage

again as Kent hurled his script to the floor and said for the third time, "I don't get it. It just doesn't seem right for Proctor."

Brenda, who was onstage also, playing Abigail, glanced imploringly at Jan. She'd gotten her wish and had been dating Kent for a couple of weeks, but she seemed even less able to cope with his increasing temperamental outbursts in rehearsal than she had been before they'd become a couple. But Jan ignored her. Sympathize though she did with her, she was not going to interfere with Mrs. Nicholson's directing unless Mrs. Nicholson asked her to help. Besides, she thought Kent probably understood what Mrs. Nicholson wanted, even though his brooding eyes seemed to belie it. She felt sure it was just that he didn't agree and that he wanted his own way.

"Transitions, Kent, transitions," said Mrs. Nicholson tiredly, pushing herself up from her front-row seat. "Surely you know what a transition is?"

"I guess," Kent answered sulkily, shoving his hands into his pockets. He moved upstage to the improvised bed where a junior named Gail Torson, playing little Betty Parris, who was supposedly bewitched in the beginning of the play, lay uncomfortably.

"A change," Gail said helpfully, lifting her small freckled face; Betty Parris was only ten years old in the play and Gail was the smallest girl in the junior class. Jan didn't know her very well, but she was in a couple of Kerry's classes; Kerry said she was smart, and popular with both boys and girls. "You know, Kent, like in English class."

"I asked Kent," said Mrs. Nicholson dryly.

"Yeah, well, I know." Kent sat on the edge of the "bed"— it was three chairs, seats lined up like a bench—and dramatically cradled his head in his hands. "Look," he said, standing again, "Proctor's no fag. He's still thinking how much he likes Abigail in this scene. I don't care what else is on his mind, as soon as he sees Abigail, he . . ."

"That's right," interrupted Mrs. Nicholson, one hand on the step unit's wooden banister, the other pulling her black wool cardigan closer around her body and buttoning it. "But only for the first few lines. You're doing the whole scene as if you wanted to be in bed with her, and . . ."

Two or three people in the back of the auditorium tittered, and Ted muttered to Jan, "Not so far from the truth. You should have seen him and Brenda at the movies Saturday night. Kent's no fag either."

"Maybe he's trying to prove that," Jan muttered uneasily, thinking again of the conversation in the cafeteria and what Kent had said about the gay men during *Streetcar*.

"I thought," said Mrs. Nicholson, turning to face the auditorium and projecting her voice clearly out over its empty seats to the small group from which the titters had come, "that I asked all of you to be quiet while we worked on this scene. Anyone who can't be, or who is going to be silly, can leave. I thought you were all mature enough to do this play."

There was an uncomfortable silence while Mrs. Nicholson glared out at those who had laughed. "That's better," she said finally, turning to go up the steps to the stage.

And then she fell.

Fell, and didn't move.

It was so quick Jan didn't really see it happen, and it was so quiet afterwards in the hushed auditorium that there was hardly a sound following the thud and the rustle of Mrs. Nicholson's long skirt.

Kerry was the first to react. With a gasp, she shot out of her seat behind Jan and ran to Mrs. Nicholson. "Someone call a doctor," she said quietly. "An ambulance, something. They'll know in the office. Kent, why don't you do it?"

"I will," said Brenda when Kent remained staring, statue-like, down at Mrs. Nicholson. Brenda put her hand briefly on Kent's shoulder, then ran up the center aisle and out the door to the lobby. Mrs. Nicholson didn't move; she barely seemed to breathe.

"Jan, get me some water, would you, in case she comes to?" asked Kerry, still calmly efficient. She opened the top buttons of Mrs. Nicholson's sweater and blouse, loosened her belt, anxiously scanned her still, white face. "Someone see if there's a blanket backstage; I think I saw one the other day. She's breathing but she's unconscious, I think. Maybe in shock."

Jan had stood, but was frozen in the aisle with most of the others; now Kerry's competent voice giving her a job to do freed her to move and to think more clearly. As the others in the cast began whispering and moving forward, Jan ran out into the hall for water, half her mind thinking, *Cup; I should get a paper cup for the water;* and the other half fervently praying, *Please, oh, please, let her be all right!* The strain on Mrs. Nicholson's face at tryouts came back to her; her shaking hands; her thin, tired appearance; Ted's ominous concern—but she pushed those thoughts aside, and found a cup and water.

When Jan got back, there was a tight knot of people—Nanny, Will, Gail, Kent, most of the rest of the cast—around Kerry and Mrs. Nicholson. Jan had to force her way through, holding the cup high so no one would jostle it. Damn the heat's being off, she thought, shivering—but then she saw

Ted with a blanket and moved aside after handing the cup to Kerry.

"Thank you," Kerry said to both of them, putting the cup down behind her and carefully covering Mrs. Nicholson with the blanket, tucking it around her with great politeness.

I love you, thought Jan, watching Kerry, barely noticing the thought at first. Then it came again, and she caught herself almost wishing that she were Mrs. Nicholson, so Kerry would be touching her so gently.

Overflowing with guilty confusion, Jan turned away.

Someone touched her arm—Ted. "It'll be okay," he was saying kindly. "She'll be all right."

Jan felt herself tense, unable of course to tell him it was Kerry, not Mrs. Nicholson, who had suddenly made her unable to face the group near the stage.

"Look," he was saying soothingly, "it's a tough play, right? And old elephant-ego Kent's been giving her a hard time. Even though they like each other a lot, it must be hard for her to have him defy her the way he's been doing. We've all noticed that she came back tired from the summer. So maybe this'll make her rest a couple of days, and then she'll be herself again. And then . . ."

"Look!" Nanny shouted suddenly.

Jan spun around and saw Mrs. Nicholson struggling to sit up, half supported, half held back, by Kerry.

"Well," Jan heard Mrs. Nicholson say thickly but clearly, "I certainly didn't know *that* was in the cards, too." She sounded surprised.

Ted let go of Jan's arm and they both moved closer. What does she mean by "in the cards, too," Jan wondered.

"Mrs. Nicholson," Kerry was saying, "don't you think you'd better rest some more? Brenda went to get a doctor and I'm sure he'll be right here. You had a terrible fall. How's your ankle?"

"My *ankle*?" Mrs. Nicholson looked bewildered, one hand at her head. "My *ankle*?"

"Well," Kerry said uncomfortably, "I think you must've fallen on it. It was sort of twisted under you, and . . ."

Slowly, Mrs. Nicholson struggled to get up. "Now that you mention it," she said, "yes. It hurts. But . . ."

"Please." Kerry caught her arm. "Please."

Jan eased her way past Ted, Nanny, Will, and one or two others. "Mrs. Nicholson," she said, kneeling, trying to avoid Kerry's dark and anxious eyes, "please take it easy. Would you like me to call Mr. Nicholson?"

"What?" Mrs. Nicholson's hand went to her head again; she seemed dazed. "Who—oh, hello, Janna. No. Robert? No. He'll—worry. Just bother. It said. I—fine. Fine."

Out of the corner of her eye, Jan saw Ted and Nanny exchange a look. She's just come out of shock, Jan told them silently, trying to believe it. Of course she's not quite herself.

"Mrs. Nicholson," Kerry said firmly, "excuse me, but I don't think you are fine. I don't mean to be rude, but really—please wait for the doctor."

"Yeah, you'd better wait." Ted knelt beside Kerry. "Hey, look, think of the school, for Pete's sake, Mrs. Nicholson. Suppose you fell again, you know, just sort of slipped or something, and then Mr. Nicholson got mad and sued the school." He clapped his hand to his head in mock horror. "Wow! Suppose he sued us kids! You know what that'd do to us!"

The nervous laugh that followed seemed to cheer Mrs. Nicholson a little. "Perish—the thought," she said weakly, with a slight smile. Then her smile faded and she slowly raised her left arm and scratched her nose. "Where's my John

Proctor?" she asked, her speech clear again. "If I have to sit here like a lump, waiting, I can at least finish what I started."

Kent brushed past Jan and knelt next to Kerry. "How're you doing?" he asked Mrs. Nicholson awkwardly. "I'm sorry if I . . ."

"What I meant," said Mrs. Nicholson quickly, as if she wasn't sure how much time she had, "was that you're not changing enough in the scene. Proctor's"—she winced as if something hurt, and Kerry hovered, ready, Jan could see, to support her again if she needed it—"Proctor's a chameleon in that scene—doesn't know his own mind. That's pivotal about him, Kent. Not weak—or—as you—crudely put it— faggy—ugly word. Most of the play—once he . . ."

She's losing the thread again, Jan thought painfully. What is wrong with her? And where's that doctor? She saw Kerry move closer again and put her hand behind Mrs. Nicholson's shoulder, supporting her once more.

"Nurse Kerry," Mrs. Nicholson said. "Thank you, my dear. One minute," she went on, to Kent again, "Proctor lusts for Abby. Next minute—feels guilty about it. Thinks of Elizabeth, and morality. Loves Elizabeth. Though she's cold sometimes. Understand?"

"Okay." Kent took her hand; it looked even thinner in Kent's large one. "You just take it easy, Mrs. Nicholson. You just take it easy."

Mrs. Nicholson leaned against Kerry and closed her eyes as Brenda and two men—Mr. Taylor, who was Southview's principal, and a man carrying a black satchel—burst into the auditorium and hurried down the aisle.

"You take over, Jan," said Mrs. Nicholson. She spoke clearly, but her eyes were now closed. "You know what I mean about Proctor?"

"I think so," said Jan. Sure, she thought, lust and guilt and morality—yeah, I understand! Quickly, she squelched the thought.

"All right, everyone," boomed Mr. Taylor; no one had ever heard him speak quietly. "Step back now." He bent over Mrs. Nicholson, who opened her eyes and then closed them again, murmuring, "I'm sorry, Michael. I didn't think it would be this soon."

"You just rest, Elvira," Mr. Taylor said. "Take it easy now. The doctor's here." He squeezed Mrs. Nicholson's hand, then straightened up and shouldered people out of the way. "Move along now," he said impatiently.

"Thinks he's a freaking cop," Ted muttered.

"Thank you, Kerry Ann," Mr. Taylor went on. "We'll take over now." Without really giving Kerry a chance to curl her feet out from under her, he pulled her up.

"She's been helping," Jan said angrily. "If it hadn't been for Kerry . . ."

"Good girl." Mrs. Nicholson opened her eyes again. "Thank you. Good little Elizabeth."

"It'll be okay now, Mrs. Nicholson," Kerry said. "The doctor'll fix you up." Jan saw tears glistening in her eyes, though, and longed to touch her, but she remained still, rigid, by Kerry's side.

"I'm sure she twisted her ankle when she fell," Kerry said to the doctor.

"I'll see to it." He knelt beside Mrs. Nicholson. "Nice job," he said to Kerry, nodding at the blanket and the cup of water nearby. "Looks like you know some first aid."

"Girl Scouts," said Kerry.

"Cookies and all?" Jan whispered, trying to cheer Kerry up as the doctor bent to examine Mrs. Nicholson's ankle, asking her questions in a soft voice.

"Okay, everyone," said Mr. Taylor. "Time to go. Come on, let's . . ."

"No," Mrs. Nicholson interrupted. "Rehearsal's still going on—still time. Finish the scene. Jan, you take over, I said."

"All right," said Mr. Taylor, "later, but for now in the lobby, all of you. Come on." Briskly, he herded them out.

"Cookies, badges, the works," Kerry whispered nervously to Jan when they were waiting by the door for Mr. Taylor and the doctor to bring Mrs. Nicholson out. "And I worked in a hospital one summer. Oh, Jan . . ."

Jan finally let herself touch Kerry's hand. "You were great," she said.

"I think she's terribly sick. I think she fainted and then fell, not the other way around."

"No," Jan said. But she knew she was denying it too quickly. *"Didn't know that was in the cards, too . . . didn't think it would be this soon"*—it did sound as if Mrs. Nicholson had suspected something like this would happen. But aloud Jan said stubbornly, "She's tired," trying to convince herself as well as the others. "She's been tired since school started. She'll be okay. She's tough. You'll see."

Kerry's sympathetic eyes told Jan she was just being kind when she said, "Yes, you're probably right. You know her better than I do."

"What badges?" Jan asked, desperately changing the subject; why were they taking so long in there?

"I wanted to get all the outdoor ones, but my mother made me get the cooking ones and the arts and crafts ones, stuff like that. She said she couldn't teach me housewifey things because she's no good at them, but she thought I ought to know how to do them and this was an easy way to learn. She said I could go for the badges I wanted later. But, except for working on the first-aid badge, I hated the whole thing."

"Then how come . . ."

"My mother, the doer. Look."

The doors opened and the murmur in the lobby stopped as Mr. Taylor and the doctor, wrists and hands clasped to make a human chair, came out carrying Mrs. Nicholson. Her arms were hanging limply around their necks.

But Mrs. Nicholson gave them a weak salute. "Carry on," she said almost cheerfully. "The show must go on, you know. Good luck, dears. I'll be back soon. Jan knows what I want. She'd better, anyway."

Smiles, laughs. Then Ted—bless him, Jan thought—stepped forward, saying, "Come on, everyone. A big hand for our director, for good luck."

Obviously relieved to have something to do, they all clapped.

And Mrs. Nicholson exited on a wave of applause.

EIGHT

༄

BUT WHEN THE OUTSIDE door closed after Mrs. Nicholson, the applause died away and everyone except Kent turned expectantly to Jan.

"Well, let's go," she said, shaking off the tears that threatened and her desire to run after the doctor and grab him, begging like a small child, "Make her well, oh, please, make her well!"

"We've got about half an hour left," Jan told the cast after glancing at the lobby clock, "and I guess Mrs. Nicholson wanted us to go on with the same scene." She held the heavy auditorium door open, then followed the others back in and down to the stage. "Act One," she said, picking up her clipboard. "From your entrance, Kent."

Brenda, Gail, and the others in that scene quietly went up the steps and got into position, but Kent, who had been the last to leave the lobby, stayed behind, glowering moodily at Jan.

"Look," said Jan, trying to avoid his angry eyes, "I think what Mrs. Nicholson meant was . . ."

"Stow it," Kent snapped. "Just stow it. You're the stage manager, not the director. You'll take us through our lines, nothing more, till she comes back."

It was as if everyone else in the auditorium had suddenly stopped breathing.

"I love Mrs. Nicholson, too," Jan said as steadily as she could. "But I think we ought to do what she asked, which was go on with rehearsal."

"I'll walk through my lines." Kent's voice was like stretched steel. "That's all."

"That's not what she meant and you know it," Jan told him quietly, trying to hold back her anger. "Come on, Kent. I know how you feel, but she wanted to get the scene right, and . . ."

"Kent," put in Gail from the stage, her freckled face looking very earnest, "she did say she wanted Jan to work out the problem with Proctor and everything. I think we should all . . ."

"*I'm* playing this part," Kent shouted, whirling around to face her. "Not you, not Jan, not anyone. Not even Mrs. Nicholson. No one's telling me how to play my last big part in this school, no one. Maybe my last big part forever," he added dramatically; Ted snorted.

"Kent, let's go out in the lobby for a minute," Jan suggested, feeling that she might be able to reason with him better without an audience. "Come on." She started down the aisle, but Kent stayed still.

"Just because of one lousy summer in stock," he said nastily to Jan, "you think you're some great director, Stanislavsky himself or something. Well, you're not. You're an actress, not a director. I'm not taking direction from an actress, and that's that."

"Right," Brenda said under her breath.

Will gave a couple of tentative claps, but no one else joined in. Still, Jan felt everyone's eyes on her, especially Kerry's. To gain time, she kept herself from looking at Kent as she walked slowly back to her front-row seat. Then she picked up her prompt book, opened it carefully to the right page, and said slowly and distinctly, "Places for Act One, Proctor's entrance. Abigail, Proctor, Mercy Lewis, Mary Warren, Betty Parris— right, Gail, on the bed. Rebecca Nurse, Reverend Parris, Mrs. Putnam, Giles Corey: ready to enter—a little closer, Ted— good. Kent, places, please," she said briskly, directly to him. "Let's really see it this time, the whole thing; I know you can do it. You know, the lust for Abby in the first few lines, the realization that she still wants to sleep with you but that you can't because of being married to Elizabeth, then the anger when she keeps at you. Underneath everything—what was the line from that dumb one-act you and I did last spring? 'The two things war in him until he knows not who he is'? That's how Mrs. Nicholson sees Proctor, I think, for the whole play."

Jan turned deliberately away from Kent to the group on-stage and then to the rest of the cast, waiting out front. "Listen, there's something I want you all to know. I'd rather Mrs. Nicholson were doing this than me. And all I'm going to tell you to do is what I think she wants. If you don't agree, tell me, and if *I* don't agree—if I don't think Mrs. Nicholson would agree—we'll just have to save it for when she comes back. But meanwhile we've got a show to rehearse and that means someone's got to watch to make sure everything fits together the way the director wants it to. Okay, everyone, places."

Kent didn't move.

"Oh, come on, Kent," Gail said, beckoning to him impatiently. "We all want to do the scene."

"Yeah, Kent, let's go," the boy playing Reverend Parris said from backstage. "I'd kind of like to get through Act One today."

Jan felt Kerry, next to her, tense; she herself stopped breathing.

Kent swore under his breath at Jan. But he stomped up the step unit, glared at her, and moved into position for his entrance.

"Curtain," said Jan.

Kent entered, and the scene began.

Jan felt herself breathe again.

"Well done," Kerry whispered. "Well, well done!"

For the next couple of rehearsals, Kent was surly but cooperative and there were no more open arguments. There was no news of Mrs. Nicholson, though Jan tried several times to call her husband and stopped by the school office at least once a day to see if anyone there had heard anything. Finally, on Thursday, Mr. Nicholson answered his phone, and after an awkward moment when Jan had to explain who she was, he told her brusquely that Mrs. Nicholson had been in the hospital but now was home and would be back in school on Monday.

"What happened?" asked Jan. "I mean, when she fell and everything?"

"She sprained her ankle," Mr. Nicholson said with obvious reluctance, as if he didn't want to talk to her. "Not badly. She'll be using a cane for a while, that's all."

"No, I meant—why she fell and—well, why she fell. She's—some of the kids thought she might be sick. It's just that we're worried. I don't mean to pry or anything like that."

There was a long silence.

"Mr. Nicholson?" Jan said cautiously. "We really are worried. She's my favorite teacher. Other kids', too."

"She must have tripped," Mr. Nicholson said gruffly. "You'll have her back on Monday." He sounded bitter, as if he resented his wife's going back to school. Jan was sure, as she sent Mrs. Nicholson her "best wishes" and hung up, that there was something he was deliberately keeping from her.

Saturday was the dance, and Kerry and Jan figured out on their way in Jan's mother's car to see Olivier's *Hamlet* that everyone involved in *Crucible* except themselves would be there: Ted with Nanny, Kent with Brenda, almost everyone else with someone from the cast or crew. "Wow," said Kerry, counting on her fingers after Jan had found what had to be the last parking space, way in a back corner of the theater's small lot, "it'll be just like a rehearsal. Hey, do you realize there are ten girls and eleven boys in the cast?" She got out of the car. "But if you count the crew . . ."

"Matchmaking?" Jan got out, too.

"Nope. Just an exercise, I guess. Like if Team A has seven members and Team B has eleven members, what's the color of Team C's uniforms?"

Jan laughed.

"It was a dumb exercise anyway, figuring out how many kids in the cast and crew. It's almost like I'm nervous or something." She paused for a second. "Are you nervous or something?"

"Umm-hmm." Jan realized that she was and that she was glad Kerry was, too, even if it didn't make much sense. After all, even though this was the first time the two of them had

73

gone anywhere special together, there was nothing inherently odd about it. So what if most kids were at the dance? They both really did want to see the movie—Mrs. Nicholson had even recommended it—and it was only playing once; it was a very old movie. It's not our fault, Jan thought, that the art-film theater scheduled it for the same night as the dance.

"Look." Kerry pointed to the sky, and shivered under her suede jacket. "There's that old moon again, our good moon."

Jan looked up at the bright, cold moon, full now. Then, shivering herself, she pulled Kerry toward the theater. "Hey, crazy woman," she said, "come on, I'm freezing. And look. There's a long line."

The movie, black and white with frequent mist swirls and dramatic camera angles setting off what seemed to both of them to be a near-perfect performance, made Kerry and Jan huddle very close together in the dark theater and finally, in an especially moving scene, reach for each other's hands. After a few minutes, when Jan's mind strayed from the screen long enough to be fully conscious of it, she thought, *What if someone sees?* But Kerry's hand felt good in hers, not awkward like Ted's—not awkward at all, in fact, but as if it belonged there. She didn't let go till the film ended and the houselights went on. Friends touch each other, she told herself; we're both emotional about the movie; it doesn't mean anything.

But in the fresh air of the parking lot, back in the far corner in the cold car, it was as if they were both silently embarrassed.

Or scared.

"I think I'll wait till the other cars clear out a bit," Jan said, putting her key in the ignition without turning it. "I hate traffic, especially at night." She rubbed her hands together to warm them, then turned the key partway, just to start the heater going.

Kerry leaned back, gazing outside. "You know the one thing I'd change," she said as the cars around them coughed, roared, or purred into motion, and left, "is that bit at the end when the moon's on Olivier's face. You know, when he's dead and being carried up to the top of the castle or wherever."

Jan agreed. "Melodramatic, right?"

"Like Kent."

"He'd love it. If he were playing Hamlet, there'd have to be a spotlight called the Kent Norris Special, just the right color to bring out his brooding features . . ."

"Brooding even in death . . ."

"Perfectly chiseled . . ."

"Perfectly accented . . ."

"With Max Factor Number Something to make his beautiful cheeks glow palely in the moonlight. Oh, Kerry, I . . ." Jan stopped herself in time. "I *like* you," she said.

"I—like you, too," Kerry answered slowly, her voice clear but so quiet Jan had to strain to hear. "You're a very special friend. Like Horatio was to Hamlet. When Hamlet said to Horatio, 'If thou didst ever hold me in thy heart,' I thought of you. Of me. When Horatio called Hamlet 'sweet prince,' too."

"So did I." Jan felt she was being slowly mesmerized and could no longer hold thoughts in her head, except she wondered absently why her heart was pounding so uncomfortably. She wished, from a great distance, that it wouldn't.

Neither of them moved and then at the same moment they both leaned toward each other. Kerry's lips lightly brushed Jan's cheek, then found her mouth.

It was a quick, soft kiss, over soon, but Jan felt all her muscles melt and feelings she had never had before stirred in her. She felt as if she were waking out of a long sleep into something new and wonderful—scary, too.

They were still holding hands, but when Kerry leaned her head against Jan's shoulder, Jan changed hands quickly so she could slip her arm around Kerry. She bent her head and kissed Kerry's hair, then knew she wanted to touch it, to take it out of its braid, to bury herself in it . . . could she? The thought intruded till she felt Kerry turn closer against her, felt the softness of Kerry's breast against her arm and then Kerry's arms tightly around her, holding her closer than she'd ever been held, pulling her away from the steering wheel. They moved at the same time to kiss each other again, a little clumsily, but the clumsiness didn't matter, and Jan felt that her dizzy heart was going to burst. Her hand went up to Kerry's face, moved Kerry's head slowly back so she could see her, and found her own awe and wonder and fear mirrored in Kerry's eyes. Kerry's cheek was smooth and warm; Jan's hand slid down to the curve of her throat, and then lower, nearly to her breast—and though Kerry seemed to lean against her hand, Jan pulled it away suddenly, as if to punish it or herself, and gripped the steering wheel. It was too much, much too much too quickly; she was going to explode with it.

Jan could feel Kerry shaking and realized she was shaking, too. "I'm sorry," she said. "I don't know what happened. I got—sort of carried away."

"Sorry!" Kerry whispered. "Don't be." She touched Jan's face. "Jan, I liked it. I didn't want you to stop."

"I know," said Jan. "But . . ."

"I know."

They sat in silence at the far edge of the lot until the lights went off on the theater marquee and they were left with only moonlight.

"If we don't leave soon," Kerry said, her voice unsteady, "I don't know what'll happen."

"Oh, Kerry, neither do I." Jan turned the key the rest of the way in the ignition.

"A fine pair," said Kerry.

Jan could tell from her voice that she was smiling; she, too, felt more in control now that the familiar sound of the engine had broken their mood.

"Weird," said Kerry. "Well, we knew that long ago."

"Weird," answered Jan. She felt suddenly elated, strong, powerful, as she backed the car around in a huge swoop and drove out onto the nearly deserted road. With Kerry beside her, with Kerry having touched her, kissed her, with Kerry . . .

"Jan," Kerry whispered. "Jan—Jan."

Jan shifted her eyes momentarily away from the road. Kerry's face was in shadow now that the moon was behind them. "H'mm?"

"Just your name. And could you still drive if I moved over? I want to be close to you. It's lonely way over here."

Jan held her arm out till Kerry had snuggled under it. "Okay?"

"Okay."

Jan drove in silence, realizing after a while that she was gently stroking the sleeve of Kerry's jacket, as if she wanted to go through the suede to the skin, and realizing, too, that she was growing more and more conscious of Kerry's head nestled in the crook of her neck, of her breathing, of the warmth of her breath. "Kerry," she said, stopping at a light, kissing her quickly on the top of her head, "Kerry, it's no good. I can't concentrate."

Kerry reached up and kissed Jan's cheek just before the light changed. "Okay." She moved back. "I know what you mean. It was nice, though."

"Maybe with practice."

"Right." Kerry clasped her hands in front of her, stretching. "Oh, can't we drive all night? Can't we never go home, or back to school, or to rehearsal, or anything? Can't we go down to the river, and . . ." She broke off, fidgeted with a loose button on her jacket, looked everywhere but at Jan.

Jan pulled onto a side road and stopped, turning off the ignition. "It's just hit you like it's just hit me, right?" she said after a second or two of silence. "Right? When you said that about the river? Because that's where everyone goes to make out? It's just hit you that that's what we're doing."

Kerry nodded.

"So I guess it's true," said Jan, avoiding Kerry's eyes. "What we talked about after Ted asked me to the dance. You know, when you said about me wanting to be with a girl instead of a boy. Kerry?"

"I—I'd rather not think about it like that."

"I know. Neither would I. It's sort of like giving it a label. But maybe we ought to talk about it."

"I just want to feel," said Kerry. "I just want to feel."

The memory of the evening by the bike rack came vividly back to Jan and it was as if it twisted inside her. "Just want to *experience* it?" she asked harshly. "Like Faust? Is that it?"

"Oh, no!" Kerry gripped Jan's arm. "No, no, it's not like that. It's only, only . . ."

"Only what?" But Jan found herself reaching for the key, turning the ignition on again anyway.

"Only nothing," said Kerry dully. She let go of Jan's arm and moved farther over on the passenger side. "I guess we'd better go home."

"Right." Jan had to swallow hard and blink against her sudden tears. Why hadn't she remembered Kerry's *Faust* thing earlier, and stopped in time? It fit so well!

At Kerry's house, Jan parked and then sat stiffly in front of the steering wheel. "I'll stay here till you're inside, just like a good date," she said sarcastically. "But I guess I'd better not walk you to the door and kiss you good night."

"You could kiss me here."

But Jan didn't, couldn't, move.

"Jan, don't be like that! Believe me, I—oh . . ." Kerry threw her arms around Jan and kissed her hard. "I love you," she whispered. "I'm not experimenting! I'm not being Faust now. I'm being Kerry Ann Socrides, and I love you. Do you hear me? I love you!"

Light shot onto the front path as the house's heavy front door opened and a plump woman in a dark red bathrobe and hair rollers emerged, framed by the porch columns and roof. "Kerry Ann, is that you?"

Kerry moved away from Jan and rolled down the car window. "Yes, Aunt Elena," she called breathlessly. "Be right there." She gripped Jan's hand tightly. "Do you believe me? Oh, please, please believe me!"

"Is that your girlfriend with you?" Kerry's aunt came partway down the porch steps. "Jan What's-Her-Name from school?"

"Darn," whispered Kerry. "Yes, it's Jan What's-Her-Name," she called to her aunt. "Quick, Jan What's-Her-name, do you believe me?" she whispered again.

79

Jan had to laugh then, and as soon as she did she began to let herself believe. "I'm sorry," she said. "I guess I got scared—look out, your aunt's coming down the path. Yes, I believe you. And I—I feel the same way about you."

Kerry dropped Jan's hand as her aunt came up and peered into the passenger-side window.

"Da-dum," sang Kerry, switching on the inside light. "Aunt Elena, this is Jan Montcrief. Jan, this is my aunt, Ms. Socrides. How's that? Real Amy Vanderbilt stuff, huh?"

"How do you do, Ms. Socrides," said Jan politely, trying not to laugh at the absurdity of the situation and at this red-haired woman with her bird-like wrinkled face, greeting them in hair rollers and bathrobe and makeup.

"Pleased to meet you, dear," chirped Aunt Elena, thrusting a faintly liver-spotted but carefully manicured hand toward Jan. "Do call me Aunt Elena. Ms. sounds awfully school-teachery, don't you agree?"

Jan reached awkwardly across Kerry and took the woman's hand. It was so limp Jan almost felt she ought to kiss it, like an old-fashioned European courtier.

"Do come in for some cocoa," Aunt Elena said brightly. "That is, if you gals haven't already stopped off for a big goopy sundae—which I bet you did," she said, wagging a knowing finger at them, "because the movie let out an hour ago. Oh, it's all right. I always used to do that, too, when I went out with a girlfriend. I remember. Somehow we never quite felt we could do that with a boy, have a sundae, I mean, but we felt we could with another girl; that was different. But, ladies, it's cold out here! Do come in, Jan, anyway."

Jan hesitated. It was late, but she didn't want to leave Kerry yet, even if she'd have to put up with Aunt Elena in order to stay with her a while longer, and to see where she lived.

"Oh, come on." Kerry opened the passenger door. "It's not that late. You can always call your mother."

"Well, okay." Jan climbed out of the car. "Thank you."

"I was unpacking a new shipment," said Aunt Elena cheerfully, leading them up the front path. Jan remembered Kerry's telling her that her aunt ran a shop and she noticed the gilt-lettered sign—GIFTES—swinging outside what she had at first thought was the garage but which she now saw was a small single-story building behind and to one side of the sprawling yellow house.

"It's such fun and of course it gave me something to do while you were out, Kerry Ann. I've gotten so used to Kerry's company," Aunt Elena said to Jan as she opened the front door, "that I hardly know what to do with myself when she's not home. Here." She reached for Jan's jacket. "Make yourself at home. Kerry Ann, please hang your guest's jacket up, and I'll put on some milk."

Jan saw, now that they were inside, that Ms. Socrides—Aunt Elena—was wearing tattered bunny slippers on her feet. She looked even older than she'd seemed outside. Despite her heavy makeup (Jan wondered if she slept in it, since she seemed ready for bed), she seemed at least old enough to be a grandmother.

"You should bring friends here more often, Kerry Ann," Aunt Elena said. "It's such fun! Take Jan into the shop if you want. You girls can help me unpack, what a *treat!*" With a swish of bright red robe, she left.

They looked at each other.

"Hi." Kerry touched the tips of Jan's fingers with her own. "Okay?"

"Okay. Hi yourself."

"I meant what I said."

"I know. I meant it, too."

They moved apart quickly as Aunt Elena's voice came caroling out from someplace beyond the living room. "Marshmallows?"

"Sure," Kerry shouted after Jan said yes. "She's silly," she said, "but she's sort of a dear."

"She seems to like you. Your father's sister, right?"

"Yes, but much older sister. My mother hates her, but I don't mind her, and there was no one else for me to stay with. Besides, she's kind of lonely."

Jan scanned the living room, trying to confirm her first impression. Yes, there actually was at least one china figurine, or a planter with a fussy plant, or a glass animal, or a garish ceramic bird, on almost every available surface.

"Appalling, isn't it?" Kerry grinned. "She moves her surplus in here—anything she can't sell. But even so, you should see the shop."

"I don't know if I could stand it," said Jan.

"Oh, come on." Kerry tugged her toward a bright yellow door at the far end of the living room. "After all, she did ask us. And unpacking's kind of fun."

"I better call Mom first," Jan said, and Kerry led her to the phone.

Her mother was fine about her staying at Kerry's, at least for a little while. "No more than an hour or so, though, Jan," Mom said. "Promise?"

"Okay. Promise."

When Jan hung up, Kerry bustled her through the yellow door and across the yard and a small parking lot to the shop, which was even more of a jumble than the living room. Glass animals filled two shelves that ran the length of one wall, with china ones on the shelves below, interspersed at random with mugs, butter dishes, cereal bowls, and other small pottery pieces. A huge table in the center of the room held needlepoint and crewel kits, an enormous heap of next year's calendars, wrapping paper, and recipe books, with a full greeting-card rack against a nearby wall. Wooden canes, fireplace bellows and tongs, handmade brooms, and other tall treasures were thrust into one corner; jewelry lay on black velvet in a glass case beside an ornate old-fashioned brass cash register; unclassifiable china and wood objects—small toys, dollhouse miniatures, ashtrays, napkin rings, coasters— were on an el jutting out from the cluttered counter. Ugly wood-inlaid pictures hung on the walls, sporting scenes mostly: hunting, football, sailing—and below them marched a row of ceramic tiles that went, almost in order, from floral-attractive to floral-hideous.

The floor was covered with S-shaped Styrofoam packing worms that had obviously been tossed unceremoniously out of the large crate that stood near the table amid a bevy of fake Dresden china shepherdesses, more or less guarded by a heavenly array of fat gray-white cherubs with gilt wings.

"Good lord!" Jan picked up a cherub in disbelief.

"Isn't he darling?" cooed Aunt Elena, coming in bearing an Oriental-looking black lacquer tray that was set with gold-edged demitasse cups, a matching chocolate pot, tiny spoons, a plate of pale cookies, and a crystal bowl heaped with miniature marshmallows. "I thought we could be elegant." She giggled, setting the tray down near the cash register. "Isn't this fun?" She hunched her shoulders in apparent excitement as she poured, and then handed Jan a full cup topped with two tiny floating marshmallows. "I adore midnight feasts— not that it's *really* midnight yet, but we can pretend." She passed Jan the cookies before Jan had figured out where to put the cherub and while she was still trying to balance her cup and saucer in her other hand. Kerry took the cherub just in time.

"These cookies are from England," Aunt Elena said. "I just opened the tin. It's wonderful how tins keep things fresh. I've had these nearly a year, I think, but they're yummy, aren't they?"

Jan bit politely into a cookie, found it was nearly as hard and as tasteless as its tin probably would be, and saved herself from choking only by downing half her tiny cup of chocolate. Too late she realized that it and its melted marshmallows were still too hot to swallow. She tried not to wince obviously as she felt the skin on the roof of her mouth pucker with the burn.

"You okay?" Kerry asked.

"Careful," warned Aunt Elena. "The cocoa's hot."

"I'm—fine," Jan gasped, exploring the roof of her mouth tenderly with her tongue. "Just—took too big a swallow, that's all."

"Kerry Ann tells me you're helping direct the play she's in." Aunt Elena refilled Jan's cup and passed her the cookies again. "How wonderful! I always dreamed of going into the theater myself," she went on with a faraway look. But"—she spread her hands in front of her, palms down, for effect, Jan was sure, but it didn't work because it looked as if she was examining her nails—"alas, no talent. I do envy Kerry Ann so! *I* was reduced to shopkeeping, and in a talented family, that's not much. But Kerry Ann—she'll do something grand, I just know it. Like her wonderful mother—although Kerry Ann's more artistic, I think, while her mother is a real scientist, even though she's in theology now."

"Oh, Aunt Elena," Kerry said, struggling with a cookie, "you know you love the shop. And I'm really not very talented. Here, let's unpack." She put the half-eaten cookie down behind a shepherdess and rummaged in the crate. Jan heard what sounded like either a burp or a concealed guffaw and then Kerry held up a pink china pig, its belly studded with tiny magnets. A moment later she held out her other hand, a litter of tiny piglets, matching magnets on their mouths, nestled in her palm. "Oh, Aunt Elena," she exclaimed with what Jan knew was mock admiration, "these are so cute!"

Jan had to put her cup down very quickly.

"Do you think so, dear?" asked Aunt Elena thoughtfully. "You don't think they're just the tiniest bit—risqué?"

"Oh, no," said Kerry solemnly. "They'll even help teach kids, you know, the facts of life."

Jan stuffed another dry cookie into her mouth to keep from laughing.

"Then they're yours, dear, if you like them. I'm not sure I should teach the facts of life in my shop. I know!" Aunt Elena pushed up the sleeves of her robe. "Why don't we each pick one thing we'd like to keep as we unpack? That way we'll have a real incentive, and it'll be heaps of fun, don't you think?" Without waiting for an answer, she thrust her arm into the crate. "Oh, now this is really fab!" she gushed, holding up a thickly stuffed lemon-shaped potholder mitt. "Isn't it darling? And look, girls, it's got a slice out of it, just the right size for a pot handle. Well, I can't keep that, much as I'd like to; it'll sell wonderfully. Too bad there isn't another." She rummaged deeper in the crate. "No. An orange and an apple—how clever. No more lemons. Your turn, Jan." She put the pile of felt fruit aside and settled back on her heels on the floor.

Pick anything decent and I'll disown you, Kerry's eyes signaled mischievously to Jan.

That's easy; there's nothing decent to pick, Jan signaled back as she bent to hunt for something to rival the piglets.

"How about this?" suggested Kerry, holding up a plastic outhouse with GONE FISHIN scrawled on the door.

"Oh, we've got one at home," Jan said casually.

"Really?" Kerry cried, instantly falling into Jan's game. "Hey, that's super! Aunt Elena, did you hear that? Jan says she has one of these adorable outhouses."

"Kerry Ann," said Aunt Elena, wagging her finger, "I wouldn't be surprised but what you're having just the eeniest joke on me, now am I right?" Before Kerry could answer, Aunt Elena let out a shriek of laughter that sounded to Jan like the noise the piglets would probably make if someone yanked them away from their mother's magnets.

"Aunt Elena," explained Kerry, "likes a good laugh."

"Oh, you're right there, Kerry Ann, you're right there." Aunt Elena wiped her eyes. "Even when it's on me. But I'm on to you girls; you can't fool me for long. I know some of this stuff is terrible. I simply *loathe* those outhouses, but I have to stock them. Do you know they sell almost better than anything else? Can you imagine?"

Just as Jan was beginning to think there might be some hope for Aunt Elena after all, Aunt Elena picked up a large water-lily-shaped purple bath sponge. "Now, how about this, Jan?"

Jan gulped, avoiding Kerry's eyes. "Gorgeous. Absolutely gorgeous."

"Then it's yours." Aunt Elena beamed, handing it to her.

"Oh, I couldn't," said Jan.

Kerry kicked her. "Oh, but you must."

"Well—wow—thank you," Jan sputtered. She put the sponge next to her, wondering if Aunt Elena wasn't having her own private joke on them, or if running a "gifte" shop had made her so tolerant of other people's bad taste that her own taste had suffered.

Later, after Jan had said she had to leave and she and Kerry had run through a thick drizzle to the house so Jan could get her jacket, Kerry said it was lack of taste. "For instance," Kerry said in explanation, "she used to have a poodle, a miniature white one, and the poor dog had a collar to match every outfit Aunt Elena wore. Had her toenails painted, too. And she had a pink satin cushion in the living room that Aunt Elena used to call 'Little Poo-Poo's beddie-bye . . .'"

"Kerry Ann Socrides," said Jan, "you are making that up. Next you'll be telling me that she took little Poo-Poo out in a doll carriage with a satin coverlet and . . ."

"And a rattle—pink—dog-, no, cat-shaped, dangling from it; she did. And she knitted her pink booties at Christmas . . ."

"And a matching coat for the winter," Jan supplied promptly, trying not to laugh, because Kerry seemed to be making a game of that, "with idiot mittens . . ."

"Four idiot mittens, of course, attached to the coat's sleeves with pink crocheted strings . . ."

"Which darling Poo-Poo kept chewing off . . ."

"So Aunt Elena was always having to make new ones, and finally she just crocheted one that was yards and yards long and . . ."

"And someone thought it was a leash and offered to buy it . . ."

"And that's how the gift shop started." Kerry clapped her

hand over her mouth, then burst out laughing. "You win," she gasped, clutching her stomach. "You broke me up."

"Thank heaven." Jan let herself laugh at last. "I couldn't have held out much longer. Hey, tell me there never was a poodle named Poo-Poo?"

"Oh, but there was," insisted Kerry, her eyes round and solemn, "and she had little gold dishes with her name on them, and . . ."

"Stop!" Jan protested helplessly. "I can't keep it up. Please, ma'am, mercy. I've got to go." She opened the front door.

"It's really raining now," Kerry remarked, coming close behind Jan and looking out over her shoulder.

"Astute observation," said Jan, very aware of Kerry's body pressing against hers. "Kerry . . ."

Kerry moved away. "In fact, it's raining cats and dogs, you might say. Sorry."

Jan put her hand on Kerry's shoulder. "Don't be sorry. But your aunt's still around, and I don't think she'd be too happy to see us—well, close together."

"Yeah." Kerry dipped her head and kissed Jan's hand. "Cats and dogs," she said loudly. "Poodles and fox terriers and Abyssinians and Siameses . . ."

Jan kissed Kerry's cheek quickly, then said, "And little ceramic cherubs with gold wings."

"And outhouses that say GONE FISHIN . . ."

"And magnetic pigs and piglets . . ."

"And—and—oh, Jan!" Kerry dropped her voice and leaned against the door. "Besides all the rest of it, I have such *fun* with you."

"Here," she called a minute later when Jan was running to the car. "Don't forget your bath sponge!"

NINE

❧✕❧

IT WASN'T UNTIL LATE Sunday night that Jan finally finished the homework she'd neglected all week because of substituting for Mrs. Nicholson. By then it was too late to call Kerry.

Dummy, she thought, getting up from her desk and going to the window. Just one day without seeing her and you miss her like crazy.

She lifted the window shade, wondering if Kerry was looking at the moon. "I love you, Kerry Ann Socrides," she whispered against the windowpane. "I love you and I don't dare think about it any more than you do."

But she knew she was thinking, even so.

Jan returned to her desk and took out a clean sheet of paper. "Dear Raphael," she wrote at the top, and then sat staring out the window. Pushing that piece of paper aside, she took another and wrote:

Dear Kerry,
   I just finished my stupid homework and looked out the
window at the moon and told it I love you. Or told you, via

89

the moon. My mother's gone to bed and Dad's away again and the house is very quiet. I ought to go to bed myself, but I don't think I could sleep anyway.

I don't really have anything to say, do I?

Yes, I do. I have to say that I love you, even though I don't think I really came right out and said it out loud to you yesterday. I don't know quite what that means or what's going to happen next and I'm trying not to worry about it or think about it too much, but suddenly, even after being around my gay friend Raphael that I told you about, all summer . . .

Jan crumpled that piece of paper violently and went back to the first one:

Dear Raphael,

Guess what, I think I'm in love. And if I am, I guess I'm gay. I bet you wondered about that last summer. I look back on it now and wonder myself. Listen, what did you think about Corrin? I mean about me and Corrin? I didn't think anything about it, but I do wonder now. I mean I never touched her or anything, but now I think I must have sort of wanted to, I don't know. I know I thought she was beautiful, but I also know straight women like my mother and sister sometimes think other women are beautiful, so I guess that doesn't mean much.

But when I look back on myself, I see that I always liked being with girls best. Sometimes I was a tomboy and sometimes I wasn't, but the idea of having to someday go out with boys or get married always seemed weird to me. It just never seemed to fit me, except I knew it was what I was supposed to do, to want to do, too.

Anyway, I keep having this dream with you and Corrin in it, only now sometimes this other girl is in it instead.

See, the thing is that I feel about this other girl the way I guess I felt about Corrin, only much, much more so, and this time I know it. Is that how it starts? Is that how one finds out? I always felt I wasn't quite like other people. If I am gay, maybe that's why.

Raphael, remember I told you about that guy I grew up with, Ted? Sometimes he's in the dream now, too. He tried to kiss me, I mean in real life, not the dream, and I hated it. But last night I kissed this girl—no, not "this girl"—this wonderful girl, maybe I should say "woman," except she's my age and I'm not used to calling myself that. She's great—funny and kind and deep and intelligent and talented and strange— not as beautiful as Corrin (no one could be), but pretty, especially her eyes, which are very dark brown and show almost everything she feels. She's a little weird, too, but we've decided we both are.

Oh, Raphael, I never felt this way about anyone and I don't know what to do. I sure never felt this way about Ted or any boy. (Funny, I thought I was going to like you that way at first, isn't that dumb?) If this is how you felt about Don Jeffords last summer, then I can see how come I had to poke you sometimes to get you to hear what I was saying.

By the way, I'm stage managing Crucible. *(Right, I didn't get Elizabeth. Kerry did. Kerry's the girl. It's okay about Elizabeth. She plays her better than I could. And I love her so much I'm not jealous. Where was I? Oh: Parentheses.) There. We'll have two performances, the third weekend in December. Can you come?*

The thing is, Raphael, I can't think except about Kerry. I can't study. I can't even worry too much about Mrs. Nichol-

son, our director, who seems to have something wrong with
her but no one will say what.

    Kerry says she loves me, too.
    Raphael: AM I GAY?

Love, Jan

Quickly, before she could change her mind, Jan stuffed the letter into an envelope, addressed it to Raphael's apartment in New York City, stamped it, and put it with her clipboard so she'd be sure to mail it in the morning.

Then she took the crumpled letter she'd started writing to Kerry, tore it into tiny pieces, and went to bed.

Mrs. Nicholson was sitting front-row-center when Jan, Kerry, and Ted went into the auditorium Monday afternoon. The rest of the cast was already clustered around her. Nanny was pretending to sign the bandage on her ankle as if it were a cast, and Will was clowning around ineptly with the gold-headed cane by her side. Jan thought Mrs. Nicholson still looked pale and tired and thin under her makeup, but not much more than she had before the accident. Her wide and happy smile, anyway, was reassuring, as was the fact that she showed no signs of the mental confusion she'd had right after she'd fallen.

"I hear you and Kent had a little altercation," Mrs. Nicholson said to Jan while the cast got into position for Act One.

"Oh, it's okay now," Jan answered, not wanting to worry her, but hoping that it *would* be okay now that Mrs. Nicholson was back. "I think he's finally figured Proctor out, at least." She hesitated briefly. "I'm kind of nervous about what you'll think, and I sure am glad you're back!"

Mrs. Nicholson patted Jan's hand affectionately, but

quickly withdrew her own, which Jan realized felt oddly fragile. "Janna, thank you for taking over for me," she said. "It must have been hard."

"It was fun, Mrs. Nicholson, really. It was only hard at first. I liked it. More than I thought."

"Did you, Janna? Good! Well." She settled back, smoothing her skirt and draping an extra sweater carefully over her shoulders. "Call places, please, stage manager. And"—her voice rang out in almost the old vigorous way—"entertain me, cast. Let's try to run through the whole thing—no interruptions, just notes at the end of each act. I want to weep over this play, over the injustice that is done to these innocent people. I want to be at the edge of my chair by the end of the first act, and in tears by the final curtain."

"Places!" Jan called. "Act One. Ready? Curtain."

Jan watched Mrs. Nicholson anxiously as much as she could while the first act progressed, but as in auditions, her face was unreadable. During the Proctor–Abigail scene, Jan tried to see Kent's familiar performance freshly, as Mrs. Nicholson would be seeing it. Was he angry enough? Did his mood shift cleanly and clearly as well as quickly? Was he really communicating?

But except for a faint smile at the end of that scene, Mrs. Nicholson gave no sign of approval or disapproval.

At the end of the act, she sat still, making notes on the large legal pad attached to her clipboard, until the cast had come back down off the stage and were seated in the auditorium. Then she slowly got up and faced them. "All right," she said. "All right! It's going well. I see you've been working hard, all of you. Kent, you've got it now."

Jan closed her eyes in relief and leaned back; Kerry, sitting beside her, punched her triumphantly on the shoulder.

"Whew," breathed Ted. "*That's* over."

"Kent, come here, please." Mrs. Nicholson sat down again. "Take five, everyone. Then we'll go on to Act Two. No, Jan, you might as well stay with me."

Without looking at Jan, Kent got up from his seat and stood in front of Mrs. Nicholson.

"How do you feel about Proctor now?" Mrs. Nicholson asked, studying him intently, as if trying to see beyond his swagger.

"Okay, I guess," he said indifferently. "I guess I sort of worked it out while you were away. I just didn't want him to seem weak, that's all."

"No, Kent," Mrs. Nicholson said. "I think *you* didn't want to seem weak, playing him. Don't identify so totally with your character. Proctor *is* weak at times. Norris isn't."

Kent looked embarrassed but not entirely convinced. He scratched his chin and Jan noticed it was stubbly, as if he hadn't shaved for a while.

"Anyway," said Mrs. Nicholson dryly, winking at Jan, "I agree that you've probably worked it out. Not growing a beard, are you?"

Kent looked startled, as if he hadn't expected anyone to notice. "Just haven't had time to shave," he said evasively. "It's an idea, though, don't you think?"

"Not for Proctor, it isn't," Mrs. Nicholson answered, then called briskly to the cast. "All right, everyone. Back to work."

They succeeded in running through the whole play that afternoon, breaking only briefly between acts. About halfway through, Jan realized that Mrs. Nicholson had gone to the back of the auditorium and that she herself had been too absorbed in what was happening onstage to even turn the pages of her script. I *am* on the edge of my chair, she realized excitedly, hastily finding the place, just as Mrs. Nicholson said she wanted to be!

After Kerry, as Elizabeth watching Proctor's execution, had said the play's ringing last line, there was absolute silence in the auditorium. Then Mrs. Nicholson's voice came quietly from the back row. "Thank you, ladies and gentlemen. I think we have ourselves a play."

But there were still scenes to polish, still problems to solve, still parts of the play to rehearse over and over again, out of context, before Mrs. Nicholson would let them run through it again as a whole. Jan found herself being fascinated at the way Mrs. Nicholson shaped scenes bit by bit, resolving one problem and then, when the actors had grasped whatever it was and done it smoothly several times, building on the change, deepening characterizations and clarifying action.

"She's amazing," Jan said to Kerry at the end of that week as they walked to the parking lot. "Just amazing. She can get more out of an actor than anyone I've ever seen, even in stock."

"She sure can get a lot out of me." Kerry buttoned her jacket and shivered. "Brr! That wind's cold!"

"I'll drive you home," Jan said; they'd just reached her mother's car. "Can't have you getting sick!"

"My mother says you can't catch a cold from *being* cold." Kerry opened the passenger door when Jan unlocked it. "But I accept. Any excuse to be with you a little longer," she said when they were both in the car.

"I know," said Jan. "But we really don't need excuses, do we?"

Kerry lay back against the seat. "Nope. Sometimes I wonder how I existed before I knew you," she said as Jan pulled the car out of the lot. "I used to dream of having a perfect friend, someone who'd be almost a second self, or another half of me, a friend I could say anything to, who'd accept me and love me and not expect me to be someone else. But I never thought I'd find that person." She leaned over and gave Jan a quick kiss on the cheek. "Thank you," she whispered.

"Hey," said Jan, "don't thank me. I've dreamed of a friend like that, too."

"A lover," Kerry said. "That's what we both really wanted, isn't it? Only since boys somehow didn't fit, we thought what we wanted was a friend. You had Ted, though . . ."

"Ted's wonderful, but there was always something missing. Since I grew up, anyway." Jan glanced at her watch, then said hesitantly, "Want to come to my house for a minute?" she asked. "It's only five-fifteen. Your aunt doesn't expect you home till after six, does she? I can't believe I haven't asked you there yet. The play—"

"I've been hoping that's the reason," Kerry said, smiling, "not that you didn't want to invite me. I'd love to see where you live."

Jan turned the car around in someone's driveway and back-tracked to her street, then pulled into her driveway. She studied the house and the yard critically as she got out, trying to see them as Kerry would.

"What a neat garden!" Kerry exclaimed, heading straight for Mrs. Montcrief's perennial bed, which formed a half circle at one edge of the lawn. Most of the plants were frost-bitten and withered, but a few chrysanthemums, asters, and sedums still bloomed.

"It's a sheltered spot, Mom says," Jan explained while Kerry examined the flowers. "I don't know much about it, but she usually still has something flowering at Thanksgiving."

"I'd like a garden like this someday," Kerry said. "Can we have one?"

"Sure!" said Jan, startled and then excited at the thought of living with Kerry, of Kerry's wanting to live with her.

"And a little gray house with a big maple tree on one side, and a white picket fence . . ."

"Or maybe a gray split-rail one . . ."

Kerry shook her head. "But a dog can go right through a split-rail fence. Can we have a dog?"

Jan grinned. "Of course we can! I've always wanted a dog, but my mother's allergic. What kind?"

"What kind have you always wanted?"

Jan was about to answer when her mother called from the front door. "Jan! There you are," she said, coming down the steps. "I thought I heard voices, and I was waiting for the car; I've got to go to the store." She smiled at Kerry, and Jan introduced them quickly. "Kerry's the one who's playing Elizabeth," Jan explained, and her mother asked, "How's it going?"

"Okay, I hope," said Kerry. "Largely thanks to Jan."

"I'm sure thanks to you, too," said Jan's mother. "And now I'm afraid I'm going to be very rude and run off. Keys, please." She held out her hand to Jan. "I'm in the middle of making a complicated recipe for Thanksgiving, but I've run out of butter."

"Keys," said Jan, handing them to her. "Gas is low!" she called after her.

Her mother waved in acknowledgment, and drove off.

"For Thanksgiving?" said Kerry as Jan led her up the front steps. "Isn't it a little early?"

"She makes stuff ahead and freezes it. Pies, usually, and rolls. Come on in. Golden retriever, by the way."

"I was hoping you'd say that," Kerry answered without hesitation, as if Jan's mother hadn't interrupted their conversation at all. "My favorite kind. I like your mother . . ."

". . . and I like your room," she said a few minutes later when Jan had taken her up to it. "But"—she put her arms around Jan—"not as much as I love you." She kissed Jan, and for a long moment they stood there, holding each other.

"I'm still sort of nervous," Kerry whispered. "It's so new. Sometimes I feel I might burst with feeling, with love." She kissed Jan again. "It's okay, though. It's fine. It's wonderful." She moved out of Jan's arms, did an awkward pirouette, stumbled against Jan's desk chair and, laughing, sat down when Jan said, "Madame, a chair?"

"Did you really mean it," Jan asked, sitting on the edge of the desk to be close to her, "about the garden and the house and the golden retriever and all?"

"Of course!" said Kerry indignantly. "Didn't you?"

"Yes," Jan said softly. "A thousand times yes."

Right before the Thanksgiving break, when everyone in the cast was exhausted, Mrs. Nicholson let them have another run-through, and despite everyone's fatigue, Jan felt the same electricity coming to her from the stage then as she'd felt the day Mrs. Nicholson had come back.

But Mrs. Nicholson, though she seemed even more tired than the cast, was still not satisfied. "There are still rough spots for us to work on separately," she said. "But I don't want us to do any more run-throughs till close to technical rehearsal. I don't want you to lose your spontaneity. Janna, let's work a bit on the end of Act One, the Abigail–Betty scene, where they start accusing people of witchcraft. I don't need the men in that scene, just the two girls. The rest of you can go home if you want. Kent, I trust you'll find time to shave over the holiday. Happy Thanksgiving, all."

But no one moved except Gail and Brenda, who got quietly back into position.

"You have to *build* this scene, ladies." Mrs. Nicholson leaned against the apron. "You have to start small and build high," she said. "You're starting well, but you don't take the scene anywhere. Brenda, what happens to Abigail? What does she want here?"

"Well, she wants Proctor, of course," Brenda answered. "Like who wouldn't?" That got a laugh, quickly stifled by a glare from Mrs. Nicholson.

"What else?" asked Mrs. Nicholson.

Brenda hesitated, then said, "She suddenly sees her chance to get rid of Elizabeth? Like she thinks if she starts calling other people witches, she can get away with calling Elizabeth one, too, and get rid of her that way. Right?"

"Right enough for the play," said Mrs. Nicholson. "But for the scene, remember she's more or less been accused herself, and she wants to save her own skin. Understand?"

"I think so," said Brenda, after a quick glance at Kent, who was sitting in the third row, watching.

"Good," said Mrs. Nicholson. "Now, Gail. What about Betty?"

A frown creased Gail's freckled face. "Oh. Well, I think Betty just gets hysterical when Abby starts yelling out names. And so she yells out names, too. She doesn't really know what's going on."

"What's she feeling?"

Gail's frown deepened. "Excitement? Sort of—sort of like she gets carried away? Till she can't keep from screaming?"

Mrs. Nicholson straightened up, holding her hands high

as if for emphasis. *"That's* what I don't see yet," she told them. "That rising excitement, that growing hysteria—I don't see it enough. One girl's hysteria feeds the others', back and forth, and it rises, rises . . . Kerry Socrides, are you still here?"

Kerry, next to Jan, seemed surprised. "Yes," she said.

"Good. Janna, Kerry, on stage, please."

Kerry raised her eyebrows inquiringly at Jan, but Jan felt bewildered, too. She scrambled up onto the stage; Kerry followed.

"You know how to improvise, Janna," said Mrs. Nicholson, following them and leaning against the proscenium. "Kerry, I'm sure Jan's told you about doing improvs in stock. That's when you take a basic situation and some characters, and play the situation out, making it up as you go along. Sort of like children pretending. Nothing to it, really. All right," she went on, addressing the four of them. "Let's see. You are— ah—not quite yourselves, but younger girls, twelve or thirteen. You giggle a lot, you're imaginative, and you're very susceptible to suggestion."

"Like the girls in Salem, right?" asked Gail.

"Exactly. You and Brenda can think of yourselves as Betty and Abby, if you like, but, Brenda, you be a younger version of Abby." Mrs. Nicholson bowed her head, as if thinking, and then said, "All right. You're outside, and it's night, very dark. You've all been going somewhere, a party maybe, but you've lost your way. You've come upon a barn and you decide you'd better stay there for the night. I don't care what you do with the improv except for one thing." She lowered her voice dramatically, as if telling a ghost story. "At some point, Kerry, you think you see—something. That something, whatever it is, must never emerge corporeally, never enough so any of you actually see it. It may not even be there, of course; it

100

may be nothing, but you think it is, all of you. Understand?"

"Yes," said Jan, but the others just stood there looking nervous and confused. Although she was sure she knew what Mrs. Nicholson was after, Jan realized she was nervous herself, suddenly onstage again with so many people depending on her. "Okay," she said, trying to sound confident. "You guys ready?" she asked the others.

When they said they were, Mrs. Nicholson waited a few seconds longer, then called, "Ready—curtain."

Gail and Brenda immediately started walking aimlessly around the stage, Brenda poking at her hair and both girls looking vaguely up at the lights and out into the auditorium. Kerry stood upstage for a minute, then joined them. They're still outside, Jan thought, watching; okay, we'll have to start there. She walked, too, for a moment, with as much purpose as she could muster. Then she stopped and said, "Hey, look! Isn't that a barn up ahead? Maybe we could go in and get warm. Come on!" She walked a few steps farther, and then peered around, saying, "It looks deserted." She pantomimed pushing open a heavy door and holding it for the others. "Sure is dark in here," she whispered, groping, her hands out in front of her, fervently wishing that someone else would say something.

"Sure is," said Kerry, as if she'd read Jan's mind. "I can see a little, though."

"Yeah, me, too." Jan sank down onto an imaginary pile of hay. "I'm so tired," she whined. "I think we'd better stay here. I can't go another step." Come on, Jan, she scolded herself. Can't you think of anything better? This is terrible!

"I'm hungry," moaned Kerry, sitting next to Jan.

"So'm I," said Gail at last, and then Brenda said, "I'm scared."

101

Jan saw Mrs. Nicholson nod and go slowly back to her first-row seat, near Ted and Kent and Will and the others, all of whom were watching intently.

"Well," said Kerry, getting up. "Um—maybe there's something to eat somewhere." She started walking around, searching behind curtains and flats.

Jan hugged her arms around herself, deciding it was time to inject some atmosphere. It was odd, half directing an improv when she was also participating in it. "I'm so cold," she said. "Kerry, I don't see how you're going to find anything in this light. You'd better be careful. Hey, watch out! You never know what you might . . ."

Kerry screamed as if on cue and ran back to Jan, huddling next to her, her eyes huge as if she were really frightened. "I saw—I saw a—a mouse, or a snake, or—I don't know, *something* over there—in that corner . . ."

Jan peered fearfully in the direction Kerry was pointing. "You're right," she whispered. "Something just moved! Abby, Betty, can you see anything?"

"I saw it *again*," squealed Kerry. "It's a mouse. I just know it's a mouse. I *hate* mice. I'm so scared!"

"Me, too," Gail said timidly. But she didn't really sound frightened yet.

Jan got up and walked cautiously to the corner, pretending to peer into it. Then she shrieked and ran back. "It's not a mouse," she cried. "It's a snake. I know it's a snake!"

"Maybe it's a ghost," Kerry suggested. She clutched Brenda and screamed, staring into the corner. "It is, oh, it is! It's a ghost. Betty, look—is it?"

"Don't make me look," Gail moaned in the little girl voice she used for Betty. "Abby, I'm scared. I don't want to. Don't make me. Don't make me look!"

Brenda, finally in character as Abby, pushed Gail roughly

toward the corner. "You look, Betty," she said severely. "You look."

Gail hid her eyes. "Oh, it is, it is! I saw it, too! I saw it, too!"

"Use the line," came Mrs. Nicholson's voice quietly. "Jan, use Abigail's line."

"So did I," said Jan, her voice controlled but rising as she worked into the line from the play. "I saw it—I saw—'I saw Sarah Good with the Devil. I saw Goody Osburn with the Devil.'" She turned to Brenda; Abigail still had one more accusation to make.

"'I saw Bridget Bishop with the Devil,'" said Brenda, low but intense, staring at Gail.

Kerry, glancing at Jan, who nodded, moved away.

"'I saw George Jacobs with the Devil,'" Gail answered in character as Betty mimicking Abigail. "'I saw Goody Howe with the Devil!'"

Jan made her voice deep so they would know she was playing Parris and then Hale, both of whom had lines in this scene. "'She speaks! She speaks,'" she said, and then, in a slightly different but still underplayed voice, "'Glory to God! It is broken, they are free!'"

Brenda and Gail were facing each other; they hardly seemed aware that Jan and Kerry were still onstage. "'I saw Martha Bellows with the Devil,'" Gail said, her voice rising, beginning to lose control.

"'I saw Goody Sibber with the Devil,'" Brenda said, topping her.

"'The Marshal, I'll call the Marshal,'" said Jan, quietly playing still another character. She moved aside and stood close to Kerry, who by now was far upstage.

"'I saw Alice Barrow with the Devil!'" Gail cried.

Brenda answered without giving Jan time to provide the

last intervening line. " 'I saw Goody Hawkins with the Devil!' "

" 'I saw Goody Bibber with the Devil!' "

" 'I saw Goody Booth with the Devil!' "

"I saw . . ." screamed Gail, "I saw . . ." Her voice trailed into silence and she dropped her arms, which she'd been flailing wildly over her head. "Oh, my God," she sobbed. "I got so caught up in it I didn't even realize it was over."

Brenda flopped down on one of the chairs that served as part of Betty's bed in rehearsals. "Whoa!" she said weakly. "I think we did it, huh?" She peered out front. "Mrs. Nicholson, did we? I feel like—I don't know. A wet towel, maybe."

"So do I," said Gail.

There was scattered applause from the auditorium, from Ted, Jan saw, and Kent, and one or two others.

"My good girls." Mrs. Nicholson, beaming, came up to the stage. "My good actresses. Yes, you certainly did do it. Thank you. *That's* the way to play the scene. Thank you, Janna and Kerry, also. Fine work, all of you. We'll stop now. Have a good Thanksgiving, girls. The rest of you, too," she said to the other cast members.

Mrs. Nicholson gathered up her script and pencils and clipboard and notes and sailed out of the auditorium.

"See?" said Kent when Jan, still shaken, returned to her seat. "See? *Actress*, not director. You were good, Jan; you got them going. Your experience showed. Ever hear the saying that the cobbler should stick to his last?"

"Oh, dry up," said Kerry, dropping down beside Jan. She pointed at Kent's bristly chin. "Why don't you go shave yourself?"

Jan laughed.

TEN

꩜

THE POLISHED APPLES gleamed brightly among the oranges
and grapes in the Montcriefs' Thanksgiving centerpiece. The
old papier-mâché turkey, which had topped it for as many
years as Jan could remember, glowered down at the family
all through their early-afternoon dinner, as if he resented having been placed so far away from the nuts that Jan's mother
had strewn plentifully on the tablecloth. Dinner was perfect:
the roast turkey golden brown and succulent with moist, rich
bread-and-apple stuffing; the sweet spicy yams, topped with
melted, lightly browned marshmallows; the tiny onions, the
peas, the turnips for those who liked them. Jan ate as if nothing else mattered, perhaps to hide from herself that something did. Still, she tried to make the expected flattering
comments about Anita's new red corduroy maternity smock
and about Hal's diligent preparation for the law-school entrance exam he was planning to take. She dutifully helped
her mother clear the dishes and bring on the pies; she carried
in the coffeepot and passed around the cream—thinking, as
she had since yesterday when she'd gotten Raphael's answer

to her letter: I am different from them; their world isn't my world.

And underneath that was the constant ache of missing Kerry, who was far away in Connecticut, visiting her grandmother. Four days without Kerry, four days without talking with her, touching her, hearing her voice and seeing her smile—and next year, she thought, next year when I'm in drama school, where will she be? Next year—heck, what about January, when her parents come back from their trip?

I wish, she thought, looking around as her family finished their desserts, chatting about the new baby, about Hal's test, about who was going to have everyone for Christmas—I wish I could tell them about Kerry. Then she thought: Maybe I could!

But now everyone was getting up from the table. Mom was stacking dishes; Anita was eating a walnut, saying, "I wonder if nuts are okay for babies"; Hal and Dad were loosening their belts and heading for the living room and the usual football games on TV, Dad with his pipe and Hal with one of the terrible cigars he'd recently started smoking. "The boy can't even wait till his kid is born," Dad had joked earlier.

Where do I fit, Jan wondered, a sudden catch in her throat. Where do Kerry and I fit? If we stay together, end up together, could we make a place for ourselves here?

Anita tossed a pecan at Jan, who ducked but caught it. "Here, dreamer. I bet you didn't hear a thing I said."

Jan shook her head and tossed the pecan back.

"I said why don't you join Daddy and Hal or read or do homework or something, and I'll help Mom with the dishes? You helped a lot during dinner, and before, and"—Anita pushed herself heavily away from the table, her pink face pinker with the effort—"and I am *not* an invalid, in spite of how all of you've been treating me. Go on," she said, giving Jan a gentle push. "Scram!"

Gratefully, glad to escape, Jan hugged her sister quickly and went up to her room.

Upstairs, she closed her door and took out the letter from Raphael, even though she'd already read it three times:

Dear Jan,

I assume it was you writing that oddity—I can't quite bring myself to call it a letter. Honeybunch, you are so far gone I could barely read your name! Congratulations! Have you done IT yet? (You know what I mean, sweetie, so stop blushing.) I bet you haven't; girls take so long. Oh, well, you just go right on being soulful, sweetikins; I think it's lovely.

Now I'll be serious, so please listen.

First, baby, take it easy, take it slow (forget what I said in Paragraph One, too). Do what you feel okay about doing, but don't jump to conclusions. Maybe she's not gay; maybe you're not. Now, you're right that I wondered about you last summer. You seemed to have such a thing for Corrin, and you didn't for any of the guys (except, ahem, for me, but I hardly count, lovey, though I'm flattered!). Corrin, by the way, just wrote me to say she lost her virginity on Halloween to a boy named Edgar (Allan Poe?). I guess that won't destroy you now that your affections are elsewhere.

Listen, honeybunch, I don't want to be cruel, but you've got to think of everything. It might be love (it probably is, if I know you), but I feel it my duty as your gay uncle (not auntie yet, I hope!) to tell you that it could be one of those things called an Adolescent Crush. Girls get them, too, I believe. So have fun and feel what you feel right now, but be honest with yourself and don't go putting yourself for all time into a little lavender box marked "gay" until you're really sure. I'm sure, but I'm almost twenty. You're only—what are you? Sixteen? Seventeen? I came out in high school, too, and you better believe it was pretty damn rough. Maybe kids are more understanding where you live, but don't count on it! School's not show biz, hon. So be careful, okay?

AM I GAY? you asked me in big letters. I can't answer that. Only you can, and maybe you won't be able to till you've done a lot more living. I am *trying* to say, though, that I think there's a pretty good chance of it. There's Corrin, and there's the fact that you were the only girl on the plantation last summer who wasn't chasing my ass (you really weren't, you know) or some other boy's. I never got the impression that you really had the hots for old Teddy back home, and you weren't shocked when I told you about me and Mr. Donald Jeffords. (Who, by the way, has left me for a dancer, of all things. I believe you mentioned that he seemed fickle. You were right.) As for your thinking at first that you "liked" me—well, maybe you did a little, and maybe I did a little; the point is who you like *best* usually, not who you like at all. I think I read someplace that there really aren't very many 100% straight or gay people in the world (I speak as a 99% gay, however, I hasten to add!), so don't be shocked if you're not 100% anything either. Did I ever tell you that I slept with a girl once? It was nice, too. But I like guys better, in all ways. Like it's guys I relate to emotionally. I can talk to girls, sure, but it's guys I fall in love with, guys I want to spend my life with. No offense, but I could live without ever seeing another woman, but I'd die if I couldn't ever see another man.

Baby, I feel like your father or something! I mean I bet there's not a soul for you chickens to talk to up there in darkest New Hampshire—what's the name of that hick town you live in?—*Southview.* If you were in a city there'd be places you could go, people you could talk to. All I can say is be kind to each other, and fair, and as honest as you can be, because even if you don't end up in each other's arms forever, that could be your gay sister you're in love with now. Even if she turns out to be straight, she's still your sister—another woman and a human being who deserves to be respected and cherished. (Don't we all?)

And if you do turn out to be straight (I write, slanting off the page in horror, pouring myself another glass of vin ordinaire—I always take vin ordinaire with difficult letters)— if you turn out to be straight, well, c'est la vie; that's not so bad either, and maybe you'll both grow up to be nice ladies who don't dish gays.

Honeybunch, got to go. If you ever want to talk more, write again. Or call. If my cat answers, hang up.

Love, Raphael

P.S. I do want to come to your show. Particulars, please.

P.P.S. This is even more embarrassing. Lesbians can get AIDS, too, a dyke friend of mine reminded me when I mentioned you (no, not in any real detail; trust me). She said to tell you that if you haven't slept with anyone else, boy or girl, and if your girlfriend hasn't either, and if neither of you does drugs, which I'm sure you don't, you're probably pretty safe. But if you have ANY DOUBTS and you do you-know-what, you should, um, protect yourselves. She mentioned condoms, and Saran Wrap and something called a dental dam, but the details elude me. Thank God she said you could write her. She's Margie Zamack, and she lives in the apartment upstairs from me, so you've got the address. For God's sake write her if you have questions!

Jan put her head down on her desk, on the letter, and stayed there motionless, listening to a squirrel chattering outside and to the distant scrape of someone raking leaves. That last P.S., incomplete as it was, was more than she wanted to know; it made her feel queasy.

She closed her eyes, trying not to think, until her mother called up to her, "Jan, telephone! Mr. Nicholson. Your teacher's husband, I guess."

Immediately Jan went cold inside. Reluctantly, she went downstairs and, full of dread, picked up the phone.

"After first year," Dad was saying to Hal in the living room, "law school gets a lot easier. But, boy, do I remember . . ."

"Hello?" Jan said into the phone.

"Jan?"

"Yes." The dread increased, threatened to overpower her.

"This is Robert Nicholson—er, Mr. Nicholson. Mrs. Nicholson's husband."

"Yes. Hello."

"Jan, Mrs. Nicholson asked me to call you."

Then she's not dead, Jan thought; it's just something about rehearsal, just some message.

"She asked me to tell you she'd like you to take over rehearsals for the next couple of weeks."

Jan sat down abruptly. "But—but," she stammered, "what's wrong?" Then, panicking, she exclaimed, "There's only a couple of weeks left till the technical rehearsal. And that's the week of the show!"

"I know. She told me that. She said to tell you she's sorry. She said you know what to do, that you can do it, that she believes in you and that you've been doing fine. She also said to tell you that it's been cleared with the principal. You know, Mr.—er—Mr. Taylor. He says it's all right for you to take over."

110

Jan barely heard the last part of what he said. "But, Mr. Nicholson, what's happened? Please, what's wrong with Mrs. Nicholson?"

"She's in the hospital," he said slowly. "She—she's had some surgery. She'll have to stay there awhile."

"But what's wrong? Can you tell me what's wrong with her? It's not just her ankle, is it?"

"No." There was a pause. "I guess you do have to know," he said at last. "I know she'd rather keep it quiet; she doesn't want a lot of people fussing over her, but . . . I guess you do have to know. She has cancer, Jan."

Jan closed her eyes. Somehow she'd known it since tryouts, someplace way down inside where she didn't have to face it till it faced her, the way she'd known somewhere inside that she was gay, that she loved Kerry and had been attracted to Corrin.

"I'm sorry," she managed to say politely. "I'm so sorry. Is she—in pain or anything?" That's what you ask, she remembered; that's what Mom always asks.

"Some. We've known for quite a while." Mr. Nicholson's voice shook slightly.

Jan nodded silently, remembering Mrs. Nicholson's words to Mr. Taylor the day she collapsed: "I didn't think it would be this soon."

But she'd recovered; she'd been all right after that; she'd been fine . . .

"Can she have visitors?" Jan asked finally.

"Not right now. Maybe in a week or so. I'll let you know."

"Thank you." Jan struggled for control. "Could you—could you please tell her everything'll be okay, with the show, I mean? It'll be fine. She's already done the hard part. We'll keep it going the way she wants it. Tell her not to worry."

Tell her not to die. Oh, tell her not to die!

111

"I will. Thank you, Jan. You've been very helpful to her, I know. I want to thank you for that." He cleared his throat as if he didn't know what else to say, said, "Er—happy Thanksgiving," and hung up.

Happy Thanksgiving, thought Jan. Sure.

ELEVEN

IT WAS A BLEAK DAY, neither fall nor winter, when school started again after Thanksgiving. The wind rustled dry leaves across the ground; the sky threatened snow but no snow fell.

Jan, early because she hadn't been able to sleep, had trouble starting her mother's car. Finally, after the third try, the engine turned over and she backed out of the driveway through billows of gray exhaust.

If it weren't for Kerry, she thought once she was out on the main road, I'd cut school.

And if it weren't for rehearsal.

She swung the car slowly into the street leading to Southview High and drove into the parking lot. But it was still early enough for the lot to be empty, grayly bleak like the day.

Maybe if Kerry's walking I could pick her up, Jan thought, backing out as another early student pulled in.

A small group of kids from *Crucible*—Kent, Nanny, Will —were walking toward school on Kerry's street when Jan turned the corner. Jan waved, amused at the surprise on their faces, and she laughed aloud when Nanny gave her a friendly smile and shouted, "Wrong way!" The day seemed better then, and since she hadn't seen Kerry walking to school, Jan decided to find out if she was still at home. She parked outside Kerry's aunt's house, and ran up the porch steps to ring the bell.

The house was tightly closed, still sleeping—or still empty. For a moment Jan was afraid Aunt Elena and Kerry weren't back yet from Connecticut. But when she checked in the garage, she saw Aunt Elena's car, and when she went up onto the porch again and knocked, Aunt Elena sleepily answered the door.

"Jan! How nice," she said, and then launched into a non-stop stream of worry. "Come in. What time is it? Have we overslept? Oh, dear, I'm sure we have! We got home so late last night. The traffic was terrible and we left later than we'd planned. Kerry Ann!" she called up the stairs, then self-consciously smoothed the skirt of her red bathrobe. "You're going to think I never take this off. Come on into the kitchen and I'll make some coffee. Or—no, why don't you go upstairs and see that my lazy niece gets up? Goodness, I hope you'll be on time for your first class. Will you?"

"We'll be a little late, I guess, if Kerry's not up yet. But not very." Nervously, Jan started up the stairs, aware that this would be her first time in Kerry's room. And Kerry would be sleeping there, still in bed . . .

"Second door to the right when you get to the top," Aunt Elena called cheerfully. "You'll probably have to shake her. She sleeps like a rock."

Jan felt the smoothness of the highly polished banister as she climbed the stairs; felt the thick carpet under her shoes, the dryness in her mouth. *Take it easy, take it slow;* she heard Raphael's voice saying his written words. *Be honest—be kind to each other, and fair.*

The second door to the right was exactly like the first door and the one opposite it, except the other doors were open and this one was closed. Funny, that Kerry's door should be like any other.

Jan knocked.

There was no answer.

I should knock again, she thought, pushing the door open instead.

The room was still dusky, even though one shade and the window behind it were partway up. It was a small room, cluttered with books and strewn with clothes; not neat at all, though Kerry herself was always neat.

Jan closed the door quietly behind her, thinking, I probably should leave it open, and went to the heap of quilts and blankets that now moved on the bed.

"Kerry?" Jan said awkwardly. "Hey, Kerry, it's me. Jan."

Kerry grunted and turned over.

Well, Jan said to herself defensively as she bent tentatively down, her aunt said I'd have to shake her. She touched Kerry's shoulder gently. "Kerry, sleepyhead, wake up."

Kerry's eyes fluttered open, then opened wider. "Jan! I was dreaming about you, and here you are!"

"It's late," Jan explained. "Your aunt said to wake you." She realized her hand was still on Kerry's shoulder and loosened its hold, but Kerry seized it quickly and held it to her lips. "I missed you," she whispered. "I missed you more than I ever thought I would."

"I missed you, too." Gently, Jan touched Kerry's face. "Understatement."

There didn't seem to be anything else important enough to say.

"Your aunt's making coffee," Jan said at last, realizing someone had to be practical. But she felt Kerry pulling her closer.

"Jan . . ."

"Kerry, I—you should get up." But she knelt by the bed and put her head down near Kerry's.

Kerry smoothed Jan's hair, and Jan felt her muscles melt. "I wish Aunt Elena weren't downstairs," Kerry whispered.

"Raphael said we should be—honest, that maybe we can't be sure yet."

"You heard from him." Kerry still smoothed Jan's hair.

Jan barely managed to nod.

"Well, I'm sure," Kerry whispered. "I spent the whole weekend thinking about you, dreaming about you, writing you long notes." She moved to one side and reached down to her suitcase, which Jan now saw was on the other side of the bed, and handed Jan a bulging envelope. "Here. Entertain yourself while I get dressed." She got up—she was wearing, Jan noticed, red-and-white-striped pajamas—and put her hands on Jan's shoulders. "The top note," she said, "is the one where I tell you I asked Aunt Elena if I could ask my parents to let me stay here the whole year, not just till January."

Jan felt her heart speed up.

"Okay?" Kerry asked.

"Of course, yes!" Jan said, finding her voice at last. "That's wonderful; I . . ."

"Kerry Ann, aren't you up yet?" Aunt Elena shouted from downstairs. "You're going to be terribly late. *Shake* her, Jan!"

They looked at each other and then both laughed so hard tears came to their eyes. Jan stood, stuffing the envelope in her pocket, and put her arms around Kerry, feeling the smooth warm skin of her back under her thin pajama top. "Kerry, you are very, very pretty," she whispered, holding her. "And I love you very, very much. But would you be hurt if I said I think I'd better go downstairs and talk to your aunt while you dress? Okay?"

Kerry kissed Jan's nose. "Okay." Hugging her again, she said, "I don't have any doubts, Jan. That's why I asked to stay. Aunt Elena said yes, by the way." Kerry's voice dropped and Jan had to strain to hear. "I never wanted anyone to touch me before. And nobody ever has. I've only kissed a boy a couple of times, last year, but it—I don't know. Didn't feel right, I guess. But it's different with you. It does feel right, and I don't see how loving someone can be wrong, like some people say. How can it be? What could be immoral or sick about love? As I said before, I'm scared and I don't know— you know—anything about it, really, but . . ." She hugged Jan harder. "I've never felt anything like this. My head's spinning, I'm dizzy, I . . ."

Jan felt her clinging, felt Kerry's body pressing tightly against her own, felt her own dizziness, and her own nervousness. But the feelings weren't really disturbing—just new.

"I know," Jan whispered. "I know."

They stayed far away from each other in the car on the way to school. But when Jan told Kerry about Mr. Nicholson's call and about having to take over rehearsals, and asked Kerry to assist her between Elizabeth scenes, it was as if she were talking to another part of herself.

That's it, too, she realized as they went inside, got late slips, and separated to go to their respective homerooms; she felt warm inside, thinking about it, and remembering the house and the garden and the golden retriever.

The day dragged, except for the two or three glimpses she got of Kerry, and Jan's mind was too much on her and on rehearsal to be able to concentrate on her classes, or to concentrate on Ted when he asked her how her Thanksgiving had been, or even on Mr. Taylor's words when he talked to her about taking over rehearsals. She tried to write a poem to Kerry during history, but she wasn't able to translate what she felt into words, and finally she decided to go to the auditorium to calm herself down and focus her thoughts before rehearsal.

" 'I wish the long ship Argo . . .' " she whispered when she got up on the stage, but it was no good. It wasn't acting she had come to think about, not even *Medea*.

It was Mrs. Nicholson, as well as Kerry. And it was directing.

All day, when she hadn't been thinking about Kerry, she'd been feeling *Crucible* almost as if it were in her hands, and she a sculptor, shaping it. It was true that Mrs. Nicholson had done most of the hard work already, but Jan knew it was also true that she herself had helped, and that some of the ideas incorporated in the production were hers. Now that she had complete responsibility for it, she realized that the whole had come to matter more to her than any of its parts, and she wondered if she would ever again be able to see a play from the perspective of just a single character. What was it Mrs. Nicholson had said so many weeks ago? That she'd someday want to do something more creative than acting?

And here it was.

It felt right, as right as loving Kerry did.

In a way, Jan realized, Mrs. Nicholson had given her both.

When the cast came straggling in for rehearsal, Jan was sitting, outwardly calm, in her front-row seat, clipboard on her lap, pencil behind her ear. She'd rehearsed the speech she was going to make to the cast; she'd swallowed her nervousness earlier, alone onstage, and by the time Kerry walked in with Ted, she felt confident and ready.

When everyone was quiet she stood next to the step unit and began. "You've probably heard rumors all day that Mrs. Nicholson is very sick, and by now you probably know they're true. She is very sick, in the hospital, and . . ."

Jan saw Kent wave his arm, about to interrupt. Still the beard, she noticed with annoyance; why hadn't he shaved it off over Thanksgiving as Mrs. Nicholson had asked?

"What's wrong with Mrs. Nicholson?" Kent asked. "You could at least tell us that."

"I'm sorry," said Jan. "I got the impression from Mr. Nicholson that she didn't want everyone to know. He said she didn't want people fussing over her."

"Do you know?"

"Yes."

"Well, how about that?" Kent glared at her. "Extra-special you, huh? Since when does the stage manager keep things from the cast?"

"When the director wants it that way," Jan answered.

She went quickly on with the few other things she had to say—that they'd keep the rehearsal schedule as it was, that Mrs. Nicholson wanted them to go ahead and that Mr. Taylor did also—but by the time she was finished, Kent was whispering to Brenda, and several of the juniors plus one or two other seniors, including Will, were frowning.

"Okay, Kent," Jan said, deciding it would be better to get whatever it was out in the open. "Spit it out."

Kent got laconically up from his seat and stood next to her. "Mind if I address the cast, Madame Stage—er, Madame Substitute Director?" he asked sarcastically.

"Suit yourself." Deliberately Jan left him to face his audience alone; she sat back down in the front row.

Kent made a deep, theatrical bow. "Thank you. Hi, there,"

he said, waving at the others in the cast. "Remember me? I'm the star—er—*lead*—in this show. How could you forget, huh?"

Everyone laughed uneasily and Jan saw Kerry close her eyes as if thinking "Oh, no."

"And so, ladies and gentlemen, I think what I have to say might be more representative of the *cast*, of the way the *actors* feel, than what you've just heard. I mean, we're up there together, and she's out front—well, you know." He cleared his throat, made his voice squeak in an exaggerated fashion, and said, "Unaccustomed as I am to public speaking . . ." That got another laugh.

"Get to the point, Kent," Ted growled, and one or two others, Jan was glad to hear, joined him. Someone else said, "Yeah, come on, Kent. We haven't got all afternoon."

Immediately, Kent held up his hand. "Let me have the stage," he said, reaching around and thumping it, "and you all know I won't give it up without a struggle." His face suddenly became more serious, and he dropped his voice, as if confiding in the cast. "And that's the point. Jan's done a good job of stage managing—yes, Jan, you have—but a director she's not. We all know you're an actress, Jan. That's okay; it's not your fault! But the point is, I think, and some of the others in the cast think, that this play is in bad trouble and that we need our *real* director to straighten it out. I think we should ask Mr. Taylor if we can postpone the performances till after Mrs. Nicholson comes back."

"But Jan said Mr. Taylor approved of us going on," said Nanny, her round face troubled. "Maybe Mrs. Nicholson won't be back in time. I mean, Jan said she's *very* sick. Suppose she's going to be out for months or something?"

"Well, if Jan would tell us what's wrong with her we might

be able to figure out what to do more accurately, Nanny, but since she won't, we'll just have to guess about it. Right, Jan?"

"Right." Jan felt trapped. It would be so easy to say "She has cancer; Nanny's probably right"—but how could she without Mrs. Nicholson's permission?

"I think Kent's got a point," Brenda said, pouting. "Why shouldn't we find out about postponing it? Besides, maybe Mr. Taylor will tell us what's wrong with Mrs. Nicholson even if Jan won't." She faced Jan. "Kent won't say this, so I will. He's not sure that your interpretation of Proctor is the same as Mrs. Nicholson's."

"Then Kent and I should discuss that," Jan said evenly.

Kerry stood up. "I'm not very experienced in plays, but I have a lead, too, and I don't think the play's in trouble at all. I think it's just the way Mrs. Nicholson wants it."

I love you, Jan thought.

"You don't have a very *long* lead, Kerry," Kent said with an air of long-suffering patience. "And as you say, you don't have much experience."

"Well, what's wrong with the play, then? You tell us. Maybe we can fix it ourselves."

"Pace," Kent said grandly, looking bored. "Timing."

"Oh, for Pete's sake, Kent!" Jan exploded in disgust. "That's wrong with almost every play at this stage and you know it as well as I do!"

"And you're going to fix it, right? All by yourself? You, an actress, are going to fix it. Well, I don't think you can, and this play is too important to me and to Mrs. Nicholson for me to want to risk your fooling around with it."

"Why don't you fix it, then, Kent?" Ted asked quietly.

"Because, pal, I'm in it, onstage nearly every minute, in case you hadn't noticed. That's why."

"That," said Nanny, shooting Jan a sympathetic look, "must mean that if the pace is off, it's got a lot to do with *your* pace, Kent!"

There was a nervous laugh.

"Jan's got a lot of experience," said Kerry. "And she's not onstage. I don't see why she can't help us with pacing and timing, if that's what's wrong."

"You wouldn't, Kerry," Kent snapped. "You think Jan can do anything. We all know that."

Jan quickly scrawled "Thanks, but leave it" on a scrap of paper, got up, and handed it to Kerry.

"Love note?" said Kent under his breath to Jan. "H'mm?"

Will, close enough to have heard, raised his head, his eyes round and startled. Brenda gave Kent a thinly disguised thumbs-up sign.

Jan felt a momentary stab of fear, but she managed to retort, "You're going to turn into a dirty old man if you don't watch out." Pushing Kent's words and his friends' reactions away, she faced the cast herself. Immediately Kent made another sweeping bow and said, "Ladies and gentlemen, the great Janna Montcrief will now give us the benefit of her predictable opinion."

"Look," said Jan, trying to restore reason, "instead of sitting here all afternoon wasting time, let's take a vote. Some of you seem to agree with Kent, so let's see how many. If most of you do, then I guess we should ask Mr. Taylor about a postponement. Maybe we could get him to find out how Mrs. Nicholson feels about one, or if there's any way of telling when she'll be back."

Jan heard an approving murmur from most of the cast, but Kent cut it off. "And who's going to count the votes, Madame Director?"

"I will," said Kerry quickly.

Kent gave a short, bitter laugh. "Not you, doll. You're just a little too involved, don't you think?"

Jan heard a suppressed snicker and asked quickly, "How about Nanny?" She felt her hands making fists and found herself wishing she could punch Kent into silence. "Will you accept that?"

"I didn't even say I'd agree to a vote," Kent answered.

"Come on, Kent," Gail said impatiently. "You're wasting a lot of rehearsal time."

"How about this?" said Ted. "All in favor of having a vote, and having Nanny count, say aye."

Everyone but Kent, Brenda, and Will shouted "Aye!"

"Opposed? What's the matter, Kent?" Ted asked when there was complete silence. "Cat got your tongue? How about you, Brenda? Will?"

Brenda poked Kent, who slouched back to the front row and sat down. "Paper ballots," he said. "And if Nanny counts, Brenda helps her."

"Right," Will said emphatically. "That's only fair."

"Okay," said Ted. "Write 'Go on' or 'Postpone' on your ballot, depending on how you feel. Okay, Jan?"

"Sure." Jan scrawled "Go on" on a scrap of paper, handed it deliberately to Brenda instead of to Nanny, and walked rapidly up the aisle and out to the water cooler in the lobby.

Ted followed her, after handing in his ballot.

"Thanks." Jan gulped down a cup of water she didn't really want. "That would have gone on forever."

"Jan," Ted said anxiously, "you'd better be careful. I don't know why—maybe some kind of power thing—but I think Kent's out to get you. And if he loses this vote I wouldn't put it past him to do something really rotten."

Jan crushed her paper cup fiercely and threw it away. "Like what?"

"Like—I don't know."

"You do know. I can tell that you think you do, anyway. Come on, Ted, what?"

"Well, for instance, Nanny told me that this morning she met Kent and Will when she was walking to school, and that all three of them saw you driving to Kerry's house. She said Kent made some kind of crack."

Jan froze; her stomach lurched, and for a moment she was afraid she might have to run to the bathroom and be sick. *I came out in high school, too, and it was really rough . . . so be careful.* She wished she could stop remembering scraps of Raphael's letter—wished she could stop remembering Kent's comments about fags, too.

But, aloud, she managed to say "What kind of crack? Kids pick each other up for school all the time. Look at you and me—"

Ted took a cup from the side of the water cooler and filled it. Jan had never seen him blush in all the years she'd known him, but now his face was almost purple. "Some garbage about the hottest romance of the century," he blurted out finally, and then quickly hid his face in his water cup.

"Oh, good grief." Jan felt sick again. And cold. And frightened. That most of all.

"I thought you should know," said Ted miserably. He shoved the empty cup down into the wastebasket as if he wanted to hide his face there, too. "Jan, I don't think I want to know what's going on, okay? But—well, just watch it. Kent's a real pain, but some kids listen to him. Will, for instance. And obviously Brenda will go along with anything he does, and some girls listen to her. Maybe only a couple in the cast, but there are all her other friends, too." Abruptly, he yanked open the auditorium door, then called back, "Looks like they've finished."

"I'll be right there."

Jan stood still for a minute after Ted left, trying to force her mind to work again. But it wouldn't, so she went slowly back into the auditorium and sat down next to Kerry, careful not to touch her or even brush against her.

"What's wrong?" Kerry whispered.

"Tell you later." Jan kept her eyes on Nanny and Brenda, and on the two piles of paper, one a bit larger than the other, on the stage behind them. But she wondered if she really cared anymore.

"Okay," Nanny said. "It wasn't even close. I guess I should say it quickly. The 'Go on's' win. It was sixteen to six."

Kerry gripped Jan's arm, but Jan shook her off roughly, almost in a panic, and pulled away. The shock on Kerry's face made her feel almost physical pain. She started to scrawl Kerry an apology and explanation, but Kent came sauntering up to them. "Congratulations," he said to Jan coldly. He started up the step unit, but then pivoted deftly on his down-stage foot so that he was facing the auditorium three-quarters front.

"By the way," he said crisply, looking straight at Kerry and rubbing his chin with the tip of one forefinger, "I've decided not to shave off my beard. As I said before, Proctor's no fag, and I just thought I'd let you know in advance that you're going to have to get used to kissing a real man in our Act Two scene."

TWELVE

❧

AFTER A SHORT REHEARSAL Friday afternoon, Jan and Kerry went to the Southview public library, which was only a few blocks from Aunt Elena's house. While Kerry examined the picture collection, Jan sat at a table under the mullioned windows of the reference room, surrounded by costume books and history books, along with books about Salem and Massachusetts Bay Colony. None of them really answered her question, but the illustrations—mostly photos of old paintings—showed her that although most men in those days were clean-shaven, a few had worn beards. And that meant Proctor could have worn a beard, too.

So that won't work, she thought tiredly, unless Kerry finds something in the encyclopedias and historical dictionaries and the picture collection to contradict it. But that's unlikely. Maybe Mrs. Nicholson can think of something. Jan had permission to visit her in the hospital in a week, on the Saturday before the final week of rehearsals, to give her a progress report on the play, and she'd gotten Mr. Nicholson to ask her if Kerry could go, too, on the grounds that Kerry was acting as her assistant when she wasn't onstage herself. Mrs. Nicholson had agreed.

Jan pushed aside her notepad and put her aching head down on the table. All week she had tried reasoning with Kent and kidding him, but no matter what she tried, he resisted, as if he were silently saying, "Make me shave it off. Go on. Prove you're really the director!"

How dumb, she thought. How stupid, childish, and petty. Dumb.

But even though she believed that, she could see that Kent's defiance was beginning to weaken the cast's confidence in her. On Thursday, Ted had heard Will and Brenda talking about postponement again, and the pace, especially in Kent's scenes, was still sluggish despite two rapid-fire line rehearsals. It was as if Kent was deliberately putting the show in trouble to prove he'd been right about its problems all along.

Jan felt Kerry brush her shoulder and she leaned against her for a moment while Kerry rubbed the back of her neck, as if she knew how stiff it was. But then someone came into the reference room and they moved apart.

"Find anything?" Jan asked as Kerry sat down opposite her.

"Not really. A couple of beards in one or two pictures, none in the rest. No mention of Proctor in the text. The picture collection's good, but we can't prove anything with it. Most of the books didn't have any pictures at all from that period." Kerry straightened one of Jan's stacks of books. "I looked up about us," she said.

"Huh?"

"You know. Homosexuality. In the encyclopedias."

Jan raised her eyebrows.

"They don't say much." Kerry sighed. "The old ones call it

arrested development or mental illness and the new ones give a lot of conflicting theories—you're born gay; you're not born gay—that kind of thing. Some of them talk a lot about law reform and stuff like that. I guess teachers are right when they say encyclopedias really aren't that great."

"There must be books," said Jan, "if you want to read about it."

"Before the stuff about homosexuality," Kerry went on, "in one of the new encyclopedias, there's this little paragraph about homophobia. Fear of homosexuals, it says, or of homosexuality. 'Prejudice, sometimes leading to violent acts,' it says, too." Kerry fiddled with her pencil. "It says sometimes the most homophobic people are that way because they're scared of being gay themselves. Guys, mostly, it says, so they try to act extra-masculine."

"Kent," said Jan.

"I thought that, too."

Something in Kerry's voice made Jan look up sharply. "Hey, what is it?" she asked.

Kerry brushed her hair back. "Oh, nothing." Her chair made a scraping sound on the floor as she pushed it away from the table. The person who'd come into the room earlier, a middle-aged woman, frowned disapprovingly.

"Can we get out of here?" Kerry whispered. "Are you done?"

"Only if when we leave you'll tell me what's wrong."

"Okay."

Jan gathered up her notebook and schoolbooks, flung her jacket over her shoulders, and followed Kerry out into the dark early evening.

"Your mother'll be here soon," said Kerry evasively. "She's picking you up, right?"

"Kerry." Jan dropped her books on the steps and sat down. "Come on."

"It's just Kent, I guess." Kerry shifted her books and sat, too. "It's getting harder to play those two scenes with him. He really doesn't react anymore. Even after you told him today that he doesn't, he just stood there staring at me with this weird look on his face, and—well, you remember when I pulled away from him in the second-act scene and said ouch?"

"Yes. What happened?"

"I know I shouldn't have stopped like that, but he kept rubbing his cheek on mine, like some huge cat. Like he was trying to scratch me, to make a big point of that dumb beard."

"Jerk," muttered Jan. "Okay, look, I'll say something next time if I see him do it. I honestly didn't notice today."

"Maybe you shouldn't say anything. I just wanted you to know. But—oh, never mind."

"What?"

Kerry's gaze shifted to the sidewalk, where an Irish setter, burnished copper in the glow of the streetlight, was sniffing industriously at a pile of leaves. "Nothing."

"Come on."

"Well, when we did the kiss again," she said, still watching the dog, "he stuck his tongue in my mouth. And then he said something like 'I bet a girl never kissed you like that.'"

Jan winced, groaning inwardly.

"If he does it again," Kerry said, "I'm going to bite him, okay? Even if he is doing it to prove something."

"Yes, okay! Bite his stupid tongue off!"

Kerry smiled faintly. "I didn't know you'd be so jealous."

"It's not that so much—well, sure, it is. But it's also that if he's got something to say about us, I wish he'd come right out and say it. I mean, he doesn't really know anything's going on; he can't. And he knows that's no way to rehearse a kiss. Besides, Proctor wouldn't kiss Elizabeth like that. Abby, yes, but Elizabeth, no."

"I know. I hate him so," Kerry said under her breath. "I wish he'd leave us alone."

"Maybe he'll stop if we don't react." Jan waved as her mother drove up blinking her headlights. "But the trouble is that he's obviously trying to screw up your performance along with trying to play Proctor as if he were Stanley Kowalski; I think you might be right about the reason for that." She told Kerry what Kent had said about the gay men during *Streetcar.* "I don't envy you up there onstage with him. But I really do think we shouldn't react. I think we should treat him like a fourth-grade bully."

"He *is* a fourth-grade bully. And I don't envy you having to direct him. It's you who have the brunt of the beard fight, plus the whole show." Kerry stood up. "I'd better go. I'm getting morbid. Call me later?"

"Sure." Jan stood and tried to see Kerry's eyes in the dim light on the library steps, but couldn't. "You know you're going to be very, very good as Elizabeth," she said, wanting desperately to hug Kerry, but putting her hands in her pockets instead; her mother was waiting right there—and what if someone should come out of the library? "Kent or no Kent. You do know that, don't you?"

Kerry smiled, faintly again. "I hope I'm going to be good. I want to be, for you and for Mrs. Nicholson. I'm sure trying. Like you're trying to win the beard fight with Kent."

"It's such a symbol of everything else," Jan called as Kerry ran down the steps. "I've got to win it," she added under her breath. "I've got to."

130

But by the end of the next week Kent still showed no sign of giving in.

"Good grief!" exclaimed Jan's mother Saturday morning at about ten-thirty, at the door to Jan's room. "I didn't know it was still the hurricane season!"

"I can't find anything clean," Jan grumbled, "to wear to see Mrs. Nicholson." She sat down on the edge of her bed among the heaps of jeans, shirts, turtlenecks, and even a couple of skirts she'd pulled out of her closet.

"Far be it from me to criticize," said her mother, "but as I've said before, there's this wonderful modern invention in the cellar, called a—now let me see. Machine of laundry? No, that's not it. Laundry machine? Nope." She snapped her fingers. "I've got it! Washing machine, that's it! Amazing thing, really. You don't even have to put quarters in it. You push a button, and the darn thing fills itself up with water, wiggles the clothes around . . ."

"Oh, Mom," Jan moaned. "I'm meeting Kerry at twelve."

Her mother picked a pair of brown corduroy jeans up from the floor. "What's wrong with these?" she asked. "They're a dark color, anyway."

"I've worn them so much they reek."

"Well, dear, if you called Kerry and changed your lunch date to twelve-thirty, you'd have time to do a small load of whatever you want to wear, just so you wear all darks or all lights. We've got a dryer, too; did I tell you that?"

Jan snatched up the brown jeans with a dark blue turtleneck, and pelted down the stairs.

There was an odd, unpleasantly sweet smell in Mrs. Nicholson's hospital room when Jan and Kerry walked in after a

131

quick sandwich lunch. At first they stood uncertainly in the doorway, not sure whether Mrs. Nicholson was awake or not. Then she moved and Jan was stunned to realize that part of what she'd thought was the pillow was really a bandage on Mrs. Nicholson's head.

"Mrs. Nicholson?" Kerry said softly.

Mrs. Nicholson's eyes, dull when she first opened them, brightened, but that couldn't distract Jan from her taut cheeks or her pallor. As Mrs. Nicholson lifted a thin hand to straighten the bandage, her bed-jacket sleeve fell back and Jan noticed with shock that her arm had wasted away almost to bone. Of course, Jan thought; that's why she wore long sleeves all fall, even on hot days . . .

"Janna, Kerry, how nice," Mrs. Nicholson said weakly, struggling to raise herself.

Kerry went swiftly to the bed and put her hands under Mrs. Nicholson's shoulders, helping her move higher on the mound of pillows. "I could roll your bed up more," she said.

"No, dear, this is fine, thank you." Mrs. Nicholson waved in what would have been a strong, unmistakable invitation a few weeks ago, but was now only a vague flutter, as weary as her voice. "Sit down and tell me about the show. How are you, my Elizabeth? How is my Proctor?"

Jan cleared her throat, still too shocked at Mrs. Nicholson's appearance to speak. She glanced desperately at Kerry.

"Jan tells me I'm doing okay," Kerry supplied promptly, "and your Proctor's being his usual childish self, but he'll be brilliant when it matters, we're all sure. The Betty–Abigail hysteria scene is terrific now. That improvisation really helped. And . . ."

Jan found her voice at last. "It builds the way you wanted," she said. "At least I think it does. One of the secretaries from

132

the office wandered in the other day when we were doing it and she said it gave her the shivers. The pace is a bit slow still, in some places, but it'll pick up by dress, I'm sure."

"Oh, yes," said Mrs. Nicholson. "I'm sure it will. But don't panic if it doesn't. With high-school shows, it doesn't always get sorted out till the first performance. Line rehearsals do wonders, of course, but you know that."

"We had one just the other day," said Kerry.

"There you are, then." Mrs. Nicholson shifted position tiredly and her gaze strayed to the window. "You're sweet to come and see me. The cast was so nice to send those flowers, too." She pointed to a huge bouquet on the windowsill.

"I'm glad they got here," Jan said. The flowers had been Nanny's idea, and they'd all chipped in; Jan had forgotten about it till now. She made a mental note, though, to tell everyone that Mrs. Nicholson had mentioned them, and that they were beautiful.

Mrs. Nicholson pulled herself up higher in the bed and bent her head toward them. "I've talked my doctors into letting me come to first dress rehearsal," she said, and some of the old sparkle leapt back into her eyes. "That is, if the director will have me."

"Of course!" said Jan.

"I shall sit very quietly and unobtrusively in the back of the auditorium. And I shall have Robert wheel me out as soon as the curtain falls. It would be bad luck to scare the cast with a *real* Salem witch a few days before the first performance."

"But they'd love to see you," Jan said quickly. "I wish you'd come to both dress rehearsals."

"Both performances, too," added Kerry.

"I'm not sure I could manage that," said Mrs. Nicholson.

"And I don't think I want the cast to see me." She touched her bandaged head again. "I can disguise a great many things—any actress can—but not this. They shaved off some hair, you see. To operate," she explained.

"We could get you a hat," Kerry said, "or make you a wonderful stylish turban. Look—I just happen to have . . ." Kerry ran to the door, on whose handle she had draped her jacket, and pulled a green-and-brown scarf out of the pocket. "We could use something like this," she said, holding it up. "May I try? Does your head hurt?"

"No," said Mrs. Nicholson, with a faint shadowy smile. "Nothing hurts very much at all anymore. They told me they just took a look around inside and did something to relieve some pressure, and then they put my head back together again. It was rather like making a trapdoor in a stage floor. And they give me wonderful pills and shots, so nothing hurts. Yes, you may try. What a marvelous girl you are!" she said as Kerry draped and twisted the scarf skillfully over the stark white bandage. "Isn't she, Janna?"

"She sure is," said Jan fervently. She turned quickly away, though, struggling to conceal the tears that persisted in rising in her eyes no matter how much she blinked. The contrast was painful—young, strong, attractive Kerry, beside Mrs. Nicholson's wasted, feeble body. And yet she loved them both and couldn't resent Kerry's strength. She knew she could never do what Kerry was doing, could never be so accepting of what obviously was a terminal illness, could never adjust so easily.

Her eyes moved back to them again—Kerry like a little girl playing hairdresser, Mrs. Nicholson submitting almost merrily, helping hold the turban in place while Kerry tucked it in, laughing . . . Or was it the other way around, with Mrs.

Nicholson the little girl and Kerry the understanding adult?

Suddenly Jan wanted desperately to leave.

"There." Kerry stepped back. "Got a mirror?"

"On the dresser," said Mrs. Nicholson. "But I'm not sure I want to see, scarecrow that I am."

Kerry had already found the mirror. "It's up to you," she said cheerfully, holding it. "But I think you look terrific. You can't see the bandage at all, can you, Jan?"

"No," Jan answered with difficulty. "No, not at all." But Mrs. Nicholson did look like a scarecrow. It was grotesque, the painfully prematurely old face beneath the cheerful scarf.

"With makeup," Kerry said gently, "you'll look grand."

"Oh, all right. Let me see," Mrs. Nicholson decided. "I saw myself in a mirror a few days ago. I can't look much worse than I did then."

Kerry took the mirror to her, tactfully holding it, Jan noticed, to show more of her turbaned head than of her wasted face.

"Umm," said Mrs. Nicholson. "Not bad." She poked the turban. "I wonder if Robert could figure out how to do this."

"I'll do it," offered Kerry, "if you let me come early, before I have to be at school for dress rehearsal. I'll be glad to do it for you. And maybe, since I'm not on till the second act, I can even be late to rehearsal."

"If you promise to be there by the time the curtain goes up," Jan said.

"I promise."

"Accepted." Mrs. Nicholson touched the turban again, this time patting it gently. "I shall meet my public—well, my cast—radiantly transformed. Now take it off, dear; the nurses wouldn't understand. It would spoil their wonderful hospital decor. Did you know that white is for funerals, too? Now,

Jan," she said with a hint of her old briskness while Kerry obediently unwrapped the turban, "what's this about Kent? From your face earlier and from what Kerry said, I gather things aren't perfect with him."

As lightly as she could, Jan told Mrs. Nicholson about the beard, trying to make it seem less important than it really was. But she felt, when Mrs. Nicholson nodded approvingly when Jan told her about the research she and Kerry had done at the library, that Mrs. Nicholson was too shrewd and knew Kent too well not to understand.

"It's okay," Jan finished, anxious not to worry her; she suddenly seemed very tired. "I'll think of something in time. It's just annoying, that's all."

"Appeal—to his—manly pride." Mrs. Nicholson closed her eyes as if listening had exhausted her. "His—vanity. For what it's worth, I cast him as much for his face as for his acting." She paused a moment, then opened her eyes. "He's got a—wonderfully expressive face, especially—mouth. Kent's mouth—is Proctor's. Couldn't see it, though, through a beard. You may quote me."

Kerry poked Jan's arm and pointed to the door.

Jan nodded. "Thank you," she said, standing beside the bed. "I'll tell him that. But we should go now; you're tired."

Mrs. Nicholson took Jan's hand; Jan tried not to notice the way her fragile bones showed through her thin, dry skin.

"It'll be fine, Janna." Mrs. Nicholson gripped Jan with surprising strength. "I know it will. I'll be proud of all of you. If only I could shake Kent! He makes me so angry. He . . ." She closed her eyes again, then opened them; Jan couldn't believe she wasn't in pain. "He's—a troubled boy, I think. Trying to be a man. Doesn't—yet know how. Jealous, too. But—but you'll manage; you will. And—I'll come to dress,

136

protected—disguised—by—your costume, Kerry. Now, go, dears—please. Please go."

Mrs. Nicholson's voice broke. Impulsively, Jan bent down and kissed her.

Kerry kissed her, too, and then they left.

Jan strode to the elevator, fighting tears. She bumped into a bin marked "Laundry," then kicked it fiercely. "It's not fair," she shouted, not caring that there were people around. "It's just not fair! She's always been so strong, so alive."

"I know." Kerry took Jan's arm when the elevator came, propelled her into it and then out of it when it reached the ground floor, among passengers who were obviously trying not to stare.

In the lobby, Jan spotted a cigarette machine and fed it quarters.

"You don't smoke," said Kerry as they went through the swinging doors into the pale December sunshine.

"I do now." Savagely Jan ripped the pack open. "Why does it have to be a nice day? What right has the sun to be out when she's up there dying?"

"You don't know that."

Jan lit a cigarette, tried to inhale, and immediately coughed. She shook out the match and ground it against the pavement. "Oh, come on, Kerry, look at her!" She headed briskly for the parking lot, groping in her pocket for her keys; Kerry followed. "People don't get that thin when they're going to be okay. And that bandage on her head—come on!" She thrust the wrong key into the car's lock, jamming it.

"What do you mean?" Kerry eased the stuck key out. "About the bandage?" She took Jan's key ring from her, found the right key, and unlocked the car.

"Her falling down at rehearsal, the way her hands shook

sometimes, the way she couldn't talk quite right when she fell. Her husband just said she had cancer, but—well, what do you think she meant about their looking around inside her head?"

Kerry stared at Jan for a moment. "Oh, no," she said quietly. "Oh, no."

"Right." Jan squashed the cigarette out and got into the car. "A brain tumor," she said, when Kerry got in beside her. "What else could it be? I don't know why that would make her so thin, unless she just doesn't feel like eating. Or maybe they've given her chemotherapy or something and it's made her feel sick. But if they relieved some pressure in her head and put it back together again, that must mean they couldn't take the tumor out. Which also must mean she's—finished. She's going to die, Kerry, I know it. And she must've known it, too, or suspected it, all this time." Jan leaned her head for a moment against the steering wheel. "She must've known back at tryouts. She must've known then that she might need someone to take over. Maybe she even asked Mr. Taylor way back then if I could. Oh, God . . ." She let the tears come at last.

"Jan—Jan." Kerry put her arms around her, rubbing her shoulders, stroking her hair. "I could try to convince you that miracles happen, or that we don't know for sure she's dying, but I think you're probably right. I know you love her, I know . . ."

"She was—is—the only teacher who ever meant anything to me, who ever made me feel I could do anything. She trusted me, Kerry, I mean, she believed in me. If it weren't for her I probably wouldn't have dared even dream that I could be in theater someday. I certainly wouldn't have tried out for stock. I'd—oh, I don't know." She wiped her eyes, trying to stop the flow of tears; Kerry handed her a tissue. "I wouldn't ever have thought of directing, and now I really like it, even though I was mad at first when she didn't cast me."

"I know," Kerry said gently. "I know."

Jan beat her fist on the steering wheel. "It's just that I feel so helpless! Someone I love is dying and there's not a single thing I can do."

"You can give her a terrific dress rehearsal," Kerry said. "We all can. And you can try to get Kent to shave off his beard, because of Mrs. Nicholson, not because of me or even the play. You can't make her live, Jan, but you can help make her dying easier."

" 'That's not an office for a friend, my lord,' " said Jan, quoting Shakespeare.

"Oh, yes, it is! When there's nothing else a friend can do, it is." She turned Jan toward her and ran her finger under Jan's eyes, wiping leftover tears away. "And you'll do it, too; I know you will."

"With your help. You're the one who convinced her to show herself at dress."

"A turban is nothing."

"Wrong. It's a lot. She'd never have agreed to meet the cast without it. And I could no more have made that—thought of it, even—than I could fly. So there."

"Well, I could no more direct a play than I could fly, so we're even. Jan—okay, she's probably going to die, maybe even soon. But because of you she's going to die knowing the last thing she did was a fine production of *The Crucible*. She called it a great play, remember? And she said the school's never done a great play. Doing one is worth a lot to her, I bet. If only Kent . . ."

"Precisely." Jan started the car. Her eyes were dry now, and her mouth was grim. "If only Kent."

THIRTEEN

⟨ornament⟩

THE NEXT DAY WAS Sunday, the day of the first technical run-through, to be followed by a dress parade to check costumes and makeup, and then a run-through with costumes, primarily to make sure the actors could work in the clothes they'd be wearing and to practice the few costume changes. Jan was thankful that she already knew about lighting and that she'd taken the time to learn the sound system—thankful, too, that she'd made it a point to work backstage in stock as well as onstage. For the first time in weeks she would have to be more of a stage manager than a director, giving cues and supervising the scene changes that Ms. Grillo had worked out with the crew. At least she wouldn't have to worry much about costumes or makeup; Nanny had been working with Ms. Grillo all along on costumes, and had been doing makeup since sophomore year. She was really good at it, and had even taught some of the cast to do their own.

Kerry handed Jan a note as soon as she arrived:

> *Ms. Elena Alexandra Socrides*
> *and*
> *Ms. Kerry Ann Socrides*
> *cordially invite*
> *Ms. Janna Montcrief*
> *to dinner*
> *this Sunday evening*
> *at 6:30 p.m.*
> *RSVP*   *Informal*

Hastily, Jan folded a lopsided paper airplane, scrawled "Ms. Montcrief accepts with pleasure" on it, and tossed it to Kerry, making a mental note to call her mother, who she was sure would let her go. Then she said, patiently, to the junior who was going to be running the old light board, "Let's try that again, Marianne. I'll count it this time. Ready? Remember, all 'warn' means is to get ready to take the cue. Don't actually do it till I say 'go.' Okay. Warn cue six." Jan paused for a slow ten count. "Cue six—*go*. Slowly, Marianne, slowly. Move the dimmer handle up while I count. Let's try it again, on a count of eight. Warn cue six . . . Cue six, go. One—two—three—four—you should be at half now—seven—eight." Jan peered into the auditorium at the big Leko spotlights that were shooting blue and amber light onto the stage. "Perfect," she said. "Do it just like that and it'll be fine."

The technical run-through without the actors was long and tedious, for Jan made the crew rehearse each scene change until it went smoothly, and had Marianne and the boy doing sound go through their cues several times. When at last she was satisfied, the cast had already assembled for the dress parade, and the costumes were fine, except for a couple of minor problems like missing buttons and sagging hems.

Jan decided not to call the run-through with costumes a dress rehearsal, because she wanted to be able to stop to repeat light cues and scene changes. She did stop a few times, but the actors for the most part bore the interruptions patiently. At first, Jan was still concentrating too much on technical details to notice the show as a whole, but gradually she realized she *was* noticing, and soon her exhilaration grew to the point where she could no longer ignore it. It became clear to her that despite Kent's antics, one or two sloppy light cues, and a couple of misplaced props, all *Crucible*'s parts showed clear signs of fitting together as smoothly and tightly as a perfectly cut jigsaw puzzle. Once again she realized Mrs. Nicholson had been right; it was hard now to imagine limiting herself to playing a single character when she might be capable of staging an entire production.

But the hardest test was still ahead of her.

She'd worked it out carefully, lying awake half the night, drawing on all her knowledge of Kent, going over the words she planned to say, rehearsing them like lines.

When rehearsal was over and she'd finished giving the cast and crew the notes she'd taken about things they still needed to work on, she put her clipboard down, said, "Wait a sec," to the two or three people who'd started to leave, and made sure she had a smile on her face when she began.

"I've got good news," she said, "and I've got one more note, a costume note, to give. That's for Kent; you don't all have to stay for it. The good news is that Mrs. Nicholson is coming to first dress . . ."

There was a whoop—except from Kent, who was staring blankly at her.

"She's very sick, still," Jan warned them. "She looks—well, she looks pretty awful . . ."

"I didn't know anyone was allowed to see her," Kent said.

Jan found herself glancing quickly at Kerry. "I had to talk to her about the show, Kent," she said quietly.

But Kent must have seen her glance, for he said, "You and your sidekick, right?"

"Kerry did come." Jan tried to keep her voice steady. "You know she's been assisting me."

"Yeah, right," Kent snarled. "So what's the costume note? You might as well give it to me in public. *I* don't have secrets from the rest of the cast."

"Okay." Jan looked at him levelly. "The costume note is to shave off your beard by first dress." She forced a smile. "As if you hadn't guessed."

"Is that from Mrs. Nicholson?" Kent asked. "Or from you?" He got up from his seat and stood facing Jan. "I mean, did you go running to her whining, 'Ooooh, Kent won't shave and I don't know what to do . . .' "

Jan saw Kerry's angry face and said quickly, "No, Kent, I didn't. She asked about you, and I told her. Kerry and I also looked up about beards in the 1690s and I'm sure you'll be glad to know that some men wore them. So maybe you're right; maybe Proctor would have. But Mrs. Nicholson said she finds your face 'wonderfully expressive'—I think those were her very words—and she said that your mouth, especially, looks like Proctor's. Now, I don't think anyone's going to be able to see your mouth under all those whiskers, even if we aimed every Leko in the house on you, up full. But it's up to you. I'm not going to hold you down and shave it off for you."

"Might not be a bad idea," Ted muttered.

"I'll volunteer," said Nanny, who was sitting next to him. "Hey, it's part of my job," she said innocently when Kent glared at her. "I'm the makeup person, remember?"

"Damn you, Jan," said Kent. "Damn you! Since Mrs. Nicholson's coming to dress, she must be a lot better. I bet we could have postponed the show. I bet we could . . ."

Ted got up from his seat, shot a quick look at Jan as if apologizing, and said quietly, "What if she's not better, Kent? What if this is her last show, and she wants to see it before she dies and that's why she's coming? Did you ever think of that? You heard Jan say she's very sick and she looks awful. Put it together, man." He leaned down, his face close to Kent's. "I think Mrs. Nicholson might be dying. And she wants a Proctor without a beard. You figure it out." Ted went back to his seat, leaving Kent slumped angrily in his, subdued, but obviously still seething.

There was a growing murmur among the others in the cast, and finally Gail asked timidly, "Is that true, Jan? About Mrs. Nicholson dying?"

Jan saw Brenda get up and try to touch Kent; he ignored her, but she sat down next to him. Will, on Kent's other side, said, "Well, is it?"

Jan took a deep breath and made her decision quickly. "Yes, I think it's true. She has cancer. I didn't tell you because, as I said, when her husband first talked to me about it, he said she didn't want a lot of fuss. She herself didn't specifically ask me not to say anything, so I guess it's okay that you know. But I still don't think she wants a fuss made over her."

"I'm sorry," Ted said gruffly to Jan. "It's my fault you had to tell. But that jerk . . ."

Brenda jumped up. "What do you know about jerks?" she shouted. "Always sticking up for that—that—for Jan! Kent has as much right to know about Mrs. Nicholson as she does. He loves her."

"So does Jan," Ted said. "We all do. Brenda, look, I'm sorry, but . . ."

Jan went up to Kent. "Kent, Kent," she said miserably. "Maybe I was wrong not to tell earlier, especially not to tell you, but I thought I shouldn't because of what her husband said. Please let's stop all this. Let's just do a fine show for her."

He looked up at her and for a moment honest feeling seemed to penetrate his swagger. "Oh, God," he said. "I—Jan, I've been—fooling around with this play so much, I . . ." But then his eyes blazed again as if something else had taken over. "You could have told me," he said. "It still comes down to that. But no. You always have to be first, you have to be the important one, you have to win every argument. Mrs. Nicholson and I have disagreed before; *I* could win this argument if I could just talk to her. And I could have directed this play as well as you." He pushed himself violently away from his seat and strode rapidly up the aisle toward the lobby, with Brenda close behind.

Will glowered poisonously at Jan.

"So that's it, too," Jan said under her breath in the stunned silence that followed. "Jealousy. Right again, Mrs. Nicholson."

But, she thought, there's still the beard, and what happened to him last summer.

Later, after dessert at Kerry's, Aunt Elena excused herself, saying she had to work on her Christmas display. Waving cheerfully to Jan and Kerry, who were still at the table, she went through the yellow door and outside into the shop.

Kerry got up from her chair. "Come on up to my room. Let's forget the dishes."

"Won't she expect us to do them?"

"We can do them later. Or I can." Kerry went around Jan's chair and put her hands on Jan's shoulders, massaging them gently. Jan leaned back, closing her eyes.

The house was very quiet.

"Kent was so hurt," Jan said after a while. "He does love Mrs. Nicholson, and aside from everything else, it's got to be super-hard for him that we saw her and he didn't. It's funny; I shouldn't be sorry for him, but I am. I'm even sorry about what happened to him last summer—assuming that a couple of gay guys really did make pests of themselves."

Kerry knelt beside Jan and took her hands. "But maybe they didn't. I have a feeling Kent would get almost violent if a gay guy so much as said hello to him. And," she said, "you're sorry for him because you're a decent person. Deep down anyway," she added lightly, pulling Jan up and putting her arms around her. "After you get past the rough edges."

"Oh, Kerry, Kerry." Jan held her tightly. "You always make things seem so much better; you always . . ."

But by then Kerry's mouth was on her mouth, and there was nothing more to say.

There was only a single light on, across the room on Kerry's desk, when Jan opened her eyes later. She froze in panic, not remembering where she was. Then she felt Kerry's warmth beside her on the narrow bed, felt her own cramped muscles, and knew.

She wondered vaguely what time it was and let her eyes close again for a moment; her throat ached with unwept tears, but not tears of sadness.

When she opened her eyes once more she found Kerry watching her in the dim light, touching her gently. "Hi," Kerry whispered.

"Hi." Jan felt herself tremble, melting closer to Kerry, re-membering how they'd lain down together, holding each other, kissing softly and talking till they'd fallen asleep. Now

Jan touched Kerry gently wherever Kerry touched her, wanting to feel what Kerry felt as well as what she herself felt; it was as if her body had been waiting for this all its life and hers, as if it were suddenly coming alive on its own. It was wonderful and terrifying at the same time.

They were still slowly touching, exploring each other in wonder, when a door slammed sharply downstairs.

Kerry wrenched herself away from Jan and their fragile mood shattered like glass.

"Oh, no!" Kerry whispered. "Elena!"

Elena's voice called clearly, "Kerry Ann? Good heavens, are you asleep?"

"No, Aunt Elena, I'm not asleep," Kerry answered, switching on another light and putting her clothes to rights. "Be right down."

Jan sat up and fumbled with her own clothes. "Kerry, the door," she whispered sharply when she heard Aunt Elena's feet on the stairs. "Your door's open a little."

Kerry pushed it shut, and quickly pulled her hair, which had come out of its braid, into a loose ponytail. "I'll go out to her. It'll give you a minute or two more. Oh, Jan—what a way to end it!" She blew Jan a kiss, then left, and Jan could hear her cheerfully talking to her aunt in the hall, something about Santa Claus and tissue paper and then hot chocolate.

"Jan," Kerry called a moment later, "we're going to make hot chocolate. See you downstairs as soon as you finish that cue sheet, okay?"

"Okay," Jan answered. My sweet liar, she thought, then wished neither of them would ever have to lie again about themselves, or have to hide.

Jan closed her eyes briefly and put her head back down on the pillow—Kerry's pillow; it smelled of her hair and Jan's, and the bedspread was rumpled and still warm where they had been lying.

"My love," Jan whispered. "My dearest love." She ran her hands over her body, remembering Kerry's gentle hands and her own, and their bodies close together, and the clumsiness, for they hadn't known what to do, and the sweet long unpracticed kisses that left her mouth aching, even now.

So this is what it's like, she thought, not wanting to leave the bed. This is what it's like. Some of it, anyway.

She was still lying there when Kerry came back in, carrying a mug of chocolate. "Aunt Elena's watching a movie," she told Jan, "but she said hadn't you better go home or call your mother or something. Then she said you could stay if you wanted to spend the night, if it was okay with your mother. There's a cot . . ."

"Of course I want to spend the night!" Jan said weakly, sitting up.

"We'd have to be pretty careful. Her room's right across the hall."

"Just sleeping in the same room with you would be—well, it would be fine."

Kerry sat on the edge of the bed and kissed Jan. Then she handed her the chocolate. "I'll get the cot while you call your mother, okay?"

Jan took a big swallow of chocolate and burned her mouth again. "Okay," she said, wincing. "You know I'm always going to remember you and your aunt passing out boiling-hot chocolate if I remember nothing else."

"You'd better remember quite a lot else," said Kerry, standing up. "But you will. I'm going to be there to remind you. Always."

FOURTEEN

RAIN DROVE HARD against Kerry's window, waking them both at dawn.

"What a thing," whispered Jan, "to wake up with you."

They lay in each other's arms and watched the thin gray light brighten.

"Let's go out," Kerry said. "Let's go out in the rain." She propped herself up on one elbow and leaned over Jan, her loose tangled hair making a dark curtain covering them both. "Let's walk in the rain," she said, "and come back and make a huge breakfast for us and Aunt Elena, and just pretend to go to school. We could come back here and stay all day."

"Rehearsal." Jan lifted a handful of Kerry's hair and let it fall again. "Your aunt."

"Aunt Elena'll be in the shop. She's having a sale today—pre-Christmas specials. And we could go to school in time for rehearsal. Oh, Jan, how can we go back to scratched wooden desks and teachers and kids after last night? I don't know about you, but I need some time."

Jan kissed her.

．　．　．

The rain dripped from bare branches onto their heads, and their feet sloshed in sodden leaves. A cold wind blew in with the morning, but Jan hardly felt it. She spread her arms wide as they stood on the riverbank watching the current rush downstream; she threw her arms to the sky and shouted, "I love you, world!"

They played tag on the riverbank before anyone else in Southview was up, and hurried back to make breakfast, only to find that Aunt Elena had already gone into the shop. "Hi, early birds," said a note propped up against a bowl of deviled ham and mustard on the kitchen table. "I saw you go out to walk in the rain. Hope you come back for breakfast before school. Take some deviled ham for lunch if you want—I made myself a sandwich of it to eat in the shop between customers. Kerry Ann, see you at dinner. The rush begins! Merry (groan!) Christmas!"

Kerry grinned. "See?" she said. "She'll be in the shop all day."

Jan grinned back, and kissed her.

"Breakfast," said Kerry.

"Right." Jan opened a cupboard. "Where does your aunt keep the coffee? Hey—I don't even know how you like your coffee. Or if you like it. Maybe you drink tea. Maybe you drink herb tea. Maybe you drink milk. Or—oh, spare me!— hot chocolate?" She paused, her hand on another cupboard door.

Kerry laughed. "Real coffee's in the fridge, instant's in that cupboard—no, the next one. Yes, I do like coffee. Light, with lots of sugar." She put her arms around Jan from behind and rested her head on Jan's shoulder. "I don't know how you like your eggs. Or if you like eggs. Or how you like your steak.

Or hamburger. Or tofu, for that matter. I don't know if you hate cauliflower."

"Scrambled. Yes. Rare. Rare. I've never had tofu. I do hate cauliflower, but I can manage to get it down if it has lots of cheese sauce on it." Jan turned, still in Kerry's arms.

At around eleven the phone rang.

"Won't it ring in the shop, too?" Jan asked. They were on the floor of Kerry's room, listening to tapes, Jan's head in Kerry's lap.

"No. The shop's another line." Kerry moved Jan's head gently. "I'd better answer it. Sometimes packages for here get sent to a gift shop downtown. I can just tell whoever it is to send them on if it's that, and if it isn't, I can hang up or say wrong number or something."

Jan wasn't sure she agreed that was a good idea, but she didn't want to argue, so she said "Okay" and lay still, dozing, while Kerry was gone.

"No one there," Kerry said cheerfully when she came back. She knelt beside Jan. "Never change," she said, touching Jan's face. "Please never change."

"The sun's out—look!"

Kerry raised her head from the pillow, then pulled the curtain to one side. "It's shining on you now," she said, kissing Jan's bare shoulder.

"And on you." Jan traced the sunspots on Kerry's body. "My golden love," she whispered.

After they dressed, they had tomato soup and deviled ham at the kitchen table. Several customers' cars, nearly soundless

151

through the closed window, drove up and parked near the shop while they sat there.

"I don't believe us," Jan said, crumbling a cracker into her soup. She was suddenly ravenous, her eyes heavy from lack of sleep. She lifted her hand and touched it to her mouth, then reached across the table for Kerry's hand. "I never knew hands and mouths could make anyone feel what I've felt today," she said.

"Neither did I." Kerry ran her own fingers lightly over Jan's. "I don't think I knew anything till today. It's like getting older and being born all at the same time." She lifted Jan's hand to her cheek and held it there. "It's almost holy, touching you."

"Touching you, too."

"I can't imagine doing anything like that with a boy." Kerry kissed Jan's hand and let it go.

"Imagine it, maybe," said Jan slowly. "But want it, feel the same way about it, no."

"It's like another way of talking with you, of us learning about each other. Of being close."

"My friend Raphael," said Jan, discreetly biting into her sandwich, "says the important thing is who you feel something for emotionally as well as physically. Who you want to spend your life with. He said in his letter that he'd slept with a girl and liked it, but that he likes boys better in all ways."

"I always liked girls better," said Kerry. "Being with girls, talking with them. You didn't. You had Ted."

"I usually liked playing with boys better than playing with girls when I was little. I didn't much like playing house and stuff like that. I don't think we have to be the same as each other, Kerry, just because we're gay. We can still be different people. We should be."

Kerry laughed and munched her sandwich. "Yes, of

course," she said. "I wouldn't want us to be the same. But it's like I expect a—a direct translation. You know, that one can put everything one's been taught about being straight into gay terms by just turning it around, making it opposite, sort of."

Jan shook her head. "I don't think it works like that. Not from what I know from Raphael, and what I feel. I mean, I don't want to be a boy, even though I liked playing with boys when I was little. I just feel as if I've always been a different kind of girl. But still a girl."

" 'A different kind of girl,' " Kerry repeated. "Yes. That's a good way to put it, I guess."

Jan lay on her back on Kerry's bed, watching Kerry unbraid her hair and brush it, long, shimmering, and dark, over her shoulder. She'd undone it from its ponytail the night before, but Kerry had twisted it quickly into a braid when they'd gone for their walk.

Kerry looked at Jan in the mirror. "You're staring at me. I like it."

"You're so pretty. Beautiful, right now."

"Garbage. You're just prejudiced. Didn't you ever hear that thing about love's being blind?"

Jan got up and took the brush from Kerry; Kerry let Jan push her back gently till she was sitting on the bed. "May I brush your hair?" Jan asked.

"Sure." Kerry reached up and tangled her fingers in Jan's unruly curls. "You're beautiful, too," she said, pulling her closer and kissing her.

"Garbage," Jan said.

The phone rang again while Kerry was in the shower, as they were getting ready to go to rehearsal, so Jan picked it up, since Kerry had answered it earlier. Still, she felt annoyed at the break in the house's comfortable stillness—nervous, too; was someone checking to see if anyone was home before breaking in? Or—she thought guiltily, just as she said "Hello?"—is someone from school checking on us?

But by then it was too late to hang up.

There was no sound, really, nothing like the heavy breathing she realized she'd half expected, or even breathing at all, yet something told her someone was listening intently.

Suddenly frightened, she said "Hello!" again, sharply this time.

There was a choked sound like the beginning of a laugh, and then a click.

Kerry poked Jan when they went into the auditorium for what was to be a quick rehearsal, without costumes, to fix a few remaining rough spots. "Look at Kent."

Kent was onstage, doing the "To be or not to be" speech from *Hamlet* to a rapt audience of most of the cast—Kent, with no trace of a beard on his arrogant face.

Jan winked at Kerry as she went quietly to her front-row seat, and Kerry went to her usual seat behind her.

" 'Nymph,' " quoted Kent, reaching the end of the speech and turning to Brenda, " 'in thy orisons be all my sins re-memb'red.' " He held up his hand, silencing his audience as they began to clap. Quickly turning till he was facing Jan and Kerry, he bowed.

"Thank you, Kent," Jan said quietly. "You look great, by the way."

But Kent, eyes flashing, stepped to the edge of the stage, bent forward, and launched into the middle of another speech from *Hamlet*:

" 'Who calls me villain?' " he quoted, and Jan, knowing the speech as well as he, closed her eyes briefly as the rest of the cast watched, mesmerized. " 'Who calls me villain?' " he repeated, shouting this time. " 'Breaks my pate across? Plucks off my beard and blows it in my face?' " He snapped his body straight and, skipping to the very end of the speech, lifted his arms above his head and shouted, " 'The play's the thing wherein I'll catch the conscience of the—king!' "

Jan saw Ted glance at her uncomfortably, heard Kerry's indrawn breath behind her—and Will's and Brenda's echoing applause.

"Places," Jan said briskly, ignoring them all, knowing she had to. "Act One. Remember this is primarily another technical rehearsal for the crew, but please give it everything you can. Let's get all the remaining bugs out before tomorrow's dress, when Mrs. Nicholson will be here." She vaulted up onto the stage; she'd be working backstage from now on. "Lights, you ready? Sound? Close the curtain, please. Let's do this right."

FIFTEEN

❦

TUESDAY MORNING, Jan woke up again to the sound of driving rain, but this time against her own window. Her room was so cold she shivered as she dressed, and when she went downstairs, her mother was on the kitchen phone saying, "I don't care if you *are* shorthanded, Mr. Riston; it's forty-eight degrees in my kitchen!"

"Furnace blower again?" Jan asked, pouring herself some coffee from the pot next to the stove. "I wonder if Mr. Riston's the guy who services school, too."

Her mother sighed. "I am so sick and tired of that—that *dope* telling me he can't find anyone to—oh, well." She kissed Jan. "Eggs? French toast? This is the big day, right? First dress rehearsal?"

"Yup. I wonder what Stanislavsky had for breakfast on dress-rehearsal days," Jan mused, opening the refrigerator.

"Probably caviar and vodka," said her mother. "For pity's sake, Jan, close that thing. It's already cold enough in here!"

Jan took out bacon and eggs and closed the door. "I'll do it, Mom; you don't have to wait on me. You've got enough troubles."

"So do you." Her mother picked up the frying pan. "We'll both do it. I could do with bacon and eggs myself, and I'd like nothing better than to be as close as possible to the stove. Bacon, maestro, please."

Jan tossed her mother the bacon. "How about scrambled?"

"Terrific." Her mother peeled bacon slices into the frying pan and then watched Jan beat four eggs with a fork. "Nervous?" she asked.

"Not a bit. No, this tremor in my hands is simply a new way of beating eggs quicker, and the weird feeling in my stomach is just hunger."

"Am I right that you don't want to go out to dinner with Dad and Anita and Hal and me Friday night before the first performance?"

"You are right. I'll have something here. Maybe I'll invite Kerry over. I don't know. I think I'd rather be alone. Hey, Mom, what happens if Anita has her baby right in the middle of the show?"

"Well, if it's a boy your father will cheer, and if it's a girl Anita will cheer, I suppose." Her mother flipped the bacon and reached for the eggs. "Honey, don't worry. That baby's so reluctant to be born I think the doctor's going to have to induce labor. I must say, I hope you'll have a more eager first baby than your big sister when your turn comes."

"Umm." Jan dropped four slices of bread into the toaster.

When she got to school, her jeans soaked below the hem of her old yellow slicker, the school secretary, her eyes wide and frightened, beckoned her into the office and said, "There's a *telegram* for you. I haven't seen one of those for years! I don't think I even knew one could still send them." She stood beside her desk uncertainly, holding out a yellow envelope. "When I was a girl, telegrams mostly meant bad news. I hope that's not what this is. I can't imagine why it wasn't sent to your home . . ."

Jan reached for the envelope, feeling warm for the first time all day. He'd remembered—early, but nonetheless Raphael had obviously remembered the pledge they'd made last summer to send each other telegrams every opening night regardless of where they were. "Oh, it's just a thing I have with a friend," Jan explained. "An old theater custom. It's okay. Not bad news at all."

She took the envelope from the mystified secretary and opened it in the hall on her way to find Kerry before classes started. She'd have to remember to send Kerry a good-luck telegram in time for it to be delivered to her Friday.

SENDING THIS NOW FOR 1ST DRESS INSTEAD BE-
CAUSE AM NOT SURE WHEN IT'LL BE DELIVERED.
WILL ARRIVE ON SATURDAY IN TIME FOR FIRST PER-
FORMANCE AS PER YOUR INVITATION. STAYING WITH
FRIEND IN MIDDLETON. MUST I GO TO CAST PARTY?
MAY CRUCIBLE BE PINNACLE OF SUCCESS FOR YOU
AND AHEM YOURS. LOVE, RAPHAEL

"What a sweet guy he must be," Kerry said a few minutes later when Jan showed it to her.

"A little lewd at times," said Jan, "and flaky, but yes, he's sweet. I'm glad you'll have a chance to meet him. And I am going to make him go to the cast party. I can't wait to see Kent's face when Raphael walks in with me. Or with us. Kerry—how're you feeling?"

"Terrified. I couldn't eat breakfast."

"You've got to eat breakfast!"

"Oh, Jan, I couldn't!"

"What's your first class?"

"Chemistry."

"You like doughnuts?"

"Yes, but . . ."

"You go on up to the lab. I'll meet you there with a dough-nut. No arguments. Go!"

It was when she stopped off in her homeroom to get a book she'd left there that Jan saw them—the words scrawled on the chalkboard.

They didn't really register right away; it was almost as if she didn't see them, couldn't read them. They made no sense to her at first:

I SAW JAN MONTCRIEF WITH THE DEVIL.
I SAW KERRY SOCRIDES WITH THE DEVIL.

Then they did make sense, and she grabbed an eraser and rubbed them out before anyone else could see.

And when she went up to the chem lab, having gotten a doughnut at the candy store across the street from the school, she found Kerry outside the door, staring at a copy of the school newspaper. Wordlessly, Kerry pointed to the gossip column, regularly written by Brenda:

What noted theatrical personage (*former* star of stage) has been seen lately flirting gaily with what upcoming young ac-tress? A new romance, perhaps?

Jan told Kerry about the words on the chalkboard then.

Kerry leaned against the wall outside the lab. "Saw?" she said finally. "*Saw* with the Devil? I don't understand. Except for that one morning when you drove to my house, who could have seen us do anything that . . ."

"Little things. We've touched each other more in rehearsals lately. And," Jan added, suddenly remembering, "the mysterious phone calls the other day when I was at your house."

Kerry's eyes were wide and full of pain. "But I don't understand," she said again. "Calls? What . . ."

"There was another call while you were in the shower," Jan told her. "I answered it."

"But . . ."

"Kerry, it could have been someone from school who'd noticed both of us were gone and was trying to check up on us. And then if whoever it was recognized my voice . . ."

"Kent," breathed Kerry.

" 'The play's the thing,' " Jan quoted. "You heard him."

"That bastard," Kerry said fiercely. "That bastard!" For a moment Kerry looked as if she was going to cry. But then she said, "What are we going to do?"

"What can we do? It's just sticks and stones, so far. Again, let's try not to give him any reaction, and let's hope that doesn't make him so mad he'll pull something else."

"What else could he possibly pull?" asked Kerry as other members of the chem class started to flock up the stairs. "Everyone in the whole school will see the newspaper."

"I don't know," Jan answered, "but I'm sure he's capable of thinking of something." She handed Kerry the doughnut. "Please eat it."

"*Hi* there, you two," said a boy who was in Kerry's class but not in the show. He grinned—almost leered, Jan thought—as he passed them. "Got today's paper, I see."

Jan saw Kerry's fists clench and murmured, "Easy. Can you get through chem?"

"Oh, I'll get through it," said Kerry, "if I don't end up killing half the class."

"Good. I'll see you at lunch, okay?"

"Okay," Kerry answered, but then, when she was halfway through the lab door, she hesitated and said, "Should we? See each other at lunch, I mean?"

"It's up to you," Jan said stiffly, trying not to feel hurt.

"I—I don't know."

Jan swore silently at Kent. To Kerry, she said, "I'll wait for you in the cafeteria. Usual place. If you don't come, I'll understand." She reached out to squeeze Kerry's shoulder, but Kerry shrank back as two girls came up the stairs, looked their way, and exchanged a significant glance.

"Right," said Jan, moving away. "See you later."

In history, Ted slipped her a note with #%$^&%$**!@!! drawn on it, and under it "The newspaper advisor must've slept through this issue. Want to talk?"

Jan scrawled "Don't know, but thanks" on a scrap of notebook paper and passed it back to him.

Ted came up to her table in the cafeteria at lunch when she was waiting for Kerry and trying not to notice that several kids she didn't even know very well whispered and giggled as they passed. Kent and Brenda, sitting by themselves at a corner table, pointedly didn't look her way, but Will, who was with a couple of *Crucible* cast members, did, and then leaned toward them, whispering.

"Hi." Ted slid into the chair Jan had made sure was there for Kerry. "Okay if I join you?"

"Unless Kerry comes," Jan said.

"I saw her outside," he told her. "Like she was going home or taking a walk or something."

Jan started to get up, then thought better of it and sat down again.

"Kent," said Ted with great emphasis, "is a seriously deficient human being, and almost everyone in the cast thinks so, except Brenda and that little nerd, Will. Nanny said none of the girls in the show are talking to Brenda since they saw the paper."

"It's probably not really Brenda's fault," Jan said dully. "He probably put her up to it. She's such an airhead she'll go along with anything someone she's dating wants her to do."

"Jan." Ted poked idly at his uneaten sandwich. "Tell me to go to hell if you want, but is it true? I mean, if it isn't, I could tell him that, and . . ."

"And if it is?"

"If it is . . . I don't know."

"Yeah," said Jan bitterly. "That's what I thought." Deliberately, she changed the subject. "I guess Kerry's not going to come. I'm going to go find her. Thanks," she said, again sarcastically, "for the company."

Ted reached for her hand. "Jan . . ."

But Jan brushed him aside and left.

She found Kerry outdoors, shivering under a tree near the parking lot, her face glistening with tears.

"Your cheeks will freeze," Jan said, rubbing them.

Kerry caught Jan's hands and pressed them to her face, then let them go guiltily and put her own hands in her pockets. "Oh, Jan," she said miserably. "I'm so sorry. I hate myself for what I said before. For—for doubting, for not coming to lunch. I'm so sorry."

"Shhh."

"I love you; you know that."

162

"Yes, I do, but thank you for telling me right now." Jan paused, then said, "Kerry, maybe we shouldn't see each other till after the show. What do you think? It's only a few days. Kent will probably calm down once the show's over and everyone tells him how great he was, and neither of us will have to see him much after that. I have one class with Brenda, but none with him, and since you're a junior . . ."

"Isn't that sort of giving in?"

"Yes, but there's the play to think of."

"How about us?" asked Kerry angrily. "Isn't there us to think of? Or is the stupid play more important?"

Jan felt as if she'd been slapped. She pivoted sharply and went back across the parking lot to her mother's car.

"Jan!" Kerry called after her. "Jan, wait!"

But Jan yanked open the car door, thumped down onto the seat, and roared out of the lot, leaving Kerry staring after her.

That night, when Jan called half hour for rehearsal, she didn't go all the way into the girls' dressing room, but she saw immediately that Kerry wasn't there. Okay, she told herself, she's not on till Act Two. But by the time the curtain went up on Act One, Kerry still hadn't arrived. And when it fell at the end of the act on Brenda's hysterical scream of " 'I saw Goody Booth with the Devil!' " Ted went up to where Jan was standing backstage and said, "Mrs. Nicholson's out front, Nanny says, but no one's seen Kerry. Maybe you're going to have to read Elizabeth."

SIXTEEN

AS SOON AS THE houselights were up full for intermission, Jan dashed to the costume room under the stage and rummaged along the racks till she found a simple long gray dress. As she slipped it on over her jeans and shirt, she tried to remember what it felt like to want to play Elizabeth. To want to play Elizabeth—read her, actually, for she'd probably need the script—opposite Kent.

But all she could find where her desire for Elizabeth had been was a hollow place rapidly filling up with fear as the minutes passed and there was still no sign of Kerry.

"I can't even be mad at her for being unprofessional," she said to Ted, pacing back and forth during what was left of the intermission.

"You care about her too much," he said simply. Then he jerked his head toward the stage, where Kent was standing and watching them, a faint smile playing about his lips. "Careful," Ted said, leaving as Kent strolled over.

"Well, well, well, well, well." Kent draped himself over the prompt desk where Jan stood as stage manager. "I see our *star* hasn't shown up." He wagged his finger at Jan. "I told you the play's the thing," he said. "Now we'll see how great you are, won't we? Sure you remember how to move in a skirt?"

Cold fury built in Jan and she wheeled on him, eyes snapping. "If what you're saying is that you had anything to do with Kerry's not being here," she said, "I'll—I'll . . ."

"You'll what, friend?" Kent interrupted, smiling. "The show must go on, after all. Pity you'll have to do Lizzie with the script."

"Pity you'll have to play opposite someone who's holding book," she retorted.

"I'll manage." He picked up the prop gun he used in the beginning of Act Two and got into position to enter. "Oh, this is going to be fun! Play's the thing," he mouthed at Jan as she, too, got into position and said, "Warn houselights."

But as she did, Jan heard something behind her and then she saw Kerry, in costume and makeup, but not enough makeup to hide her red, swollen eyes, standing beside her.

"You—you're dressed like Elizabeth," Kerry said.

"You weren't here."

"The show must go on," Kerry said coldly. "Right?"

Jan reached out and grabbed her wrist. "Kerry, for heaven's sake! Maybe you've got a good reason for being late. I'm glad you're here. And I hope you're okay. But I've got to get the curtain up and start Act Two. *Are* you okay?" She lowered her voice. "I was worried about you," she said. "That was worse than worrying about the play."

"Jan." Marianne's voice came out of the near-darkness. "I'm on a warn for the houselights."

"I know," said Jan, her eyes still on Kerry. "Kerry, I'm sorry—but can you go on?"

165

Kerry nodded, and Jan, trying to ignore the fact that she still looked angry and hurt, mouthed "I love you." Aloud, she said, "House to half. Warn curtain."

Kerry moved silently into position for her entrance. Kent, still watching from the opposite side of the stage, looked startled, then furious.

"House out," Jan told Marianne. "Warn cue eleven."

Kerry started singing softly as she was supposed to do as the act opened.

"Curtain," said Jan, and when it was open, "Cue eleven—go!"

Proctor entered, and the act began.

It was a bitter victory. The applause, tumultuous for a dress rehearsal, surprised all of them when the final curtain came down. Jan leaned against the prompt desk after the last curtain call, unable to enjoy it, still too upset and worried about Kerry's continued coldness and her lateness to go out and congratulate the cast. Then, just as she was about to, a weak but unmistakable voice came from the other side of the curtain's thick folds, and Jan remembered Mrs. Nicholson—and that Kerry had promised to help her with her turban.

"You idiot!" Jan scolded herself under her breath, reaching for the ropes as Mrs. Nicholson called, "Please open the curtain."

The cast surged forward, Kerry among them, as soon as the curtain parted. The first thing Jan noticed was Kerry's green-and-brown scarf, wound around Mrs. Nicholson's head.

"Oh, my dears!" Mrs. Nicholson held out her hands. "Oh, my dears!"

They leapt down off the stage and surrounded her wheelchair, clasping her hands and hugging.

"My dears, my dears," she said again, her voice thin and quavering, her eyes bright with tears. "Thank you. You were all wonderful. It is a beautiful play, sad and noble—such cruel misunderstanding, such evil, such courage, such ignorance—and you made it sing; you found it all, and showed all that's in it, and I am so very proud. Kent . . ."

He stepped forward, smiling.

"You were so much better without the beard, and you were splendid. Kerry," she went on quickly, "what a perfect Elizabeth, such quiet strength, such truth. Ted, excellent Giles, and Nanny, what a poignant Rebecca. And Brenda, my wonderful Abigail, and Gail, fine little Betty, and Will—what a smooth, steady Cheever, with few mistakes—oh, all of you, each and every one." Her eyes sought Jan's then, and Jan, still onstage, tried to smile, but all she could really concentrate on was how small Kerry's shoulders were under the grayness of Elizabeth's dress.

"How'd you like my scene with Hale in Act Two?" Kent asked, pushing eagerly past the others. "And the big Abigail scene—did you notice the new . . ."

But Mrs. Nicholson's eyes were still on Jan, and she cut Kent off, putting her hands together as if to clap, saying, "A round of applause for my reluctant stage manager who had to become director." Feebly, she clapped; Ted quickly covered her weakness by leading the rest of them in applause.

All except Kent. Left out, he turned away, scrubbing at his makeup with a tissue as if he wanted to tear his face off.

Then he jumped back up onstage, elbowing Jan aside as he exited.

SEVENTEEN

"I WANTED TO TELL you," Kerry sobbed later, in Jan's mother's car. "I wanted to, but you seemed so mad; you were so busy, and the curtain had to go up. And at first I didn't know what to do, and my aunt kept me so long I was almost late for Mrs. Nicholson, and then I just had to be by myself for a while, and then get dressed and made up, and . . ."

Jan tightened her arms around her. "It's okay," she said, still staring at the sign Kerry had handed her—the cardboard sign her aunt had taken off the door of her shop that afternoon:

I SAW KERRY SOCRIDES WITH THE DEVIL.
I SAW JAN MONTCRIEF WITH THE DEVIL.

"It doesn't help much," said Kerry, wiping her eyes with the tissue Jan gave her, "to know Kent's mixed up and jealous, and maybe wants to prove he's a man and all. It did at first, some, but it doesn't anymore."

"No," Jan agreed. "It doesn't." She stared out at the snow

that was now falling; they were parked near the river, and the weather had turned very cold.

Kerry blew her nose. "Aunt Elena asked me what the sign meant and I tried to say it was a joke from the play, that someone was just kidding. She was mad, though. She said it was bad for business, or would be, if a customer saw it. And then she asked me if you're popular, if you have a boyfriend, and—and stuff."

"What stuff?"

"Oh, nothing."

"Kerry!"

"Well, she asked how come I don't have a boyfriend. And how come we spend so much time together." She leaned her head against Jan's shoulder. "It's so hard to believe. So much beauty. And then this."

Jan brushed Kerry's hair back gently; Kerry closed her eyes.

"I'm so sorry," Kerry said. "About my aunt, about getting mad, about being late, about Brenda and Will and Kent . . ."

"Shh. I have it a lot easier. I don't have to play opposite Kent or live with your aunt."

"I wish we could run away."

"So do I." Jan bent her head to kiss Kerry, then thought better of it, and straightened up again. "You look so tired."

"Jan, she . . ." Kerry broke off and fell silent.

The snow, Jan noticed in the glow of a distant streetlight, was falling faster now, swirling down, but aimlessly, as if its destiny were controlled by something beyond itself. Like me, she thought; like us.

"She said she wants me to have other friends," Kerry said finally. "She wants me to ask other people to the house, to go out with other people. She said she's worried about me, that I'm too intense."

"I'm not surprised," Jan said, watching the snow and feeling momentarily defeated. I can't let myself drift like that, she thought, *we* can't; it's not right. It would be a lie . . .

She took Kerry's hand. "Like I said, I don't have to live with your aunt. And," she added, remembering painfully, "you don't either, once your parents come back. I want you to stay in Southview, Kerry, more than anything in the world. But you could go home with them in January, the way you were supposed to originally."

There was a long silence.

"It would be pretty bad for you," Jan said finally, "if your aunt figured out about us. Wouldn't it? I mean, she doesn't strike me as someone who'd understand."

"No," said Kerry. "Well, I'm not sure. Not without a lot of explaining, anyway." She hesitated. "Aunt Elena said—she said the same thing you did—that maybe I should go back with my parents after all in January instead of staying. She said she'd leave it up to me. I haven't written them about it yet. I was going to after the play. But . . ."

Jan tried to ignore the tight feeling in her throat. "I can't tell you what to do," she said carefully. "You know I'd like you to stay. But I don't want you to stay if you're going to be miserable. Maybe you shouldn't decide yet. Wait a bit, and see how things develop with Kent and the others after the show. It might all die down then. But . . ." Once again, she thought of what Raphael had said about his own high-school years and wished he'd told her more. "I guess it could get pretty bad, Kerry."

"I know. But most of me thinks it's worth it."

"So do I, my love. But *all* of you has to think so."

" 'My love,' " Kerry repeated. "That sounds so good. Funny, what I really want to say is thank you."

"Thank you?"

"For calling me that. For loving me."

Jan hugged her. "Thank you, too." She moved away gently. "But we still need to be careful."

"You mean," said Kerry slowly, "sort of protect what we have by pretending we don't have it."

"It sounds terrible that way. But—well, yes. At least for a few more days. Once the play's over, as I said, maybe things will calm down. Then Kent won't have the jealousy motive anymore. And he won't have Proctor as a vehicle to, you know, try to show how macho he is. Maybe the others won't notice us so much after the show either."

Kerry looked out the car window, intently, as if she were counting snowflakes. "I hate myself," she said finally in a very soft voice. "I hate myself for saying okay, let's try to be careful."

"Yeah, I know. I hate myself for suggesting it, and I hate both of us for going along with it. But the thing is that we can't let Kent or anyone else destroy us."

"I miss you already." Kerry stroked Jan's hand.

"Me, too. But it's not as if we'll really be away from each other. And, anyway, for now there's the play, and the cast party Saturday." She paused a moment, thinking. "Your aunt might be relieved about your going to that. And about my going with Raphael. He's a boy, after all."

Kerry nodded. "I hate it," she said. "But—but you could pretend he's—you know. Your boyfriend. That might help with Kent, too, if you did it at the party."

Jan chuckled mirthlessly. "Raphael and I used to kid about my covering for him when his parents came to visit him in stock. They're very old-world and they're worried that he isn't married yet. He keeps telling them he's married to his career, but he doesn't think they believe that anymore. When we'd go out with his parents he'd always make a big show of putting his arm around me, stuff like that. I guess we could do that at the party; I guess he'd agree."

"Hey," Kerry said, sounding as if she was trying to be brave. "Don't take it *too* far at the party. I'll be jealous."

"Don't be." Jan touched Kerry's shoulder. "I don't think you'll ever have to be jealous of anyone, Kerry."

"Nor you—oh, Jan." She flung her arms around Jan's neck. "It's snowing so hard no one could see even if there were anyone here, and it's dark anyway."

Jan slipped her arms under Kerry's jacket and for a long time they clung to each other. "Good luck for all the times I won't be able to say it properly," she whispered. "And good night for all the nights."

"To you also." Kerry hugged Jan tighter. "Until Saturday. It'll be *our* party, then."

The next dress rehearsal went smoothly; at least there were no backstage dramas and Kent seemed to be pulling in on himself, too preoccupied at last with his own performance to notice anyone else.

"We'll get through," Jan mouthed to Kerry behind Kent's back, bringing down the fourth-act curtain, and Kerry, still frozen in her final position as Elizabeth, nodded imperceptibly. Jan took the cast through their curtain calls quickly and then, without looking at Kerry, said, "Well, that's it, gang. Line rehearsal tomorrow, but we'll make it as quick as possible, okay? And then you can all take it easy Friday afternoon till performance. See you tomorrow." She picked up her clipboard and went backstage again, pleased to see that Kent was watching her and hoping it registered in his mind that she wasn't with Kerry.

And then she ran into Will near the prop table.

"Lose something, Will?" she asked, trying to sound casual.

His expression was unreadable. "No," he said. He put his hand out, laying it on her arm. "I've been waiting here for you, Jan." He dropped his voice. "Everyone knows," he said, "about you and Kerry. But it's a sin, Jan; don't you know that? A terrible, unnatural sin."

For a minute Jan didn't know whether to take him seriously or not. But his look chilled her, and she could see from his eyes that he meant every word he'd said.

While she was still trying to think what to answer, he tightened his grip on her arm. "You need to change your ways, Jan, you and Kerry. Even the Bible says it's wrong, you know. I'm trying to help," he added, his eyes boring into hers, "for the good of your soul. I wouldn't want you to be—punished."

She shook free of him, jumped down off the stage, and headed up the center aisle, shaking—and almost bumping into the school secretary, who had just come in from the lobby.

"Someone told me you'd still be here," the secretary said. "Your mother's on the phone in the office. Says it's important."

Puzzled, Jan went into the office. Why would Mom be calling me here, she wondered, when she knows I'll be coming right home? Then she thought of Anita and so wasn't surprised when she picked up the phone and her mother said tensely, "Hi, darling. The baby's coming after all. Now, don't worry. I just wanted to catch you before you left. Daddy and I are at the hospital."

"Okay," said Jan. "How is she?"

Her mother seemed to hesitate, then said, "She's having a little trouble. The doctor says it'll probably be a while, so we might be here all night. Do you want to drive over?"

"No." Then, thinking that sounded crass, Jan added, "Unless you want me there, or unless 'Nita does."

"Well, it'd be lovely, of course, but they won't let me and Daddy see her, and they're not even letting Hal stay with her very long at a time. No, I don't think you need to come. But will you be all right? Could you get Kerry to stay with you? I'd feel better if you weren't alone."

Jan allowed herself an ironic smile. "No, I'll be okay, Mom, really."

"Are you sure?"

"Yes. Give 'Nita my love if you do see her. Hal, too."

"I will, honey. And I'll call you first thing in the morning if we're still here. Oh, dear—Jan, I'm so sorry! I forgot! How was rehearsal?"

"Fine, just fine." A sudden thought hit her. "Mom, she'll be all right, won't she? 'Nita? You said she was having some trouble—"

"She'll be fine. First babies are often hard. You just get some sleep, and let us worry. You've got the play. You're sure Kerry can't stay with you? Or maybe you could go there."

Jan felt the secretary watching her. "Mom, I'll be okay."

"I'll call you in the morning, then. Don't forget to turn down the thermostat when you go to bed. Riston came after you left for school, so the furnace should be working again."

"I won't forget."

"Good night, hon."

"Good night."

"Everything okay?" the secretary asked when Jan got off the phone.

"My sister's having a baby."

"Wonderful! Boy or girl?"

"Having," said Jan. "It's not born yet. And she and her husband didn't want to know in advance."

"Very wise," said the secretary. "I always think it's better that way. Good luck."

"Yeah," Jan said. "Thanks."

The house was cold when Jan got home and seemed twice as large as it really was. She checked the thermostat but it was on 65, even though the thermometer said 42; Riston can't have done a very good job, she thought. I'll just have to freeze.

She went up to her room, dug her heavy ski sweater out of its mothballs, shook it out, and put it on. Then she went down to the kitchen, leaving a trail of blazing lights behind her. Maybe she could make an omelette. Something hot, anyway.

But there were no eggs, so she had a can of chicken soup instead, and crackers. Then, thinking of Kerry, she made hot chocolate. "Can't even burn myself on the dumb stuff when she's not around," she muttered, sipping it.

She went into the living room and switched on the TV, but was bored in ten minutes. The news was over, and there was a Western, several situation comedies and police shows, and a nature documentary. The latter was almost interesting, but she found her mind wandering, so she turned it off.

"Blast it," she said out loud to the empty room. "I wish I could call her." But she decided not to take the chance.

" 'I wish the long ship Argo,' " she intoned, standing in the middle of the living room—but *Medea* didn't work either.

She went back to the kitchen and found a root beer in the refrigerator, but then she felt too cold to drink it in the cold house, so she left it on the counter and went upstairs. Maybe a hot shower, she thought. Thank goodness the water heater works even when the furnace blower doesn't.

She was warmer after the shower, but no more cheerful. She put pajamas on instead of her usual T-shirt, and her ski sweater over them, opened her Shakespeare to *Romeo and Juliet*, and crawled between the icy sheets on her bed.

An hour later, when she'd just finished reading Romeo's speech when he thinks Juliet is dead, the phone rang.

Anita, she thought—and ran to answer it.

But it was Kerry, and Jan felt warm again.

"Where were you, Jan, where were you?" she asked. "I tried before, twice, but there was no answer . . ."

The warmth left her at the sound of Kerry's agitated voice. She explained about the shower and then said, "What is it?"

"Jan—oh, Jan, I have to see you. I can't tell you on the phone."

"Tell me what?" said Jan. "You shouldn't come over at this hour. Your aunt . . ."

"I have to see you. Aunt Elena's asleep. Can I come right over? Would your mother mind?"

"Mom's not home; no one is. Anita's having her baby. Kerry, quick, are you all right?"

"Yes. Jan, it's—it's not me. It's Mrs. Nicholson . . ."

It was as if the world had stopped and Jan with it.

". . . Jan, I'm sorry. I wanted to tell you in person. She— her husband called me when he couldn't get you. She—she died tonight. Peacefully, he said. Please, Jan, I'm coming over."

"I—okay," Jan said numbly. She couldn't move, except to replace the receiver. The words *we killed her* burst into her mind and stayed there, echoing. She saw Mrs. Nicholson sitting there in her wheelchair, Kerry's scarf on her head; Mrs. Nicholson trying weakly to clap, to tell them they'd done well. If Mrs. Nicholson hadn't come, or if she'd left right afterwards, would she still be alive?

Jan sat by the phone till the doorbell rang, and then Kerry's arms were around her and her head was against Kerry's breast. From somewhere she heard Kerry say, "Jan, my love, I'm so sorry"—but she couldn't speak herself, or cry, or even feel much. It was as if she were wrapped in cotton, insulated from her surroundings. An odd feeling, but it protected her from thinking much about it except at what seemed a great distance. She wondered, though, what it was like to die. She found lines from plays in her mind and repeated them silently, screening out everything else.

"Please, Jan," Kerry said. "Please. It'll be better if you talk."

But Jan couldn't. She found she did want to speak to Kerry, but cotton still surrounded her and it was almost as if Kerry weren't there. She was drifting like the snowflakes; everything was slipping away, leaving her chilled and immobile in an alien, too-fast-moving world. It was only when the phone rang again and Kerry prodded her to answer it that she found she was able to speak at all. Consciousness told her it would have to be her mother, and that it would fit the day if Anita or the baby or both were dead, too.

But it was Kerry's aunt, and in the shock of that, Jan began to fight back to herself again.

"Jan?" Aunt Elena's sharp voice was saying formally, as if she barely knew her. "Is my niece there? She doesn't seem to be here, and my car is gone. I'm afraid that . . ."

"Kerry's here," said Jan. With the sound of her own voice, tiredness possessed her and she had to sit down quickly; she was dizzy and felt sick. "Yes, Ms. Socrides, she's here."

Kerry gasped, "Oh, no!" and took the phone away from Jan. "Aunt Elena? I'm sorry. I should have left you a note."

As if from very far away, Jan heard Kerry explain why she'd come, gently, evenly, obviously trying to reassure her aunt. Then Kerry hung up and put her hands on Jan's shoulders.

"She was really worried," she said apologetically. "Mad, too. I think I calmed her down. But I'd better go, before she starts thinking again about my spending too much time with you. She doesn't really understand about Mrs. Nicholson. Or us either," Kerry added, touching Jan's face. "I wish I could stay, love."

"It's okay," Jan managed to reply. "I'm okay."

"Are you?"

"Yes."

Kerry kissed her quickly and was gone.

The cottony feeling descended again and, wrapped in it, Jan went upstairs to bed, closed her eyes, and slept as if she'd been drugged.

EIGHTEEN

❧

"AND THEN," HAL SAID expansively Thursday night, "the little son-of-a-gun curled his feet up in the darndest way; you should have seen him, Jan."

"He really does look like you, honey," Jan's father said to her, pouring his son-in-law a second glass of wine. "Curly hair and big eyes and all."

Jan managed a smile, but she was still too shattered to share everyone else's joy. Mr. Taylor had called a brief assembly that morning to announce Mrs. Nicholson's death, and the cast had been too shocked and strained for there to be any point in holding a line rehearsal. Except for Kent, who'd bolted from the auditorium as soon as Jan cancelled the rehearsal, they'd all hugged and cried and reminisced for an hour after school, and then Jan had sent them home. Grieving together had helped, but now, especially in the middle of her family's celebration, Jan felt hollow again, lost, and alone . . .

"Charles Dana Anthony," Jan's mother was saying with a happy sigh. She took Hal's plate, already heaped with a second helping of roast beef, and filled the rest of it up with mashed potatoes and carrots. "What a lot of names for such a tiny tyke!" She chuckled fondly. "But you know what Anita said when they finally let me see her? She said she's already decided to call him Squirt."

The phone rang sharply through the laughter and Jan nearly upset her chair in her haste to answer it.

"I worry about that girl," she heard her father say as she ran to the hall and almost answered "Hi—Kerry?" instead of her usual impersonal "Hello?"

It was Kerry anyway. "Hi," she said. "How are you?"

"Okay," Jan lied. "Not allowing myself to think. Everyone's in raptures about the baby. How are you?"

"Okay, too," Kerry said unconvincingly, after a second's pause.

"What's the matter?"

"Nothing. Really. I'm fine. Just worried about you is all."

"Why don't I believe you?"

"How do I know? Look, it's okay!"

"Kerry, come on!"

"Oh, just a couple of stupid phone calls. You know—hangups. Mostly just that."

"Mostly?"

"Well, one was a little weird. It was some guy. He said 'Watch out' in a funny voice, like he was trying to disguise it."

Jan closed her eyes. "Could it have been Kent? Or Will?"

"That crossed my mind. But I'm really not sure. Like I said, he disguised his voice. It was really deep, basso profundo."

"What did you do?"

"Hung up."

"Good. Maybe he'll stop if you don't react."

"And maybe it wasn't Kent or Will at all," Kerry said lightly. "Maybe it was a wrong number. Let's not jump to conclusions."

But later that evening, when Hal had gone home and Jan and her parents were watching TV, the phone rang again.

Jan dashed into the hall, shouting, "I'll get it," trying to tell herself it might be okay; it might be Kerry.

It wasn't.

"Watch out," a deep male voice said slowly, drawing out each word. "Everyone knows. 'The wages of sin is *death.*' Romans 6:23. Watch out."

Jan slammed the receiver down, then regretted it. "That's a reaction, you idiot," she snarled angrily at herself between clenched teeth. "Stupid, stupid, stupid!"

"Janna?" Her mother came into the hall. "Who was that?"

"Wrong number," Jan told her. "I've got homework I should be doing." And without giving her mother a chance to protest, she ran up the stairs to her room and threw herself down on her bed.

Kent's face swam dizzily before her eyes, followed by Will's and Brenda's, then Kerry's, then Mrs. Nicholson's, the images fading and returning, fading and returning as she dozed fitfully. Finally they combined in a face-collage with Ted's and Corrin's and Raphael's. The images rose up together, then separated so that Kerry's face was by itself, to one side. The others floated, first lazily, then fast and with purpose toward Kerry's, and Jan realized, as Aunt Elena's face appeared above them all, laughing, that they were all pursuing Kerry, that Kerry was calling out to her in terror, and that she, Jan, watching from her dreamer's distance, was powerless to help . . .

Jan was conscious of gentle pressure on the mattress, and her mother's voice in the dim room. "Jan, honey! Jan, you're dreaming. What is it?"

Jan, foggy from sleep and feeling about six years old again, threw her arms around her mother and held her wordlessly.

Her mother patted her hair, rubbed her shoulders, and repeated, "Little one, little one, this too will pass," over and over again, the way she had long ago when Jan really had been six.

Only I'm not six now, she thought; I'm almost three times that. She pulled herself away from her mother and sat up. "I'm sorry, Mom," she said. "I'm okay now."

"Life's a bad dream sometimes, isn't it?" her mother said calmly. "And it's being one for you right now, I think. Want to talk? I know how much you loved Mrs. Nicholson . . ."

"No—no. I'm really okay. You've got Anita to worry about."

"Anita's fine," said her mother. "And little Charles Dana Anthony Squirt is fine, too. They can look after themselves for a while. Honey," she said, "we haven't talked much since you got back from stock. You've been so busy, with the play and with Kerry." She paused, as if she expected Jan to say something, then added in a very low voice, "Troubles are better shared, Jan."

"I know, Mom. But maybe some can't be."

"You forget that I know you pretty well. My little artist," she said. "Everything's so hard for you; feelings are so strong. That's why you can act, honey, and direct. I suppose it'll always be hard, but maybe never so hard as now, when feelings and experiences are new. I'm so sorry about Mrs. Nicholson. That was a terrible blow, I know. But I also know you're going to make sure the play is wonderful, for her."

Jan swallowed and licked her dry lips. "I'm sure trying," she managed to say.

"That's my girl. Now"—her mother stood up—"how about you get undressed? I guarantee you'll sleep better." She tossed Jan the old T-shirt she usually slept in. "Hot chocolate?" she asked, standing in the doorway, her head cocked.

Jan felt herself smile. "No thanks," she said. "But really— thank you."

Her mother blew her a kiss and left.

Jan got undressed, turned off her light, and lay down again, her eyes wide open this time, staring at nothing in the pitch-dark room.

Friday was a gray, lowering day, with the smell of snow in the air. The old snow had melted, but the weather had turned cold and damp again; the forecast was for a storm by evening. "Just in time for the show," Ted said gloomily, meeting Jan as she arrived at school early that morning. "What lousy timing. Now no one will come."

"Pessimist," said Jan, then added absently, "See you," and went down the hall to Kerry's homeroom. There was still about twenty minutes before classes started.

Kerry was sitting at her desk, writing something; two other juniors sat in the back row, talking.

Jan slid into the seat next to Kerry's. "Hi," she said, scanning her face.

Kerry's dark eyes were hollow with pain. "Hi. How are you?"

Jan said, "Okay," then told her about the phone call.

Kerry handed her a crumpled piece of paper. "Taped to my desk," she said. "Where everyone could see."

ELIZABETH PROCTOR MUST HAVE BEEN GAY.
IT TAKES ONE TO PLAY ONE.
SINNER, BEWARE!

"Kerry . . ." Jan put her hand on Kerry's; Kerry slipped hers away.

"I'll talk to Kent," Jan said, trying to ignore the hurt. "Will, too."

"No," said Kerry. "Don't." She touched Jan's hand briefly. "I'm sorry I pulled away."

The PA system crackled, as if someone in the office had just turned it on, and the two juniors in the back picked up their books and left, glancing curiously at Jan and Kerry.

"Do you hate me for it?" asked Kerry.

"Of course not! I hate the situation for making us both so jumpy. And I hate Kent. Never you." Jan got up. "Kerry, what if this doesn't stop after the show? I'm not sure it will anymore. Again, maybe you should forget about staying. Maybe it's not safe."

"Don't you want me to stay? I guess it would be easier on you if I left . . ."

"No!" Jan almost shouted. "That's not what I meant. I meant for you."

"Thank you," Kerry said evenly, picking up her books. Then she turned anguished eyes to Jan. "I—I don't know anymore," she said. "I know I love you. But I don't know if I'm strong enough. I'm just trying to get through the show right now. I'm really nervous about it, Jan, about the play, aside from all this other stuff. I can't think about much else. I'm so scared of forgetting my lines or of doing something dumb . . ."

"I know, love." Jan felt a huge wave of sympathy for her. "And you'll be more nervous tonight. But take a deep breath before you go on, and waggle your arms around to relax them. You'll be okay once you start speaking, trust me."

"Yeah, but what if I do forget my lines?"

"I'll prompt you. But you won't forget them. You've been word perfect for weeks. Just concentrate on the play, on being Elizabeth. And remember that Kent's Proctor, not Kent."

"I wish I *could* remember that," said Kerry grimly. But she seemed a little better.

Jan, still aching for her, leaned forward to give her a quick kiss before anyone else came in.

But just as Jan moved toward her, Kerry dropped her notebook and ducked down to pick it up.

After school, Jan resisted the temptation to find Kerry and at least smile at her, wave at her—anything to connect with her, however briefly. Instead, remembering that she'd planned—it seemed years ago—to send Kerry an opening-night telegram, she called her mother from the pay phone in the candy store across the street from school to say she was going downtown, and then had to tell her again that she'd rather not go out to dinner before the performance. Anita, of course, wouldn't be there now, but Hal would.

"You're sure you're all right?" her mother asked anxiously. "How's Kerry?"

"I'm fine," Jan said, choking on the words. "Kerry seemed okay this morning. She must've gone right home after school; I haven't seen her. Look, I really do want to be by myself before the show anyhow. You know how I am. I know I'm not performing, but I sort of feel like I am."

"Butterflies?"

"Swarms of them."

"Well, look, why don't you come home now and come with me to see Anita and the baby for a few minutes, to take your mind off the play? It might calm you down. Then you could come back with me, have dinner by yourself at home while we go out, and take my car to school for the show instead of having us drop you off after dinner in Daddy's car."

"It's okay, Mom. I *would* like to take your car to the show—thanks. But right now I've got something to do downtown. I can see Anita and the baby tomorrow. I wouldn't be any good seeing Anita today. I'd be too nervous to pay attention to the baby. She'll understand."

There was a moment's pause, and then Mom said, "I know, and I should understand, too. Okay, honey. Good luck. We'll be rooting for you—Kerry, too—everyone. Drive carefully, especially if it's snowing. And—oh, my word, I almost forgot! Your friend Raphael called to wish you luck. He said he'll see you tomorrow after the show."

"Thanks for the message. And the good-luck wish. And the car. Give my love to Anita."

With great relief, Jan hung up. She found an 800 number for Western Union in the phone book, called it, and asked how to send a written telegram. It turned out there was no way to do that on such short notice, so she went to the art room and wrote her message out on soft yellow paper, making it look as much like Raphael's as she could:

YOU WILL OUT-ELIZABETH ALL ELIZABETHS AND
SHINE BRIGHTER THAN ANY STAR. BEST OF LUCK.

JAN

She begged an envelope from the school secretary, answered the woman's questions about Anita's baby, and, after putting the "telegram" in its envelope at Kerry's place in the girls' dressing room, she went downtown in the light snow that was beginning to fall. She wished there was something more she could give Kerry, something Kerry could keep with her always, no matter what happened after the show or in January. She walked slowly along Southview's short main street without any clear plan or purpose, peering into stores for some idea—bakery, bookstore, gift shop, auto-supply store, insurance and law office, card shop, small grocer, drugstore, fabric store, jewelry store . . .

Jewelry store.

She stopped, though she'd rarely looked in its window before, and found herself staring at a simple silver ring, three wires twisted together, and she imagined how it would look on Kerry's finger, against her clear smooth skin.

She'd be able to wear a ring always, even onstage. And even if she left in January.

You jerk, she told herself, avoiding the stab she felt at that last thought; Elizabeth Proctor probably wouldn't wear a ring!

Mightn't she wear a wedding ring? Even though this one was silver and they probably only made wedding rings out of gold back then, maybe from a distance it would look all right.

But would Kent notice it and use it against them? Or Will? Or Brenda?

How would they know who'd given it to Kerry?

Did women even wear wedding rings in Salem in the late seventeenth century?

Some director you are, she admonished herself, twisting her head to try to read the upside-down price tag.

"Thinking of breaking in or of buying the Hope diamond?" asked a familiar voice behind her.

Jan jumped, startled, and found Ted at her elbow.

"Now don't ask why I'm not at home resting before the performance," he said. "These directors! Always *at* one, never letting one call one's soul one's own." He regarded her quizzically, then put out his hand. "Why, hello, Jan! Janna Montcrief, isn't it? How do you do? My name is Theodore Woodruff, and I . . ."

Jan finally laughed and slapped his hand in greeting; he slapped back. "Woolgathering," she said.

"Silver-gathering, more like," he said. "Would you consider it some obscure form of graft if I bought you a soda or a cup of coffee or something? If it's against your principles as a liberated woman—you are a liberated woman, no?—then I'll let you buy. Or we could each buy our own."

"You're on," said Jan, realizing suddenly how much she'd missed him. "Maybe we could sneak out without paying."

"My God!" Ted looked over his shoulder as if there were someone behind him. "Can it be true? That sounded like Jan Montcrief. The old Jan Montcrief—jolly, fun-loving . . ."

"Oh, come on before I change my mind!"

They found a booth at the back of the small coffee shop at the end of the street, and squeezed in. Ted ordered a chocolate soda, Jan a root beer. When the waitress finally left, Ted peered across at Jan and said, "It's none of my business, and I know Kerry must be really nervous about the show, but—well, is Kent getting to her? That newspaper thing was awful, and she's looked pretty tense since then, and . . ."

The waitress brought their drinks, gave the soda to Jan and the root beer to Ted, then realized her mistake and came back to switch them just after they had done it themselves. "It's okay," said Jan. "Thanks. Anyone can make a mistake."

"Well, it's embarrassing," said the waitress. "I mean, the last couple that came in, the girl had the soda and . . ."

"Really?" said Ted, as if he were fascinated. "Well, we don't like to run with the common herd. Thank you. We'll—er—we'll ring if we need you."

He eyed Jan as the waitress scurried off. "Okay," he said gruffly. "Tell Uncle Ted. You haven't been looking any too relaxed yourself."

"Nothing to tell," Jan said stiffly.

"Crap. Plain down-to-earth unadulterated crap. Look, if it helps, I have no designs on you anymore. I really like Nanny. She's a great girl. We're doing fine. I might even marry her someday, for Pete's sake. We've got quite a thing going. Okay?" He leaned forward. "I know I asked this before, but it seems to be getting more important. Let me put it this way. Should I go paste Kent after the last performance because he and Brenda and Will are telling lies about you and Kerry? Or should I paste him because he and Brenda and Will are telling the truth in a dirty rotten stinking way about something that's none of their business? It's—it's okay," he added hastily. "I can deal with either answer now."

It took Jan a moment to recover, but then, with great relief, she said, "The latter."

Ted looked momentarily startled, then leaned back and said, "Well. Okay. I did wonder, sometimes. You know. After we—well, after we broke up."

"I didn't even know then," Jan managed to say. "I just knew I didn't want to—to be that way with you."

"Funny how that makes me feel better. Must be true, what Nanny keeps saying about my male ego. Anyway, look," he went on, "I read the newspapers, you know what I mean? I thought people were sort of enlightened now, about gays."

"Oh, Ted!"

He shrugged. "If it helps, I don't know too many kids, really, except Kent and Brenda and a few of their fellow turds like Will who care much if anyone's gay as long as they don't bother anyone. Hey, I didn't mean that as anything," he said as Jan started to protest. "Take it easy." He studied her curiously. "Jan—do you mind? Being gay, I mean?"

"That's not the point," she said tensely, wanting to shout. "It's not the point at all. No, I don't mind being gay, at least not so far. It's what I *am*, at least I'm pretty sure it is. What I mind is people butting in, especially Kent, and making a mess of—of something beautiful. And people like Will yelling about sin when it seems to me that ignorance and hate like his are what's really sinful, not love like Kerry's and mine. This *is* love, Ted, it's . . ."

The waitress came over again. "Will there be anything else?" she asked.

"No," Ted told her. "Thanks."

"Separate checks or together?"

"Separate," said Jan.

The waitress stood there, writing on her pad.

"I saw a three-headed hydra right outside this shop day before yesterday," Ted remarked conversationally to Jan. "One head was green, one was brown, and the other was speckled."

"Funny," said Jan, but without zest. "The one I saw had all speckled heads, four of them."

"Hydras," Ted continued as the waitress crossed out what she had added up and began writing a fresh check, "never have four heads."

"It must have been some kind of freak," Jan said. "Queer. A queer hydra."

"Not many of those around these days. Oh, thanks."

The waitress had thrown a check at Ted, and fled.

"You owe me ninety cents," he said to Jan. "She wasn't able to deal with separate checks after all. Some people have no ability to concentrate. Look," he said as they both got up, "would you please keep someplace in a corner of your stub-

190

born mind that I'm your old buddy Ted, at your service? If I can help with Kent and company if they try anything more, or with anything else—I mean it, and Nanny understands . . ."

"Oh, great! I suppose everyone in the cast who isn't on Kent's side is standing around with the stretchers and the resuscitator and everything just waiting for Kerry and me to keel over . . ."

"Now, hang on," Ted said angrily. "That's not true, first of all. I haven't said anything to any of them, and I really don't know what they're thinking. But Nanny and I are close. You don't keep things from Kerry, do you?"

Jan leaned her head against him for a moment. "No, of course not. I'm sorry, Ted. That was rotten. It's just embarrassing, thinking everyone knows. Or thinks they know. Or suspects, or even just wonders."

He put his arms around her briefly. "Yeah, it must be. Look, believe it or not, it's embarrassing for me, too. I don't want to talk about it a lot. That may not be fair, but there it is. I just want you to know I'm around if you need me. I want Kerry to know that, too."

"I might ask you to get a message to her sometime," Jan said awkwardly. "I don't know. I'll try not to. It depends on how much we think we can see each other."

"Fine." Ted held the door for her. "Did I ever tell you I wanted to be a mailman when I was about five? It's true. Want a ride home?"

"No thanks," Jan told him. "I've got an errand."

When Ted had left, she went into the jewelry store before she could change her mind and bought the silver ring.

NINETEEN

DESPITE WHAT SHE'D said to her mother on the phone, Jan's nervousness butterflies didn't start swarming in earnest till she headed home in the snow to change and eat something before the show. Stage fright was something Jan had accepted for some time as a normal part of a theatrical life. She welcomed it now and gave in to it, allowing its familiar patterns to drive all other problems from her mind.

At home, she made herself a sandwich with some chicken slices her mother had left in the refrigerator, but she wasn't very hungry and her mouth by this time was so dry that the meat stuck in her throat. Resigned, for that had always happened when she was acting, she poured herself a big glass of ginger ale instead, and went upstairs to change into clean jeans and her good-luck sweatshirt.

But, nonetheless, Kerry edged persistently into her consciousness as she drove to school. What was Kerry doing now, how nervous was she, would she be able to handle it, would the "telegram" make her smile or embarrass her?

Should she have made it in the first place?

Jan's was the first car in the parking lot and she went

immediately backstage and started checking props to give herself something to do. She checked the lights and the sound equipment also, and then went out onstage, standing down center with her head bowed.

She let it flow through her and possess her, the before-show reverence she had always felt along with the stage fright.

But it didn't work as well this time. She couldn't feel anymore that the only thing that mattered in her life was theater, that she would pledge herself with each new show to some invisible god of art through which she believed ultimately all problems, all injustices, all ugliness in the world could someday be healed, or that people could be made sufficiently aware of them through theater to know how to heal them. The dark set's expectant silence washed over her, soothing and exciting her as it always had, and she felt the same gladness she had always felt, but less intensely, less surely. In the corner of herself that was left free of that feeling, there was Kerry.

And there always will be, she thought, smiling at the irony of it. She, Janna Montcrief, a pawn of art for at least the last two years; she, Janna Montcrief, for whom love was never going to be more than an interruption; she, Janna Montcrief, was so much and so deeply in love that art was rapidly receding to second place.

And being fed by love, she thought, and the other way around, too; the one feeds the other . . .

She thought of Mrs. Nicholson and for the first time understood why she had left her career for Robert, something she had always thought weakness, though most of the other girls at school had thought it wonderful and right. "One for you again, Mrs. Nicholson," she whispered. Then, for the first time since Mrs. Nicholson had died, Jan let herself remember her as she'd been when she'd been well, her strong, sure voice booming out at her cast, her hands and body instantly showing the truth of whatever character anyone was having trouble with. "I hope you can see the show from heaven," Jan whispered. "And I hope this show will be as good as you wanted it. We tried for you, we really did. I tried for you."

She remembered what Mrs. Nicholson had said about her creativity, and, in a sharp burst, realized she'd just about said goodbye to her dream of playing Medea even as she'd said goodbye to playing Elizabeth. But I'll find someone to play Medea someday, she vowed, and direct that play. "Mrs. Nicholson," she said aloud, for no one else was there to hear, "thank you!" She held her arms out to the set, then to the act curtain, as if embracing the audience that was about to arrive. "Ladies and gentlemen," she said, "I dedicate this performance to Elvira Nicholson, the greatest lady of the theater I have ever known, who . . ."

She dropped her arms and paused.

Well, why not?

Why not make a curtain speech dedicating this performance and tomorrow's to Mrs. Nicholson, whose production, after all, it was?

She looked at her watch. There was just about enough time for her to go home and call Mr. Taylor to ask permission to make the speech—assuming his number was in the phone book—change, and work out exactly what she was going to say. And then of course she'd have to tell the cast.

Thirty-five minutes later Jan was back at school, calling "Half hour!" outside the two dressing-room doors, tense from nervousness and from driving through what was now a heavy snowfall. She was wearing a black pants suit she had dubbed her Hamlet suit when her mother had given it to her the Christmas before, with a loosely flowing white blouse—a poet's shirt, her mother called it; she'd stuffed her jeans, turtleneck, and good-luck sweatshirt into a bag to change into as soon as she'd made the speech. Mr. Taylor, whose number was indeed listed, had given his permission immediately, and had roared that he thought it was "a most fitting idea, most fitting!"

Jan went out onstage for a quick look around the set to make sure everything was still in place, and to wish the crew good luck. And then she went backstage, realizing she hadn't checked to see if everyone had arrived, annoyed at herself for not posting a sign-in sheet like the one they'd had backstage in stock.

She went first to the girls' dressing room and called "Hi— is everyone here?" before she was far enough inside to notice that the room was strangely quiet.

"Everyone's here," someone said softly.

"Hey, you look nice, Jan," said someone else.

But by then Jan's eyes were at the far end of the room. Brenda and a couple of other girls were busily fussing with their makeup, but Nanny and Gail were huddled around Kerry, who was sitting in front of her mirror, head bent. They seemed to be patting her shoulders, talking gently to her, soothing her.

As Jan approached, their voices quieted and she heard Kerry whisper to Nanny, "Don't tell Jan," so she said quickly, "Don't tell Jan what?"

"Nothing," Kerry said as the other girls faded back to their tables. Nanny returned awkwardly to her own mirror, and started drawing the lines on her face that would make her look as old as Rebecca Nurse in the play.

Jan noticed two similar sheets of yellow paper face down

195

between a jar of cold cream and an eyebrow pencil. One was certainly her own "telegram." She picked up the other one before Kerry could stop her.

It certainly wasn't a real telegram, but instead a piece of math paper made to look like one, with words printed neatly on it in black capitals.

"I guess," Kerry said with a weak smile, "Kent came in here to find Brenda and saw your—your message, and got jealous again. It's my fault. I shouldn't have left it here when I went to the bathroom. But I did and I—I was there awhile."

"She was sick, that's what happened," Nanny said furiously, half her face lined and half not. "I'd like to kill Kent."

"It's all right, Jan," Kerry said weakly. "It's all right."

"It's not all right." Jan's hand shook with fury as she read what Kent had written:

SOON MY DEAR ELIZABETH YOU WILL SEE WHAT
HAPPENS TO SUCH A QUEER GAY WITCH AS THYSELF
WHICH KNOWS NOT HER PLACE AND CONSORTS UN-
NATURALLY WITH A WOMAN MADE LIKE HERSELF. IT
IS A SIN. IT IS AN ABOMINATION. "THERE BE NO
HIGHER JUDGE UNDER HEAVEN THAN PROCTOR IS."
YOU SAY IT YOURSELF. KNOW THY PLACE, WOMAN. IT
IS MY PLAY, NOT THINE.   JOHN PROCTOR

Jan glanced toward Brenda, who shrugged, scowling, and said, "I didn't write it. It was just a joke, anyway."

"Oh, so you knew about it." Jan tried unsuccessfully to keep her voice from shaking. "Right?"

"I knew that Kent was—oh, I don't know." Brenda gestured airily. "He doesn't tell me everything. I mean, he's a pretty independent *man*," she added, stressing the last word. "I haven't seen whatever that is." She gestured toward Kent's fake telegram.

"He must be crazy," said Gail. "He must really be crazy."

Nanny pivoted angrily around, away from her mirror. "He's just plain downright mean and hateful. There's nothing in the world wrong with him except that."

"Oh, lighten up, Nanny!" Brenda spat. "Can't any of you take a joke? Geeze, what creeps!"

"There are jokes and jokes," Nanny said. "But this doesn't even begin to qualify as one."

Brenda shrugged, picking up her lipstick, and Jan, disgusted, turned back to Kerry. "Nanny said you were sick," she said. "What's wrong?"

"Oh," Kerry said apologetically, "I just lost my dinner, that's all. It wasn't a whole lot anyway; I was too nervous to eat much. I hadn't even read Kent's thing yet. I don't see how people can perform every night. I . . ." She put her head down on the table, shoulders heaving, but obviously struggling to bring her sobs under control.

"Damn him!" Jan seized Kent's fake telegram. She gave Kerry a quick, awkward hug, then turned to Nanny.

"Give him hell," Nanny said, getting up. "I'll take care of Kerry." She put her hands on Kerry's shoulders, though now they were still and steady.

Jan tore out of the girls' dressing room and barged into the boys', ignoring the startled looks and the half-jovial, half-shocked cries of "Hey, look out—a woman!"

She shoved her way past everyone till she got to Kent, who was carefully applying eyeliner.

"You've gone too far, Kent," she barked, slamming the fake telegram down in front of him.

He lifted an eyebrow at her. "Got your goat at last, eh?

Dissolved in tears, is she? Well, well, guess you'll be playing Lizzie after all. We'll see who runs who into the back wall."

"I will not be playing Elizabeth and Kerry is not dissolved in tears. And if you upstage anyone tonight, I'll play Proctor tomorrow."

"Really, dear? In drag? Don't you think the school would have something to say about that?"

Jan shook her head tiredly. "Kent, I don't know what your game is, and I don't understand how anyone with your talent can be so vindictive just out of jealousy, but . . ." Out of the corner of her eye Jan saw Ted slowly approaching and she signaled him to go away, but he stood there, not far from Kent's table, watching. "It's got to be something more than jealousy, Kent," she went on. "What's the matter? Are you afraid you might be gay?"

She regretted it the moment she said it, but then saw that it seemed to hit home, for Kent's liner brush stopped moving in mid-stroke and he gave her a look of such hatred that it chilled her whole body. Will, Jan saw, was watching both of them. The other boys were, too.

"Get out of here," Kent said under his breath.

"Not until you tell me you're going to stop this."

"Oh, baby, I'm not going to stop anything. Not now. You know what you just said about me, and about Brenda by saying it?"

Ted came up and stood between Kent and Jan. "It's nearly time, you two."

Jan looked at her watch. "Ten minutes," she said as briskly as she could. "Get onstage as soon as you can. I've got an announcement to make." She explained what she was going to say, and then ran back to the girls' dressing room, where

Nanny was supervising Kerry, who wasn't on till the second act, as Kerry smoothed greasepaint onto her face.

"Ten minutes," Jan called, repeating what she'd said to the boys about her announcement. Then she went to Kerry's table as Kerry lifted an eyebrow pencil and drew a shaky line.

"It's crooked," Kerry said, her voice shaky, too.

Jan took the pencil, and Nanny faded back to her own table, poked briefly at her whitened hair, and left. "I yelled at Kent," Jan said, skillfully and quickly doing Kerry's other eye. "It probably made things worse, but I yelled anyway." She erased Kerry's first line with a tissue and cold cream, patched the greasepaint base, and redrew the line.

"Someone will see you touching me," Kerry said.

"So what? What more can he do? Besides, it's only makeup. And most of the girls seem to be on your side. On our side. Just about everyone's gone up to the stage anyway. Close your eyes."

Kerry closed her eyes, and Jan finished making them up. "I want to ask how your aunt was this afternoon and all that, but I can't, Kerry; it's too late."

Kerry nodded. She seemed smaller suddenly, defeated, and Jan thought with irony and pain of her first glimpse of her, strong, self-assured . . .

She put her hand on Kerry's. "You can do it, love," she whispered. "You really can, you know. Kent or no Kent."

Kerry nodded again, and Jan could see that she was trying to smile.

Jan remembered the ring then and reached into her pocket for it, positioning herself between the one or two remaining girls and Kerry. "Good-luck present," she whispered, holding out the box. "Luck for now and for always. Wear it on your left hand for Elizabeth." Quickly, she opened the box and slipped the ring onto Kerry's finger.

Kerry gasped, touching the ring, then smiled mistily. "Thank you," she whispered, her eyes filling with tears. "I—I love you," she added almost inaudibly. "I . . ."

"And I you," Jan mouthed back.

"Jan," said one of the remaining girls, getting up. "Isn't it time for . . ."

"Oh, good lord!" said Jan. "I forgot to call five minutes! And I've got to make a speech. On stage, everyone," she shouted, raising her voice. "Places! Everyone on stage, please, for Act One."

She looked for a long moment into Kerry's eyes, then left swiftly, calling, "Places—on stage, please!" into the door of the boys' dressing room as she passed.

TWENTY

❧

"IT WENT WELL, MOM and Daddy told me," said Anita from her hospital bed, her face pink and happy against the pillows—a painful contrast to how Mrs. Nicholson had looked the last few times Jan had seen her. "And you should have heard Hal rave. He thinks you must be pretty terrific to have practically directed that play. I wish I'd seen it, Jan. I'm so sorry I couldn't."

"Hey," said Jan, "it's okay. You had something much more important to do." Keep it cheerful, Mom had warned, telling her that people tend to get depressed easily after giving birth and that Anita was worn out because it had been such a difficult delivery.

"You haven't said how you feel about it," Anita persisted. "Do you think it went well?"

"Sure." Jan glanced out the window to where the snow lay glittering in the sunlight along the edges of shoveled walks and plowed roads. Well, yes, Kerry had more than gotten through it and Kent had tried no other stunts; the audience had clapped enough for five curtain calls, and Mr. Nicholson, who had stunned everyone by arriving at the last minute with Mr. Taylor, had been pleased, although teary, at her dedication speech. Yes, it had gone well.

"I wish I could see it tonight," Anita said, sighing. "I even asked my doctor, but she said no."

"It's okay." Jan turned back from the window. "There'll be other shows." She forced herself to concentrate on Anita. "And, like I said, you had something more important to do." She squeezed Anita's hand. "He's cute, 'Nita, your little Squirt. He's really cute. I couldn't see much of him when they held him up, and what I did see was kind of wrinkled and red, but I could tell that he's cute. And, hey, I'm going to have to learn how to be an aunt."

Anita squeezed Jan's hand back. "I'm going to have to learn how to be a mother. A mommy! Remember when we were little girls wanting to be mommies?"

"I remember when *you* were a little girl wanting to be a mommy. At least I think I do. I never wanted to be one."

Anita stretched. "You will."

Jan felt her mouth go dry, and the thought *I'm going to tell her; I can't stand that everyone thinks I'm something I'm not; I'm going to tell her*—but then she remembered what Anita had said about pitying homosexuals, and the moment passed.

"Well, for now," Anita was saying, "do you want to be Aunt Jan or Auntie Jan?"

"Good grief, 'Nita, I don't know," Jan said, both relieved and disappointed that the conversation had shifted to safer ground. "Let's let him decide."

"Okay." Anita yawned. "Sorry—Jan, it's awful, but I'm suddenly sleepy. I think I'm going to have to have a nap before they bring Charley-Squirt in. Anyway," she went on, "I think you're going to be a terrific aunt!"

Jan put her coat on. "I'll be a lot better one when he's big enough to throw a ball around, and by the time he can read *Hamlet* there'll be no stopping me. Bye, 'Nita—Mommy."

"Bye, Auntie Jan. Good luck tonight."

It was when she drove into the parking lot, early as usual and dressed in her Hamlet suit for her before-the-show dedication speech, that she saw it: hanging outside the school was a banner that said in letters at least three feet high:

KERRY SOCRIDES IS GAY.
JAN MONTCRIEF IS GAY.

Jan sat numbly in the car, staring at it for a moment before she was able to move. Then all she could think of was getting rid of the banner before Kerry saw it—before everyone coming to see the play saw it, too, but mostly she thought of Kerry. She burst out of the car then, climbed up on a nearby dumpster, and tore the banner down.

But as soon as she got inside, she saw that there were signs all over, saying the same thing. There were signs in the lobby, signs backstage, and signs outside the dressing rooms. Some were scrawled on the walls in what looked like colored chalk; others were written on cardboard and tacked or taped in place. The ones in the lobby were written on the backs of posters, which Jan yanked down and tore savagely apart.

It took quite a while to deal with all of them, and she heard people arriving as she worked frantically. When she was through, she burst into the girls' dressing room and found Gail and several other girls in the cast clustered around Kerry's table again. Then she saw that Nanny was scrubbing with cold cream at the mirror, where the same words had been scrawled in lipstick. Only Brenda sat apart, calmly doing her hair.

"It's okay," Kerry was saying insistently as Jan came in. "Really. It's just another stupid trick. It's fine." But her voice was brittle, her eyes too bright. "It's funny, really."

Jan ignored the other girls and tried to put her arms around Kerry. But Kerry maneuvered deftly aside with a remote smile and sat down in front of her mirror. "Thanks, Nanny," she said as the girls moved away. "That's great. I can hardly see it now."

"Are you sure you're okay?" asked Jan, uncertain of how to react to Kerry's brittleness.

"I'm fine." Kerry seemed to be holding herself in, as if she were afraid that if she didn't she'd collapse. "He was bound to do something tonight. It's okay. The show will go on."

"I think we should tell Mr. Taylor," Gail said to Jan. "With the signs all over the place . . ."

Jan saw Kerry's back stiffen.

"All over?" Kerry moaned. "All over? What . . ."

Jan glared at Gail. "I got rid of them," she said. "I don't think anyone coming to the performance will see them; no audience people are here yet."

"All over?" Kerry repeated.

"There were a few," Jan said, suddenly conscious of Brenda listening to them, though her back was to them and she was making a great show of leafing through her script. "I got rid of them," she said again. "Don't tell me," she added pointedly to Brenda's back, "that it was just a joke."

"Any girl," said Nanny, moving menacingly toward Brenda, "who can't stand up to her own boyfriend when he does something wrong is a coward."

Jan saw Brenda's face go pale under her makeup. "Maybe I don't want to stand up to him. I don't know about the rest of you, but I'll be glad when this play's over and I don't have to share this room with a—a lezzie. I mean, I didn't even know what I was getting into when I tried out for this play, and I sure don't like what I've found. And Kent doesn't either. It wasn't too bad at first, but now it's so obvious it's disgusting. And I'm glad Kent had the guts to, like, expose it."

"Right on, Brenda," said a girl who had a small part and was standing next to her. "I'll be glad when we don't have to take orders from a lezzie *or* share a room with one. I bet Mrs. Nicholson would be really upset if she knew."

Before Jan could say anything, Kerry got up, grabbing a stick of greasepaint, the eyeliner and pencils and rouge and lipstick that she used, plus a box of powder and a jar of cold cream. "I don't think Mrs. Nicholson would care one way or the other," she threw over her shoulder as she marched out. "But I certainly don't want to share this dressing room with someone like you!"

"Way to go, Kerry," Gail called after her.

"You coward," Jan heard Nanny say to Brenda. "You weak, sniveling coward . . ." But Jan left, following Kerry, who had gone into the girls' bathroom.

Kerry was standing in front of the sinks, her reflection framed in another KERRY SOCRIDES IS GAY sign, written in lipstick along the four sides of a square.

"Clever," Kerry said bitterly as Jan came in. "Look. Isn't it clever the way it goes all around the mirror?"

Jan grabbed the lipstick from the pile of makeup tools Kerry had dumped on the edge of the sink and scrawled JAN MONTCRIEF IS GAY on the other mirror. Then she reached for the cold cream and erased the sign about Kerry.

Kerry leaned against the sink. "Oh, Jan," she said. "Thanks, but what's the use?"

Jan put her arms around her, but Kerry slipped out from

under them. "Better not," Kerry said, smearing a paper towel with cold cream and rubbing out Jan's sign. "You've got to stay in this school. I can leave."

Jan told herself not to react to that, that this wasn't the time to show how she felt. "Then you've decided," she said evenly.

Kerry shrugged and went into one of the booths.

"Kerry, I do understand. It's just . . ."

"It's time for you to call five minutes," Kerry said from behind the closed door.

"Kerry, I . . ."

"The show must go on."

"Damnit, come out of there!"

"Jan, please. I can't talk about it now. I can't touch you. I can't even think about it or I'll fall apart. I've still got one more performance."

Jan hung her head. "I know," she said humbly. "I know. I'm sorry."

"Kent wants me to fall apart so I'll be bad and ruin the show. Then he can be a big man and pull it together. So I can't fall apart."

"I know. I—it's just . . ." Jan turned on the cold water and splashed it on her face, then finished her sentence. "It's just that I'm so afraid he's driving a wedge between us that we're never going to be able to get rid of. I can't help thinking that if it weren't for me there'd be no signs."

"It takes two," Kerry said bitterly, "for anything we've done. I think he knows that."

There was the sound of flushing and then silence from Kerry's booth.

"It's also . . ." Jan began, feeling herself break finally, and then hating herself for it.

"What?" said Kerry.

"Nothing."

"Come on."

Jan hesitated, then finally said, "It's also that it's been hard not knowing about next year. But now I guess I know. Right? I know I shouldn't ask, but . . ."

"You shouldn't," Kerry said. "Please. I'm really not sure yet, okay?"

Jan shivered and wondered if it was the cold water. Surely not; it hadn't even been very cold. "Would you at least come out of that booth so I can wish you good luck properly?" she asked.

There was a long silence. Then, so quietly that Jan had to strain to hear, came Kerry's answer: "No."

During the performance Kent successfully upstaged Kerry twice in their first scene. Jan scrawled "Two can play that game," on a piece of paper, explained how to do it, and gave it to Ted at intermission to give to Kerry. Kerry tried it once, and from then on, Kent moved according to the show's blocking.

Kerry's last scene with Kent was better than it had ever been, and even Kent seemed too moved and too involved in it to try any more tricks. Jan felt tears sting her eyes during Elizabeth's final speeches, and when she said the line "I never knew how I should say my love" there was a pause before and after it that filled Jan with hope.

But when, after the performance, which got six curtain calls this time, Jan went down to the girls' dressing room to pick Kerry up before meeting Raphael, Kerry wasn't there.

TWENTY-ONE

❧

"LOOK, I'M A WALKING cliché," Raphael had said once in stock at a party, mincing across the room, hands dangling from limp wrists, amid friendly laughter. "Put me on a TV show and nine thousand gays would complain to the producer about stereotyping."

But he wasn't a stereotype, although he often chose to talk and act like one, and he could mimic nearly anyone, straight or gay. Jan had seen his thin, rather sharp features take on a feline coyness when he wanted them to, or, slackening, make him look like a dissipated lout, as readily as she had seen them harden into a look of resolute strength, or soften into kindness. "Rubber face," someone had nicknamed him in stock, telling him he should do film instead of theater.

Now, beside her in his rented car as they drove to Kent's party, Raphael looked attentive and concerned while she told him more about Kerry, and then about Kent and Brenda and Will, and about Kerry's idea of pretending to play straight at the party. He winced at that but agreed, and gave her a quick pat on the arm when she finished.

"Do you want to try calling Kerry?" he asked then. "See if she's home?"

Jan tugged her jacket tighter around her. "I'm tempted," she admitted. "But if she's not at the party, I'll know she's home and doesn't want to come, so what's the point? I don't much want to go myself . . ."

"Hey." Raphael slowed down and stopped at a light. "Maybe I shouldn't say this, and you can be mad at me if you like, but don't stop fighting. I mean, if you've really got something worth holding on to with this girl . . ."

"I know. I won't stop. It's just—hard sometimes."

"Right, left, straight? Where do I go when the light changes?"

"Right. Then straight for a while till the next light. Left there." Jan pulled in on herself, suddenly tired and not wanting to talk, not even to Raphael. Not anymore.

"Did I ever tell you," he asked, "about the time I was beaten up in high school?"

She looked at him, startled. "No."

"It was the end of junior year, and there was this ridiculous class picnic at the beach. And this other kid, Chris, his name was, and I had been seeing each other for a couple of months. We'd been pretty careful, but there'd already been the usual faggot jokes and stuff like that. Chris was a terrific athlete and he was on the school baseball team—you know, varsity; he was a real jock. He was also beautiful—golden hair, skin, everything. Well, he did have blue eyes." He turned his head briefly in Jan's direction. "That was a laugh line," he said reproachfully. "Golden everything, except for blue eyes?"

"Sorry."

"Okay. Watch for the next one, ladies and gentlemen. Anyway, like I said, he was a real jock, but the other guys had

209

started staying away from him in the locker room and they made cracks every time he was around. You know."

"Oh, yes," Jan said. "I know."

"Well, for some insane reason Chris and I decided to go to the beach party anyway. I don't know, some kind of weird defiance, I guess. Come to think of it, maybe it was a little like you and me going to the cast party tonight and pretending to be straight, to throw your pal Kent off the track. But only a little. Anyway, off we went, Chris and I, trying to act butch, and everything was okay for a while. But finally we couldn't stand the butch act any longer, or staying away from each other, so we went up into the dunes—for a walk, you understand." He snapped his fingers. "You missed again. Laugh line."

"Sorry again."

Raphael gave an exaggerated sigh. "You're in some mood for a party. Not that I blame you. And come to think of it, this story isn't going to do much for your mood. That's probably the last laugh line in the whole thing. Forget it. Do I turn again?"

"Not for a while." Jan struggled to concentrate on his story. "Go on. You can't stop now."

"Well, one of the straight guys was a character like good old Kent, only his name was Rodney. Hey, maybe they all have elegant names like that, huh?"

"Is that a laugh line?"

"Any time you want to laugh, honeybunch, I'll wait for it. Sure."

"Hahahaha."

"Wow."

"It's the best I can do," Jan said, but she felt herself beginning to relax a little. It was hard not to, with Raphael. "You've got to admit it's better than before."

"True. But let's face it, it wouldn't make the old laugh-ometer needle even quiver." He studied her face for a moment. "I can see I should go on with this story. Okay. So old Rodney, he saw Chris and me leave and he started making cracks to the other guys, loud cracks, and to the girls, too, showing off. You know, lots of laugh lines. But Chris and I went on walking, trying to ignore them, and then Rodney said, 'Come on, let's get the queers.' And all of a sudden a bunch of them came roaring after us." Raphael paused, and Jan could see that he was gripping the steering wheel harder than necessary.

"Go on," she prompted gently.

"A couple of the girls screamed and I heard someone yell, 'Oh, forget it, Rodney; they're not worth it.' But then someone tackled me, and as I fell I heard Chris give a sort of a choking sound—you know, like a gurgle—and I tried to look over to him but I couldn't because someone was banging my head up and down in the sand. I heard someone yell 'Eat it, faggot,' though, and later I found out that Rodney had stuffed sand in Chris's mouth. That was before he broke his shoulder."

"Oh, no, Raphael." Jan touched his arm.

"To make a long story short," he said, "Chris had a broken shoulder and a mouth full of sand, some of which he was actually forced to swallow, and I had a concussion and a sprained wrist. We both had a lot of bruises. When they were finished with us, they left, and we lay there for a while. Then we crawled over to each other and held each other, and cried. And later we somehow made it back to my car and drove to the hospital emergency room. And no, we didn't report it to the cops as a gay bashing because we were too afraid."

"What happened to Rodney?"

"Rodney? Honey, I wish I could say we went after him the next weekend and beat him up, but we didn't. What we did was go back to school Monday, terrified, and Rodney got both of us in the hall separately and said that if we told anyone about it we were dead meat, and so we said 'Yes, sir,' or words to that effect, and prayed for the end of school. Luckily, it came soon. Chris went to Camp Something-or-Other, and then his parents moved. I never saw him again. Rodney graduated, and I kept my hands to myself, so to speak, all senior year. So you see, honeybunch, I know a little about what you're facing."

"What you went through was worse, though. So much worse! I wish I could take it away, somehow."

"Yeah, me too. I wish I could find Chris and take it away from him also, and from you, and from all other gay kids who've gone through the same kind of thing." He swung the car in an angry arc around a pile of plowed snow that had spilled over from the sidewalk; then he stopped at another light. "But I guess I can't. Do I turn here?"

"Yes. It's the big white house. The one at the end of the street with all the cars. Raphael, let's not go!"

Raphael deftly fitted the car into a tight parking space. "Hey, we can do this," he said, a little grimly. "If you really want to. It's not as if we never have before. Remember all those times we played straight with my parents, in stock. We convinced them; my mom still asks about you. Someday soon I'm going to tell them the truth, but they weren't ready for it then. It's the same with the kids in your school, I guess. For now, it makes sense for you to be careful, to protect yourself and Kerry. Right?"

"I—I don't know. Maybe not. Kerry's not going to be there, probably, and even if we do the straight bit, what good will it really do? The show's over. I'm not sure it even matters anymore."

Raphael turned and looked at her; his face was more serious than she'd ever seen it. "Sweetie, I know how you feel," he said. "But it probably does matter. Even if most of the kids at your school didn't see those signs, you'd better believe word about them's gotten out. Your pal Kent may very well have started something you and Kerry are going to have to deal with for the rest of the year. If you manage to convince everyone you're straight, you might be able to nip it in the bud as far as people who weren't in the show are concerned. And that matters. Think of me and Chris."

"*I'm* going to have to deal with it for the rest of the year," Jan said. "I'm not sure Kerry is." She explained about that, too.

"Well, it's up to you, sugar. You do have a choice here. I'll go along with whatever you want to do. If you don't go, nothing will change, and things could get worse, because they'll all have a chance to talk about what they've done. If you do go, and we manage to convince them, maybe they'll leave you and Kerry in peace." He squeezed her hand. "You're doing it for Kerry. For survival."

Jan looked toward Kent's house, blazing with lights from every downstairs window. A Christmas tree, resplendent with tinsel and red, blue, green, and yellow lightbulbs, twinkled from one window and a huge wreath covered most of the front door.

"I feel about as festive as *last* year's wreath," she said, nodding toward the one on Kent's house. "And mostly I just want to be with Kerry." She sighed. "But I can't be with Kerry, and you're probably right that I should go. And that we should go ahead and pretend. Can I say I hate it, though? Putting on an act like that? A lie."

"Sure you can," he said. "Yes indeed, you can say that.

Between you and me, I'm not thrilled about it either. Never have been, not even with my folks. Maybe especially not with them. But think of it as an acting job. I'll do my too-too sophisticated Hollywood-actor routine, and you—you'd better be my adoring girlfriend. *Lover*-type girlfriend, not sister-type girlfriend." He smiled, and squeezed her hand again. "Let's have fun with it," he said, "as directors say. And speaking of directors, remember that you've got to be some kind of heroine to those kids. That was one terrific directing job. You saved that show, sugar. Remember the show?"

Jan finally smiled, too.

"Well, it was. And your Kerry was marvelous."

"Kent wasn't bad either." Resignedly, Jan got out of the car.

"No." Raphael came around to her side and hooked her arm through his. "But I wouldn't dwell on that with him, if I were you. Now come on. Remember to gaze at me adoringly and don't slug me if I paw you. We're going to make this look good and we're going to shut that bastard up once and for all, if we're lucky, and if we give a really great performance. Right?"

"Right. But, Raphael, if Kerry *is* there . . ."

"If Kerry's there, we can do the same act, except we all three leave early. You and I will be driving Kerry home, as far as Kent will know, and then going out afterwards." He winked. "Or something."

Jan walked beside Raphael up the path, her feet crunching in the snow, wondering how she was going to pretend, if Kerry was there, that it was Raphael she really cared about. She hoped Kerry would remember that they'd planned to play straight.

Of course she'll remember, she scolded herself. It was even mostly her idea.

Warmth and smoke hit them as they went in the door. "Geeze," said Raphael, "you'd think they'd open a window at least. Whew!" He shucked off his jacket, dropped it on a chair, and helped Jan off with hers. "Let me open doors, too," he whispered, "and make sure you go in front of me. We'll do all that courtly old-world stuff." He draped his arm possessively over her shoulder and propelled her into the living room. "Look happy," he said under his breath. "Come on, smile. A little radiance wouldn't hurt either. You look wonderful in that suit, by the way, but it's just a tiny bit butch, so swing your hips or something."

"Oh, come on," Jan said, annoyed, "the kids all know me, for Pete's sake, even if they don't really know for sure I'm gay." Her eyes darted around the crowded room, seeking Kerry. She spotted Ted and Nanny first, dancing near a few other couples beside a CD player at the opposite end of the room, and then Kent and Brenda, obviously playing host and hostess, near the fireplace. Brenda was passing someone a huge bowl of potato chips and Kent was poking a flaming log, unnecessarily and a bit unsteadily, as if he'd already had too much to drink. She saw Gail and Will and most of the other kids from the cast and crew and a few more besides—but no sign of Kerry.

Brenda looked up from the chips bowl, straight at Jan, and tugged Kent's arm, whispering something to him. The voices died down and suddenly it seemed as if everyone in the room was staring at Jan and Raphael.

"Well, hi, Jan," Brenda called in a saccharine-sweet voice. "Kerry's not here. We thought you two had decided to—well, you know. Party on your own, I guess."

There was a not very well suppressed snicker from some of the kids. Gail, Jan saw, seemed embarrassed, and Nanny and Ted looked furious. Will looked puzzled, then hopeful, almost as if he were relieved to see Jan with a male date.

Jan felt Raphael's elbow in her ribs. "Introduce me," he said without moving his lips. "Then let's dance. They'll stop staring then."

"Hi, everyone," Jan said as casually as she could. "This is my friend Raphael Bartrol from stock last summer. He saw the show."

With jock-like casualness, Raphael raised his hand but not his arm from Jan's shoulder, dropped his voice at least two-thirds of an octave, and gave a nonchalant single wave toward the group. "Great job, kids," he said. "Really great. Showed a lot of hard work, and it's a toughie, I know. I did it back a few years ago . . ."

Jan squelched her surprise; he'd never told her he'd done *Crucible* and she was sure he would at least have mentioned it if he had.

"What," asked Kent, unfolding himself from the hearth and coming up to them, weaving a little, "did you play?"

"Proctor," said Raphael, looking straight at him.

"Really," Kent said without expression.

"Tough part. I like the way you did it. Not my interpretation, of course, but quite credible."

"Oh?" Kent lurched drunkenly, and continued to speak without expression. "How did you interpret it?"

Raphael laughed and pressed his fingers into the small of Jan's back, pushing her toward where the kids who'd been dancing were now standing, watching them. "Good lord, not now, man," he said. "This is a party. I want to dance with my girl, not talk shop."

216

Leaving Kent openmouthed behind him, Raphael took Jan's hand and started to dance. Someone changed the music, and Jan panicked; it was very slow. But Raphael put his arms around her and murmured, "No, that's good for us; good for the performance. Come on, sweetikins, let me lead. Move closer. Relax . . . I *think* we're doing pretty well," he said a moment later. "Yes, Kent's staring at us."

"Probably trying to think of something cutting to say," Jan said in Raphael's ear.

"That's the girl. Now do something mildly outrageous but sexy if you can stand it. Nibble on my ear or look into my eyes or kiss me or something."

Accidentally, Jan stepped on his foot.

"Ouch!" he whispered, pinching her. "Not *that* outrageous! Come on, snuggle a bit. He's coming up to us. I think maybe he's going to cut in. Do people still do that? Nope, he's dancing with his own girl."

"Yeah, I can see that," Jan told him.

"No, no, no, no!" said Raphael. "Keep your eyes closed, honeybunch, while we're slow dancing, except when you open them to look at me dreamily. There's no one else in the room but us. Now, come on. Aren't I the most divine creature you ever saw?" He cupped Jan's chin in his hand and gazed longingly into her eyes.

"I'm going to crack up, Raphael," Jan whispered, feeling more relaxed in spite of herself, and trying to return his look. "Careful, you're dropping the butch act."

"The only way," he said apologetically, "that I can look at you like that—no offense—is to think of a certain man named Jacques, and that's not conducive to my being very butch. Come on. A touch more Ophelia in your Hamlet, old girl. Look at me meltingly. Think of *her*, for goodness' sake."

"If I do that," said Jan, closing her eyes and leaning against Raphael as the music stopped, "I'll probably burst into tears."

"Here comes John Proctor," Raphael murmured, kissing Jan's forehead. "Where in blazes is your hand? It should be in mine, sweetikins. Remember, we're lovers, or nearly."

Kent walked toward them unsteadily while the music changed again, this time to something faster; more kids got up to dance. Someone at the other end of the room turned off a light. Someone else spilled the chips and there was loud laughter as two or three others dove to pick them up. "Floor's clean," Brenda called loudly. "Kent's mother said she had the cleaning lady yesterday."

"Let's sit this one out," said Raphael louder than necessary as Kent came up to them. He put his arm around Jan and led her toward an empty chair.

"I thought you were so anxious to dance with your girl," said Kent, barring their way.

Raphael looked him up and down contemptuously. "We did dance," he replied finally. "Now I'd like to—er—*talk* to her."

He steered Jan around him, but Kent's voice fired at their backs.

"Just how long," he asked, "have you two been going together?"

"Since last summer," Raphael answered promptly. "I live in New York, so we haven't seen each other since then. I'd *like* to see her now. Maybe it's time to leave, baby?" he said to Jan.

Kent planted himself in front of them again; Brenda came up and stood beside him, so close she was almost leaning on his arm. Jan could see people watching, and saw Nanny poke Ted, who turned around and watched also.

"Well, if you haven't seen her since last summer," said Kent, slurring his words, "there's one or two things you should know."

"I already know that you're drunk," said Raphael, "and so I doubt that there's much of interest you could tell me."

"Kent," Brenda said, laughing nervously and tugging at his arm. "Maybe . . ."

"Shu' up, Brenda. Man," he said to Raphael, "look. Lemme do you a favor. One thing you oughta know. I mean, if I was going with a girl, I'd want to know it . . ."

Ted came up behind Kent and tapped his shoulder. "Lay off, Kent," he said. "The show's over, okay? Your little game didn't work, and you were a good Proctor anyway. No one disputes that. So lay off now."

Kent shot his arm out and caught Ted in the chest, sending him sprawling into a chair. Jan heard Nanny gasp and saw two of the boys go to Ted and help him up again.

"You mentioned leaving," Jan said quietly to Raphael, trying to keep her voice from shaking, for something ugly had come into Kent's face when he'd pushed Ted. "Good idea." She moved toward the front hall, maneuvering Raphael in front of her—and then stopped, frozen.

For there, just coming into the now silent room, was Kerry, in a pair of black pants and a blazing-red tunic, her hair tied back with a matching red scarf, her mouth set in a defiant smile, and her eyes terrified.

"Hi, everyone," she said, a little too loudly. "Sorry I'm so late." She laughed self-consciously. "What an entrance, huh? Sorry to interrupt . . ."

Jan moved swiftly toward her, hands out to take hers, but Raphael stepped in front of her. "This must be the Elizabeth," he said. "What a performance!" He patted Kerry's shoulder.

"Marvelous, dear. And Jan tells me you've never acted before. Really, you must think about going on with it. I'm Raphael Bartrol, by the way. Jan's—er—friend from stock."

"Kerry," Jan began; everyone was still staring silently, as if they were all holding their breath. "It's great you got here." She moved closer to Kerry, but Kent pushed between them. As Raphael reached out as if to brush Kent aside, Kent grabbed Raphael's arm. "Hang on," Kent said. "You oughta know Jan's been two-timing you—with *her*." He pointed at Kerry and then paused, leering at Raphael. "Bizarre, huh? Thought you'd . . ."

Raphael threw back his head and guffawed, clapping Kent on the back. "Bizarre? Oh, my poor boy, you don't know what bizarre is! But I wouldn't expect you to, stuck in a small town like this. Sonny," he said, draping a brotherly arm across Kent's shoulders, "you ever hear of the maternal instinct? Jan's a sweet, warm, motherly woman. She's told me all about her friend here." His manner changed, became angry, judgmental even, in the quiet room, with everyone still watching. "Jan told me about those stupid signs, the phone calls—everything. I don't know where you and your pals got such a crazy idea, but if anyone knows this girl, I do. There's no way she's what you've been saying she is, and if she isn't, her friend isn't either. Haven't you ever heard of friendship? Haven't you . . ."

Suddenly Jan wanted to scream. She felt even worse than she'd expected, and it was clear to her that it was all wrong. It was a denial of what she was, what Kerry was; it was almost like calling it dirty, even dirtier than Will had been saying it was.

She saw the same feeling on Kerry's face.

Kerry moved to Jan's side and, with everyone in the room watching, took her hand. "Say it," she whispered urgently.

"It's okay with me. Tell them." She gripped Jan's hand so hard it hurt.

Jan took a deep breath. "Never mind, Raphael," she said. "Thanks. It's okay." She faced Kent and, loud enough so everyone would be able to hear, said, "You were right. The signs were right. I *am* gay."

With the words came a sense of relief and liberation so great that she felt she never wanted to hide again, even though she knew at the same time that she might have to.

"And so am I," came Kerry's clear voice. "Jan and I—we love each other very much. And I don't think that's anyone's business but ours."

Jan saw the astonished faces around her—even Ted's, even Nanny's—heard the few self-conscious giggles, felt Raphael's supportive hand on her shoulder, saw his other hand on Kerry's as he murmured, "All right, sisters!"

Kent, with Brenda beside him, remained motionless, frozen in place. Will opened his mouth as if to speak, but then snapped it shut.

Ted broke into applause, and soon nearly everyone else in the room joined in, except Will, Brenda, a few kids who were whispering to each other, and Kent, who wheeled and went abruptly to the table where the drinks were, popped the top off a can of beer, and downed it in what appeared to be a single long gulp.

Brenda followed him, and Will stepped toward Jan, Kerry, and Raphael as if he still had something to say. But he stopped midway, went to an empty chair, and sat down instead.

"Come on, my brave chickadees," Raphael said. "I think this is our cue to exit. I am so proud of you both," he added quietly as he steered them toward the door. "So proud!"

Jan took Kerry's hand, suddenly exhausted. What she most

wanted to do was leave with Kerry, hold her, and sleep for days.

But as she went tiredly out of Kent's house with Kerry and Raphael, with people patting her shoulder and saying things like "See you Monday," and "That took a lot of guts," and "Hey, you know *I* don't care"—as she went out of Kent's house and down his front steps to Raphael's car, she was acutely conscious of the fact that she still didn't know if Kerry was going to stay after January, and she knew she wasn't sure she could—or should—ask.

"See you Monday," Kerry whispered, kissing Jan while Raphael discreetly looked the other way when they dropped Kerry off at her aunt's. "I promised Aunt Elena I'd go to a giftware show tomorrow. I didn't go today because of *Crucible*." She pushed back Jan's hair. "I love you. You were so brave tonight."

"So were you," said Jan.

But she wondered, as she and Raphael drove away, if Kerry was going to be brave enough to stay.

She wondered if she'd be brave enough herself, if she had the same choice. As Raphael said later, gently, when he dropped her off before driving to his friend's in Middleton where he was spending the weekend, the kids in the show were one thing, but the other kids in school might very well be another matter, once word got around.

TWENTY-TWO

SUNDAY MORNING AND afternoon went by without word from Kerry, and when Jan called several times in the evening, there was no answer. Raphael came to dinner and charmed both her parents, so much so that, after he left, her mother said, "Are you sure he doesn't like you? I mean, as more than a friend? He certainly seems interested, and he's so nice, Jan!"

"Yes, isn't he?" she said vaguely, and went up to her room, pleading homework.

But all she could do was stare out of her window at the frosty world outside and wonder why Kerry hadn't called.

Monday morning, after next to no sleep, Jan was tempted to go to Kerry's house and pick her up for school. But what if, after coming out so bravely at the party, she'd gotten scared and didn't want to see Jan anymore? Instead, Jan went to school early, but Kerry never did arrive. Kids looked at Jan curiously on and off all day, some seeming sympathetic, some just prying, but she couldn't bring herself to say anything to any of them.

At lunch, Ted plunked himself down at her table. "News," he said, spearing a sad-looking mass of noodles and hamburger with his fork. "Justice may be blind, but she's not dead. Interested?" He lifted the forkful into his mouth and chewed.

"Depends," Jan told him, trying not to watch him swallow; she herself had no appetite and had barely touched the small salad she'd chosen.

Ted took a swallow of milk and wiped his mouth. "Rumor has it," he said, "that Taylor had Kent in his office for all of third period. Will and Brenda, too, but not for as long. Rumor also has it that they're all suspended for defacing school property and 'harassing other students,' I believe is the official term. Suspended till after Christmas break." He gave her a quizzical look. "Happy?"

"Sure," she said, but she discovered she was unable to feel any reaction. "Ecstatic."

"Well, it ought to help. It'll give you time, if nothing else. And maybe it'll make them think twice before they start anything again."

"Maybe." Jan toyed with her salad. If Kerry's not around, she thought, what difference will it make if Kent shuts up?

Ted reached across the table and tapped Jan's fork. "You're killing that tomato needlessly," he said. "It's December, for Pete's sake. The poor thing's dead already. You want me to call Kerry?" he asked finally. "You said something once about messages."

She was able to smile at him then, gratefully. "Not yet," she told him. "But I'll keep it in mind."

After school, Jan drove through the icy streets, almost missing two lights, straight to Kerry's.

The house was dark, though dusk had fallen, and there

was no answer when she rang the bell, so she went to the shop. Not giving herself time to question what she was doing, she walked briskly in.

Aunt Elena was at the cash register, ringing up a sale. Jan waved at her and went quickly to the stockroom door, where she'd caught a glimpse of red—Kerry's red turtleneck, she was sure—and heard a sneeze. "Kerry?" she called, looking into the room. Then she saw her, blowing her nose in the middle of gift wrapping one of the ghastly cherubs.

"Oh, thank God—Jan!" Kerry exclaimed, dropping the cherub. It smashed, and she stepped on it as she ran to Jan —to Jan, whose heart was beating wildly, joyfully, for the look on Kerry's face answered her most important question.

Kerry flung her arms around Jan and held her as if she would never let go. "I kept sending you telepathic messages all day," she whispered. "I've got a stupid cold; I had a sore throat yesterday, and I sneezed so much last night Aunt Elena made me stay home today. We got back too late last night from that giftware show for me to call and warn you. And I overslept this morning. But I'm working in the shop to show her I'm well enough to go to school tomorrow. She—um— she's started talking again about how I should have other friends."

Jan moved out of Kerry's embrace and told her what Ted had said about messages. "If she gets too snoopy," Jan said, "feel free to call him. Kent's been suspended," she added. "Brenda and Will, too."

"Jan?" Aunt Elena stood in the doorway, looking more confused than angry.

"Hi," said Jan. "I was worried about Kerry. There wasn't any answer when I called last night, and since she wasn't in school today, I was even more worried. So I came over."

Aunt Elena laughed self-consciously. "Ruth and Naomi,"

she said. "That's what you two are. 'Whither thou goest, I will go'—from the Bible. But I think now that the play's over, we should have a big party, with lots of boys, h'mm, Kerry Ann?" Aunt Elena put her arm around Kerry. "Wouldn't that be fun?"

Kerry sneezed violently, twice.

Jan laughed in spite of herself. "Feel better, Ker'," she said casually, moving toward the door.

Kerry murmured "Thanks," sneezed again, and winked.

At about ten that night, the phone rang in Jan's house and Jan nearly upset a vase of holly as she leapt up to answer it.

"I don't know," said Ted as soon as Jan had said hello. "This message business isn't all it's cracked up to be."

"You have a message?" said Jan tensely. "Come on—what?"

"It doesn't make sense. Well, maybe it will to you. I guess it would to me, too, if I looked it up . . ."

"Ted!"

"Oh, all right. Kerry called me a few minutes ago, whispering like she was afraid she'd be overheard. Said something about her aunt telling her again to see other people, not to hang around you so much, and that she'd been about to call you but her aunt had said, 'I hope you're not calling Jan at this hour,' and Kerry said she thought of me and said, 'No, I'm calling a boy,' and her aunt said, 'That's all right, then. But don't talk long; it's late.'"

"The message, Ted," said Jan, not wanting to think about the implication of Aunt Elena's increasing firmness.

"She said, 'Tell Jan *Hamlet*, Act Two, scene two, Hamlet's letter to Ophelia.' And she said to be on the stage at school at six o'clock tomorrow night."

Jan closed her eyes in relief; she knew the *Hamlet* lines well. "Yes, okay. Fine. Ted—thank you."

"Don't mention it. By the way, I never liked *Hamlet* much. Certainly not enough to check out that message."

"Thanks for that, too," said Jan. "But I don't think I'd mind if you did. You're a good friend, Ted."

"Oh, I know, I know. True to the end and all that. Well, see you tomorrow. Wow, the intrigue!"

As Jan expected, Kerry wasn't in school the next day either, but this time, though she had almost as much trouble concentrating on her classes as she'd had the day before, she wasn't nearly so worried. She actually managed to whistle as she helped Ms. Grillo and the crew strike the *Crucible* set.

An hour more, she thought when everyone left at five. One more hour.

She opened her history book and tried to read; there was a test right before Christmas break. But though she could hear the words in her mind individually as she read them, they made no sense put together. She closed the book after about twenty minutes and went backstage to the small equipment storage room, where she found a music tape, and put it on the sound machine, with the volume low so the custodian wouldn't hear and come prying. Then she bunched up her jacket for a pillow and lay down on the bare stage, closing her eyes to listen.

And the next thing she knew, Kerry was beside her, softly touching her face.

" 'Doubt thou the stars are fire,' " Kerry was quoting, smiling down at her, " 'Doubt that the sun doth move. Doubt truth to be a liar, But never doubt I love.' Sleepyhead."

"*Hamlet.*" Jan sat up. "Act Two, scene two, Hamlet's letter to Ophelia. Kerry—how are you?"

"Fine," Kerry said. "Except for this rotten cold. Fine. And very, very proud."

"Huh?"

Kerry took Jan's hand. "Because of the party."

"Hey, I'm proud of you, too. I'd never have said anything if you hadn't told me to."

"But I wouldn't have dared actually say anything myself if you hadn't said it first. And now we're free. Kent can write anything he wants on the walls when he comes back from being suspended and it can't really do us any harm."

"Don't count on it," Jan said, remembering Raphael's beach story. "If there's a way, he or Will or Brenda might still find it. Or other kids might. And now there's your aunt . . ."

"Right." Kerry sat down next to Jan on the stage floor, and with her free hand poked absently at a bit of dust. "The way I see it, it's only a matter of time before she really catches on or before someone tells her. And I'm not sure she'd know how to cope if she knew."

"So," said Jan, trying to blink back the tears that rose in her eyes, "you're going to go back with your parents in January." She squeezed Kerry's hand. "It's okay. It's probably the best thing. I—I'm sad, but I understand. And I'd hate to see you hurt. I . . ."

But Kerry was shaking her head vehemently. "No," she said. "No. I wrote my parents. I told them about us."

Jan stared at her. "You what?"

"I wrote them about us. Saturday night, after the party. And I asked them to let me stay with Aunt Elena after January, and I suggested that maybe when they come back, we could all talk about it, I mean my parents and me, with Aunt Elena. You, too, if you want. I think Mom and Dad will be okay about it, at least after a while. And I think they'll help with Aunt Elena. They're pretty decent people."

"Now who's proud?" said Jan, letting the tears rise after all. "That was an incredibly brave thing to do."

Kerry smiled. "I think we should go on seeing each other any time we want until we know what's going to happen, at school and with my folks. And then, when whatever happens does happen, we can go on from there. If my parents make me go home, which I really doubt—well, there are letters, and post-office boxes are pretty private if someone's trying to interfere with one's mail."

"And school?" Jan asked. "Things could get pretty bad, Kerry, even dangerous, when Kent and his friends come back. I have a feeling suspension may not change them a whole lot. They'll probably blame us for it, and . . ."

"Shh. You are the most important person in my life, Jan. I'm not going to let you go. I'm not going to let people walk all over me, either. School won't last forever. And if bad things happen, we'll deal with them. A lot of kids are on our side, I think. As long as we've got each other, I think we'll be okay. It took me a while to trust that, and to sort out how I feel about not being straight. I mean, you know, there are things that one expects one's life to be, and then when it isn't going to be that way, it's sort of . . ."

"A jolt?" Jan supplied, remembering how she'd wondered what Thanksgiving would be like if her family knew about Kerry, and how she hadn't dared tell Anita. But now I will, she promised herself. I'll find a way to tell all of them. They're decent people, too . . .

"Yes, a jolt. That's a good way to put it. But it's okay, because it explains why I've always felt sort of different. And as long as I've got you, I think I can handle the other stuff." Kerry paused. "What about you?"

Jan felt the tears in her eyes, but knew she was too happy to let even happy tears spill over. "I think I can, too," she said. "But it's not going to be easy, Kerry, for either of us."

"Nothing worthwhile," said Kerry, handing Jan a small box

that she pulled from her pocket, "is easy. Even Faust knew that. Here."

It was a ring so like Kerry's Jan had to look very close to tell them apart.

"See?" Kerry said softly. "Now that almost everyone knows, it won't matter if kids at school notice they're almost the same." She put the ring on Jan's finger. "Remember that moon we saw together? It seems like years ago! But it *was* a good moon, Jan, after all. What do we care what people think of us? Some of them will probably never understand. But maybe we can try to show them the truth. Maybe we've already started."

Jan looked down at the ring on her finger, and then moved into Kerry's arms. "Right," she said. "Maybe we have."